Full Figured 17:

Carl Weber Presents

Full Figured 17:

Carl Weber Presents

Brandie Davis

and

Niko Michelle

www.urbanbooks.net

Urban Books, LLC
300 Farmingdale Road, NY-Route 109
Farmingdale, NY 11735

ISBN 13: 978-1-64556-524-6

First Mass Market Printing September 2023
First Trade Paperback Printing October 2022
Printed in the United States of America

10 9 8 7 6 5 4 3 2 1

Distributed by Kensington Publishing Corp.
Submit Orders to:
Customer Service
400 Hahn Road
Westminster, MD 21157-4627
Phone: 1-800-733-3000
Fax: 1-800-659-2436

Full Figured 17:

Carl Weber Presents

Brandie Davis

and

Niko Michelle

Camgirl Love

by

Brandie Davis

Chapter 1

Wintertime in the city was when Draya's loft looked most beautiful, especially after sunset when a blanket of white covered New York. Light fixtures dangling from the ceiling throughout her home emulated countless fireflies dancing in the dark. She felt like a fairy walking beneath the man-made stars sprinkling their peace upon her and enhancing the beauty of the flowers that sat on her end tables. Her home was her sanctuary, where she only turned on her main source of electricity while cooking or showering. She was in search of peace, and the idiot box along with social media were distractions she was sure would ultimately lead to a reoccurring downfall.

Draya's favorite part of winter was when it snowed . . . No flurries that would be erased the next day, but full-fledged snow determined to make its mark. She adored the snowflakes that piled themselves on the base of her ceiling-to-floor windows. Draya felt shut in, locked away, and segregated from the world. She felt pushed into a corner of her own and loved it. Draya sat in front of her easel sketching away in the dark while Mother Nature covered Brooklyn in a flurry of snow that fed her soul. She never thought out what she'd draw; instead, she'd allow the voice from within to take charge and cry itself out on paper. Sometimes, the paper would tear, bringing to life a hint of pain, while most of the time, it would spew a violent act of rage submerged in a rainstorm of tears.

Draya liked the latter moments. She liked when the emotions she shoved down into the pit of her belly came gushing out, surprising her like vomit staining a new toilet. For the time, she felt free and empty of the disguise she tried to hide. She felt human. Forgetting she was home and protected from men and women who mistook her for being pregnant and stared at her face's slight disfigurement, Draya tried pulling down her crop top as far as possible. The stretchy material bounced back, returning to its true form, allowing her heavy, round stretch-marked stomach to breathe. She pushed herself back on the chipped, scratched stool she feared one day would collapse beneath her 300-pound frame and took a broader look at the nightmare she brought to life.

In the middle of everyday people walking through the streets of the Big Apple, absorbed inside their own worlds, laid a plump, umber-colored woman whose nakedness was covered by her floor-length dreads. She was curled within herself. Her face was hidden, and her hair was reminiscent of an African rock python wrapping itself around her. Snatching her 4H pencil from her pencil container, she darkened the places she hurt the most, which were everywhere.

Her cell phone vibrated against her meaty thigh inside of the pocket of her stretchy pants. "Shit," she spat. Her lips curled into a snarl fitting for spit to accompany. "I forgot to turn this shit off. This is *my* time," she barked. Her voice was picked up and carried around the loft, the echo screaming back at her.

Draya caught sight of the snow's downfall increasing before turning to her phone. The flakes she remembered seeing the last time she looked out into the winter wonderland had disappeared and been replaced by boulder-size snow working vigorously at painting New York white.

She stood and walked to the window greeting her with winter's beauty. She forced herself to pick up her feet a little higher, and each time she did, she hoped her massive feet would feel less heavy and more like air. Wished upon a star that the feet mistaken as swollen while wearing flip-flops would be sleek, slim, worthy of being licked without a second thought. But sadly, there was no change in mass, only the overly familiar feeling of girth weighing her down. Draya crossed her arms, conscious to avoid touching the fat swinging freely.

"Gorgeous, just gorgeous," her lips moved, striving to catch the correct wording. "What I wouldn't do to be able to melt away."

From a distance, a figure bundled in a waist-length coat, clad with a hood, took giant steps inside the snow. He moved slow and precise, heading in the direction where parked cars were almost unrecognizable. Then he took another step and collapsed inside a snowbank. Draya snickered, the first smile hitting her face in nearly a week. She watched the stranger for a few more minutes as he pulled himself out of the pit and stumbled to his car.

Draya sat on her stool and looked over the flaws invading the drawing. What was seen surpassed crooked lines and uneven shading. Faults lay beneath the paper, inside the pencil strokes, and within the scenery.

The phone she failed to acknowledge vibrated again. Draya sucked her teeth, gave her illustration one last look over, and removed the phone from her stretch pants, her one of two connections to the outside world. On the screen, before she even opened the message, it read:

Open the

Her eyes scanned the sender's name. "Willard," she mumbled. She closed her eyes, running fingers through her dreads but was stopped right above her forehead by her yellow and blue head wrap. Eyes still closed and hand still on her head, slowly, she walked to the front door and opened it.

"What do you want?" Her eyes opened to a five-foot-four old bald man with a unibrow covered in snow. *You have got to be kidding me. So this is the fool I was watching from the window?*

"I've come with treats." Willard held a black plastic bag out to Draya, who didn't take it. Then quickly, he ripped open the bag and exposed a liquor bottle. With his free hand, he held up a bottle of vodka, smiling as flurries collected on his shoulders in the doorway.

Cold but refusing to display it, Draya repeatedly tapped her foot on the floor. "I *said*, what do you want?"

Shivering, Willard tried easing his way past Draya and into the loft; however, her wide hips acted as a roadblock and pushed him backward. "Can I come in? I'm freezing. Fell into the snow back there." Willard's arm flung behind him as he gave a yellow-toothed smile.

No longer willing to ignore the weather nipping at her skin, Draya backed away from the door and allowed her most faithful customer inside.

"You've forgotten. I knew you would. I knew I should have sent you a reminder," he chuckled, followed by a snort. He looked around and took in his surroundings . . . the wooden bookshelves against the brick walls, the marble coffee and end tables on top of the fur rug, and high-tech touch screen kitchen appliances. "Wow, this place is nice." He slowly removed his jacket and hung it on the coatrack. Before his feet stepped on another panel, Draya pointed down at his boots, and instantly, Willard got out of them.

Sockless, he headed for the kitchen and placed the liquor on the island. He pulled on the cabinet handle, and when it opened on its own, he backed up and blew out globs of air. Then catching his breath, he finally answered Draya's question. "Tonight is the night you fulfill your first old man fetish. I've been talking to a few friends who are fans of yours, and they're excited about tonight's episode."

"Dammit," escaped from Draya's mouth without her meaning it. "Tonight, I have an episode, and you've told people the theme? I told you, keep it quiet. I don't need word getting out about the upcoming episodes. I work off of shock value."

Willard pulled two short, wide glasses from the cabinet and poured some vodka. "I'm sorry." His shoulders shrugged. "I had to speak with someone about it. Plus, I wanted to ensure we get viewers. This is my first time camming." He laughed again, and Draya noticed another missing tooth on the side of his mouth.

"Don't get too ahead of yourself. Remember, you're just a prop."

"And that's all I need to be." He handed Draya her glass and sipped from his. "It's so dimly lit in here. There's a bunch of these small lights hanging around, but they give off hardly anything. Why don't you turn on the main lights?"

"Because I don't want to. I like it like this."

Draya kicked back the liquor, her mind circling and trying to grasp the fact that she had a show that night that she wasn't in the mood to film.

Willard went into the living room, his feet walking on the bottom of his pants. "Wow, now look at this. You draw?"

Draya flew over to the easel and turned her nightmare around. "What I do outside of camming is none of your business. Now, go upstairs. The second room to the right is where you can set up."

Willard nodded his head, snatched the bottle of whiskey, and headed for the winding staircase. Five steps up, his hand grazed the railing's peeling paint.

"Draya, you should really repaint this railing. I know of someone who can do this for dirt cheap. I think about . . ."

The farther Willard walked, the more he spoke, and his voice diminished. Draya listened to his small feet slap against the stairs and pushed his underdeveloped voice from her ears. Then rushing inside the kitchen, she opened the tequila. This was a liquor-mixing moment, a time to speed up the process of intoxication. She held it up to her lips and took in such an amount she scared herself. It dulled her senses, shut off her brain, and commanded her body to comply and take in the pain-numbing poison.

My main john is now my closest friend, and I'm in the camming business. My main john is now my closest friend, and I'm in the camming business. She repeated this sentence in her head while drinking. Her body began to rattle, and her eyes moistened with tears. *My main john is now my closest friend, and I'm in the camming business.* Finally, she pulled the bottle away and slammed it on the island. Coughing, Draya fought to catch her breath. She rested her palms flat on the granite countertop and told herself, "You'll be okay. You'll be okay."

Draya read the liquor bottle's label, its ingredients, and its brand. She scooped it up again, took two more gulps, and with closed eyes, set it down. Her lips curled immediately, tears dropped, and her soul ached. Wide-eyed, Draya snatched the bottle by its neck and hurled it into the brick wall decorated with hanging potted plants. She crouched down, her heavy arms wrapped around her big legs. She rocked back and forth, the rapid beating of her heart pounding inside her ears.

"Breathe, Draya, breathe," she instructed herself. "Breathe." Her fist on her chest helped her inhale and exhale. Minutes of breathing as if in a Lamaze class led her entire being to stabilize. She pushed out one final surge of air and stood up.

"Draya, I was thinking, how about I wear a thong tonight? You know, gain some views from the gays and bisexuals."

Chapter 2

The door to the video room was wide open. It had professional ceiling lights, video equipment, fans, and a king-sized bed with red silk sheets. A sixty-inch smart television connected to a laptop welcomed Draya like it was the first time she stepped into that space. Equipment and stagewise, Draya wasn't where she wanted to be when it came to holding a steady ranking and making the big bucks in the camming world. However, her viewers appeared pleased and made it their business to comment on her interior decorating during every show.

Booner: Damn, your bed is huge. Can I join you?

Onenightman: I can fuck you on that fluffy-looking carpet of yours.

Don'taskmyname: I can't stop looking at that drawing above the bed. I'm staring at that more than you. Where did you get it, Casey?

***

From the doorway, Draya watched as Willard bounced up and down on the bed, testing its durability and strength.

"When did you get a waterbed?"

"Last week."

He nodded. "Great addition. I haven't seen anyone incorporate a waterbed in their videos yet."

Draya came farther inside and closed the door behind her. "I know."

She sat beside him, the bed's movement taking her up and down while she fell back into when she was first introduced to water beds, the sheets gathering around her, covering her face.

"You thinking about Steward?"

Draya sucked in air and held her breath. The silk sheets surrounding her nose blocked off the air and slowly suffocated her. She wanted to drown within the sheets inside the bed and wake up somewhere far, far away in another universe. Instead, Willard ripped the silk off her. A rush of air touched her skin, rushing inside her nostrils.

"Huh?" Willard looked down at her. He gave her a clear view of his white, overly grown nose hairs.

Draya rolled her eyes and looked away. "How can I forget him?"

Willard lay beside her, his eyes stuck on the ceiling. The ceiling he once hoped he'd see in person one day after the first night he signed into Draya's channel. "I've known him for years and never seen him like that." He scratched at his newly grown gray beard.

"How did he treat the other prostitutes you two picked up together?"

"Regular. Based on what we paid them for is how he treated them. If we paid them to dominate us, he became submissive. If we paid them to screw, he screwed. He did nothing out of the norm." Willard frowned, the extra skin under his neck swaying back and forth.

"Until he met you."

Willard stopped speaking. He treated that night as a forbidden topic. They never talked about it, treating it like a bad dream they forced to the back of their minds and locked away in a vault. Finally, he sat up. "Let's get started. We're ten minutes behind showtime, and we're not even dressed."

"Then why did he do it?"

Willard took off his shirt and unbuckled his trousers. Gray back hair escaped from out of the corners of his dingy wife beater.

"Willard, if how he acted was out of character, then why did he do it?"

"We have a show to do, Draya. Ratings are calling."

Draya shot up. The waterbed swayed and pulled her back down on her back. Her short, chunky legs flapped in the air moments before hitting the floor.

She grabbed Willard by the shoulder and forced him to look at her. Her plump fingers sank into his skeletal frame.

Willard sat back down. "We're not gonna shoot on time, are we?"

"Why did he do it?"

Willard wiped at his beady eyes. He gave extra attention to his left eye, a nervous habit formed during tense situations. Liquid seeped out of the corners of his eyes, and he grabbed the bottom of his undershirt and dried off his face. His fingers walked up his right arm in search of the scab in the center of his shoulder.

"You were a release."

Draya watched tiny pieces of crust descend from Willard's skin and plummet to their demise.

"What do you mean 'release'? He didn't fuck me. Not from what I remember." Draya leaned over and rested her elbows on her knees. She dug her elbows deeper and deeper into her flesh.

"Not that kind of release." Willard stopped tampering with his scab and pulled at his neck's stretchy skin. "Steward's wife took him to the cleaners so bad she might as well made him get on his knees and fucked him in the ass with a strap on herself. He was pissed the hell off." Willard's voice raised. His volume caused Draya to jump, her elbows sliding off her hefty legs. "She took it all. The house, the cars. And the damn dog. Boy, did he love that dog. He spent a lot having that dog trained and every week got it groomed. Could have been one of them dogs competing in shows. You know, the ones where—"

"Get back to the fuckin' point."

Willard's fingers retreated to the wound he partially reopened and ripped off. He laid the dry patch on his tongue and swallowed. "I'm sorry."

Draya spat out air and lay her head on Willard's shoulder. She planted her palm on the small of his back and rubbed in small, circular motions. "I'm sorry, just please tell me," she said softly.

All of Willard relaxed except for his toes that wiggled out of control, pushing his pinky toe out of the hole in his sock. "That feels good."

"I know. Draya knows." Her hand slithered past his neck to the back of his small head. Her neglected nails scratched the back of his head, causing him to close his eyes and thank her.

Willard took her free hand into his. He gently rubbed the top of her hand, the action reminiscent of a man petting his cat. "Back to the divorce, once it was settled—"

"No, just tell me what I need to know. No back-story."

"I have to. You can't ask someone to jump out of a plane without first taking a breath."

Draya sucked her teeth.

"Once the divorce was settled, and Steward was left with nothing except his name and two-day-old drawers he'd worn back to back, he wanted to take his anger out on someone, a woman. Said he wanted to fuck her like he'd just been fucked. Restore the balance of power is what he called it. She'd cheated, yet she got everything."

Willard cleared his throat. "I thought what you thought that he wanted to blow off some steam in a sexual manner, wanted to dominate a woman the best way he knew how. Feel like a man again, ya know? I've had plenty of days where I felt like a bottom bitch taking a dildo in the ass, lubricant-free, and needed to regain my pride someway." He swallowed hard, recalling the countless, overly thought of memories from the past.

Draya squeezed his hand. "Come back to me, Willard. Keep talking."

"Yes, yes, oh yes, I apologize." He straightened his posture. "Steward asked if I knew of any Black prostitutes. Said he had never had a Black one before. Said it would be the perfect touch. So, I thought of you." The only clear, blemish-free part of Willard without fault welled with tears. "I recommended you, knew he'd have a good time with you. Knew you could take anything he'd throw at you."

"She's carefree, that one. No uptight prude like that ex-wife of yours. Casey likes to have fun and venture out, grab life by the balls, if you know what I mean."

"I told him all of that, and to seal the deal, even told him, *'She'll do anything. No questions asked as long as the green's right. Then everything's all right.'*"

Draya wondered when the tears would fall, wondered how it was humanly possible to contain such emotion and liquid without the plummeting bursting.

"Showed him your picture, and he was all for it. Said you were perfect, his little Black girl. I didn't know his plans for you. You gotta believe me." Willard pulled his bottom lip into his mouth before continuing to speak. "When he first started smacking you, calling you names, and violently twisting your nipples, my dumbass thought he was into that whole role-playing scene. Thought it was foreplay. Thought your screaming was just good acting skills."

"How could you have thought my screaming, 'Stop—what are you doing?' and 'Please, no,' could have been acting?" Draya questioned, surprisingly without a dash of anger in her tone.

"I've dealt with plenty of prostitutes who agreed to rough sex and faked resistance. Plus, I gave him your contact information and thought you guys worked it out beforehand. So I asked no questions, especially when it's on another man's dime that I'm getting a fuck on."

"When did you notice something was off then?"

"When he started calling you by his ex-wife's name. Now, that, that's just *not* normal, and the look on his face when he said it was everything evil. Then before I could say a word, he had dug his brass knuckles out of his pocket and put them on. I can still hear the sound, its impact when he punched you in the mouth."

Willard snatched away from Draya and slapped both palms on his head. "I *knew* I heard something crack. I just *knew* it." The floodgates opened. "He kept hitting, and hitting, and hitting you, and by the time I got him off you, he tore himself out of my hold and threw you to the floor, where he started kicking and stomping on you."

"I don't remember that," Draya admitted, her eyes now foggy.

"That's because you had already gone unconscious. I grabbed him again, but my strength was like a bunny rabbit compared to a bull. He shook me right off. I knew then there was nothing I could do. Cancer had stolen that part of my manhood long ago. That's when he started dragging you by a fistful of your dreads around the hotel room, and I knew things had gone too far."

Chapter 3

Blood sank unevenly into the cream carpet. It trailed down one direction, only to shift and go the opposite way. Its flow should have been slow and steady, a snail's movement. Instead, the pool of blood gushing out of Draya's lips, inner cheek, missing teeth, and cheekbones initiated vital fluid to leak fiercely and unapologetically.

Rage and a lack of energy pulsating through Steward's body pushed his 250-pound frame slightly backward. Barely on her feet, he used a wobbly and weak Draya to remain balanced. Sweat trickled down the bald spot in the center of his head. The hand that held Draya tightly by the collar of her shirt wore bronze knuckles saturated with blood.

Steward swallowed his saliva with as much aggression placed into the vigorous and hateful punches he used to violate Draya's face. Then slightly reenergized, he continued with his violation. His brass knuckle-decorated fist cocked back and swiftly rammed into Draya's mouth. The loud, cracking sound released by her broken teeth hit each corner of the room.

He smiled. The corners of his mouth twitched. "I did it. I broke her jaw." Then using the motivation he obtained from physically breaking her, he continued to pummel her makeup-worn face. "Bitch! Whore! Slut! Cunt! I gave you everything, yet you took it all!"

Almost halfway through his purging, Steward felt pressure wrapped around his triceps and his body separating from Draya's.

"Stew! What are you doing? Stop, man!" Willard strengthened his grip, only for Steward to pull himself from his hold with a hissing, low growl.

Determined more than before and now seeing his ex-wife's face on Draya's, he squeezed both her shoulders, straightened her so that her unconscious face faced him, and tossed her to the floor.

Mounted over her, he placed his pointer finger in the air, where he wiggled it from left to right. "You've been a bad girl. I'll show you what bad girls deserve." The bottom of the construction boots repeatedly stomped and jammed inside Draya's hip, stomach, and occasionally her legs. "There's no coming back. You've done it now!" Globs of spit and bile flew from Steward's mouth between each word, landing on Draya.

"Fuckin' bitch."

Kick after kick, stomp after stomp, Steward's aggression worsened as every pain-stricken hit perfectly aligned with Draya's head. Steward dropped his foot. His body turned right and quickly collapsed beside Draya.

Hollering, he rolled off the arm his body fell onto and grabbed at it with his good hand. His eyes shut, and when they opened, he stared into Willard's.

"You fucking faggot!" Steward pushed himself up, ignoring the pain pulsating through him.

Willard's lips trembled, and his fingers twitched. "Leave her alone."

Steward raided Willard's personal space. The instant Willard broke eye contact and blinked, Steward backslapped him. Willard's head and back slammed into the nearby wall, stopping him from flying farther across the room. Hunched over, Willard fought to catch his breath and grabbed the back of his head. The moist, sticky feeling glazed over his hand, confirming what he feared. He was bleeding.

"Pussy," Steward mumbled. He used his thumb to wipe both sides of his nose before looking down at Draya and snatching her up from the floor by her locs. "Time to go for a walk, Sleeping Beauty."

He wrapped her dreads twice around his hand and maliciously pulled. It was a modern-day reen-actment of Achilles dragging Hector's body around in circles. He dragged and pulled her in every direction. His rose-colored hand deepened in color with every move made, tightening with every angry, bitter thought centering around his ex-wife.

"Stew! Calm down, man! What you need? What you want? I can make it happen." Willard slapped both palms against the delicate chest he tried pushing out. "Stew!"

By the end of Willard's sentence, Steward ended his violent march. He released Draya's hair, and her head slapped against the carpet.

Willard tore his eyes from what he hoped was not a head-injured Draya and stared at Steward's back. His lips poked out and formed into the letter O. After capturing his meek, frightened voice, he forced it out with nerves preserved for public speaking. "Steward, calm down, man. Whatever it is, we can fix it."

Once answered with silence, Willard watched the perspiration droplets grow, which decorated the back of Steward's shirt and circled his underarms. The more Steward violently breathed in and out, the faster his sweat monsters grew. Suddenly, Steward slapped his palms against his forehead and spat out several crippling sobs designated for pain and failure. His ashy hands slowly slid down his face and balled into fists. With irregular breathing, Steward dragged his construction boots to the other side of the room, his eyes lodged on the miniature bar nestled in the corner.

Big-eyed and mouth agape, Willard crawled over to Draya and checked her pulse. The presence of her low heart rate calmed him some.

"Thank God," he whispered. Then gently, he slid one hand beneath her head. His fingertips grazed a bump forming behind her head.

"You're OK, you're OK," he softly repeated into her ear. He kept Steward in sight.

"I fuckin' hate you!" Steward yelled.

Red eyes watered with pain, his volatile tone broke through Willard's chest and hit his heart. This man was aching, broken, and checked out from the world he once took comfort in.

Draya's eyes flicked open and closed. Her mouth twitched and very slowly opened. Air escaped as she tried to speak.

"Rest, Draya, I'm here. I got you." Willard put one finger on her lips.

She took a deep breath, then shortly after released air. She tried to form words. In the midst of her struggling to communicate, the loud and irking sound of the hotel's phone disturbed the chaos Steward brought into the room. Willard and Steward's eyes met. Neither blinked; however, both communicated.

What do we do?

We answer.

Who answers? And what do we say?

"Get it," Steward demanded. He wiped the sweat cascading down his eyebrows. He licked his lips and chucked back the brown liquor, burning from the inside out.

Willard lowered Draya's head on the carpet met by countless feet over the years.

"Make them go away," Steward instructed.

He tossed back a drink. Staring at the empty glass, he refilled it and repeated the process.

Willard rotated his shoulders backward. He looked up at the ceiling and swallowed. "Hello?"

"Good evening. This is the front desk calling. We've received several complaints from guests regarding the noise. Is everything OK?"

Steward poured another round, all while staring at Willard.

"I'm sorry for the disturbance. I turned the television up a little too high. My favorite movie is on. With old age, your hearing tends to go."

Steward nodded.

"Are you sure, sir?"

"Positive."

"Then, on behalf of Kansas, we welcome you and ask that you please lower the television."

"Will do."

"Thank you, and enjoy your stay."

Slowly, Willard placed the telephone back on its cradle. His inner self hoped and cried out for the hotel to demand their departure. Sadly, without that demand, he was left to fend for himself.

"We good?"

Willard eyed the bloody footsteps leading from Draya's body to the bar. Its details, the exact replica of the bottom of Steward's boots.

"Will, are we good?"

Overwhelmed by the footprint's appearance, Willard allowed himself to check out mentally and disconnect from reality.

"Umm, no, no. We're not good. They want us out."

"Fuck, how the hell are we supposed to do that when that obese tub of lard is passed out?" Steward's head pointed in the direction Draya lay.

Willard looked at his friend's battered body. "You go. I'll stay here. I'll wait until she wakes up, and then we'll leave. Housekeeping won't come until morning."

Steward poured another glass of clear liquor. He took a sip. "I like that idea." His head nodded up and down before finishing the contents of the glass. "Who knew a fag such as yourself was bright." He looked behind him long enough to wave Willard over. "Have a drink with me before I go. Let's toast to my punching bag of an ex-wife over there, and your balls finally dropping." He laughed a hearty, accomplished laugh.

Willard looked over the bronze Buddha statue acting as a centerpiece for the room's table. "Sure. Mind pouring me a full glass? I'll have what you're having. Clean glasses are right below you."

Steward retrieved a glass hanging from the bar's lower half and acted as a bartender. "Let's do this again. Next week good? I've taken some time off work."

Willard grabbed the head of the statue.

"Next week's good. Just tell me when."

Although Willard's glass was full, Steward kept pouring, the liquor overflowing. "You think fatty would join us again? I'd make it worth her while."

Willard stood behind him. "I don't know. You have to ask her when she wakes up."

"It'll probably be best if you—"

The cracking sound let off from the statue connecting with Steward's head held no resemblance to the sound of Draya's jaw breaking. Steward fell to the floor, his hands clasped to his head as the dreadful roar escaped from the pit of his stomach. Sadly, the protection his hands provided helped none. His flesh was useless against Willard's repeated beating. Willard hit Steward until his face, hands, and shirt were covered in blood. Steward's head was completely dismantled. His insides leaked out. Willard's arms began to ache, and his running out of breath was the only reason he ended the bashing.

Willard wiped whatever blood he could from his face with a stack of napkins left on the bar. The drink prepared for him, he instantly devoured despite the blood-coated rim. Finishing each glass filled with liquor, he washed all the used glasses and wiped down the bar and wherever else he touched. He mimicked all his years of watching crime TV, his OCD instinct fresh and alive.

Minus the blood splatter, Willard did a better job cleaning than housekeeping ever had. He stood in the middle of the room, nodding in approval of his work. His head moved up and down and didn't stop until Steward's faceless body came into view.

"Last but not least."

Willard grabbed each of Steward's arms and dragged him behind the bar. He kicked aside fingers lost in Steward's attempt to protect his face in the process. With Steward out of sight and his work completed, Willard removed each item of clothing, all except his boxers that sagged and dropped at the sides. Gently, yet diligently, he cleaned off a bloody Draya. Stripping the bed of its blanket, he covered her cold, goose-bumped skin. Her swollen, heavily bruised, cut-up face left no room for his friend to be recognized. He slid underneath the blanket beside her and moved in close.

"You're safe now. Everything's OK," he whispered. His lips grazed her ear with every word. "I got you."

In one maneuver, he pulled down her leggings and panties. His groin pushed through the slit of his boxers.

"I got you," he whispered softly. "I got you."

Lost in a fog while deaf to the world, Draya stared out in front of her. The king-size bed transformed into a deserted island in the middle of nature's jungle amongst the wild who'd protect and understand her. She stood surrounded by vines and large leaf plants that supplied shade. Berries coated the ground, neighboring twigs, and grass. Coconuts dangled overhead, their shells moist and glistening from the morning's rain. Butterflies in all the colors of a crayon box displayed an aerial art show. They flew past her face, their wings tickling her cheeks.

"Breathe," a voice far off into the sky instructed. "Breathe." She took heed, closed her eyes, and breathed in and out deeply. Opening her eyes, she smiled at the sea turtle slipping inside the ocean. Opening her eyelids allowed her to witness the tide easing itself to the tips of her toes. Its cold touch shut her eyes and quickened her breathing, a knot fixed in her throat. Followed by a countdown of numbers, her breathing leveled out, and her eyes opened. Her island a mirage, and Willard her reality.

"Draya?" Cautiously he waved a hand in front of her face. "You OK?"

Draya looked around, repeatedly blinking her eyes. "Yeah, yeah, I'm OK."

"I thought I lost you there for a minute." Willard slightly moved his head in different directions while examining Draya.

"You really killed him?"

Willard's lips plunged inward before answering. "I had to," he admitted in a low tone. "He hurt you. What else was I to do?" Snot crept out of Willard's left nostril, and immediately, he wiped it away using the back of his hand.

"How'd you get us out?"

Willard diverted his stare. "It rained that morning. Stew wore a hoodie he took off before he—" He caught himself. "I wore it when we left. You were in bad shape, but at five a.m., you woke up and somehow managed to walk out with me. I put a robe on you to cover up your bruises. What really helped us was no one was in the lobby when we left. Even the front desk was empty." Willard placed his hand on her knee. "You don't remember leaving?"

"No, I remember nothing past entering the room." Draya shifted and cleared her throat. "Did he rape me?"

Willard put his hands behind her neck and squeezed the fat below her hairline. "No way. You weren't touched like that in any way that night." He locked eyes with her, then pulled her head forward to rest on his shoulder.

Eyes shut, she didn't resist the peaceful gesture for a good thirty seconds. Finally, she lifted her head and pushed her body away from his. "Good," she voiced loudly.

Willard licked his lips and lightly tapped his knee. "Well, if you ask me, you look better now than before the surgeries and jaw wiring. I don't care if you did drop weight because your jaw was wired shut." He playfully plucked her cheek.

Draya smirked. "You're a horrible liar, Will." She stood. "I'm sure they'll shit on us for being so late, but if you're still down to give a show, so am I." Draya stretched her arms and flab jiggled.

Willard hopped up. "Always!"

"All right, but fuck me naked. None of that dick poking out of your boxers slit shit. I can't stand that. Pissed me off since the very first time we screwed."

Chapter 4

"Sonny, I need Huntsman number two out on set in five minutes."

Sonny took a step back and, from a short distance, examined the silicone blisters and wounds plaguing the pale, hairy face of his human canvas. Attentively, he studied the application of his work.

"Five minutes, Sonny. Not five and a half, not six, and not seven."

Sonny held his open hand out into the air and in the direction of the clipboard-holding, headset-wearing short woman.

The small woman's pointer finger stabbed into the air. "Five fuckin' minutes, Son—"

Not halfway into her rant, her voice jammed inside her throat, followed by her placing her hand over the headset covering her right ear. Then nodding in response to the voice in her ear, she released the curtain.

Sonny's open palm transformed into a crocket's middle finger swaying from left to right. He bent down, leaned forward, and added color to the fake wounds.

"Put me on the clock. I don't give a damn if you
are the production manager. He'll come out when
my masterpiece is complete. Short, spiky-haired
heifer."

In the process of adding color to the tip of a blis-
ter, Sonny's eye picked up on a mysterious, small,
black dot staining the center of the Huntsman's
forehead. After several failed attempts to rub away
the imperfection on the villain's face, he stuck his
tongue out, licked his finger, and immediately the
Huntsman pulled back. "Don't put no damn spit
on me."

Sonny grabbed the actor by the back of his
bald cap and forced him forward. His blue bangs
roughly swayed left, then right. "It ain't gonna
kill you. Take it like a man." Sonny's moist finger
aggressively rubbed away the dark spot, leaving
the Huntsman's face tainted with nothing other
than makeup.

"And you wonder why you're left with doing
all those small pieces inside of full-on prosthetic
looks," Draya voiced out loud. She then asked
the mystical creature in her chair to open and
close her mouth and eyes. Pleased with her facial
movements, regardless of the silicone and glue
applied, she had her move her head from left to
right. "Good," Draya whispered. She brushed over
the actress's cheeks and chin. "Look up for me,
Helen."

"Ummmm, excuse me? Since I'm too busy wondering what the issue is, do a girl a favor and tell me why I'm not doing a full face, Draya. I'll wait." Sonny crossed his arms. Strands of tiny hairs, which separated from his bangs, were reunited with one swift move of his head. The brightly lit room showcased his otherwise bald head.

Draya added crystals to the lines and shapes applied on Helen's neck. She repositioned her head toward the mirror. The direction gave Helen a clear view of her special effects makeup transformation. "Damn, Draya, Jeanie was right. You *are* good. Special effects makeup is your thing."

"Little girl!" Sonny snapped, "Don't you see we're having a conversation?" He poked out his filler-filled lips.

"Right there, there's one reason," Draya replied over her shoulder. "You have no people skills. Licking your damn finger and rubbing it on a client's face like you're someone's damn grandma. Shit like that is what has you on the lower pedestal here and damn near on your way out."

"And who the fuck are you, Draya? Employee of the month? I've been doing this shit for years, so who the hell do you think *you're* trying to school?" Sonny pointed to the red-stained brush he held at her.

"Exactly. You've been doing this shit for years, yet you're right where you started, doing low-budget films because your ass can't take orders and control your mouth. So they got you here doing rookie work." Draya stepped back and gave her work a once-over. "I'm just trying to warn you so you can avoid hitting the stroll to support that vicious name-brand addiction of yours when they fire your ass."

Helen's body quivered with bouts of chuckles that escaped her. "Zing."

"She zapped your ass, Sonny," Helen muttered. Payback for how he had just spoken to her. Chuckles mixed with head nods slammed the room.

"Sonny, I have to admit you wear some expensive threads," Reese confirmed. She dug in and out of boxes stacked in the back of the room. Articles of clothing stuck out of the top of the boxes. "I've been a part of handling wardrobe on sets for a few years now, and never have I come across clothing budgets that meet your price range."

Reese's assistant nodded.

Draya shrugged. "I'm just saying the streets like an exotic tight little piece of ass like yourself. They'll stretch your shit the fuck out, then get mad at you for walking around, sagging. So watch how you move in this business, and don't fuck up your reputation."

The once light chuckles grew into heavy laughs accompanied by a few damns and hell nos.

Although laughing, the Huntsman admitted, "I don't want to hear all of that."

Sonny looked from the actors to costume designers and assistants littering the small room. With every face he looked into, they met his stare with teary eyes and joker smiles.

Each snicker made at his expense was absorbed and screaming inside Sonny's mind. They matched the entertained, high-pitched laughs that stretched across his high school years. The only difference lay in the fact that today's chuckles were more mature. Nevertheless, the intentions and insensitivity remained untouched.

Sonny tossed the stipple sponge on the mirrored table and crossed his arms, his fresh, clear polished nails hidden.

"Bitch, I thought you were a makeup artist. When the fuck did you become a comedian? And when the hell did you become a part of my damn business?" Sonny's tone transitioned from a spicy diva to a hardened prison guard. He cleared his throat, pulling back the man in him.

"When we started working the same movie, and I do the bulk of the creating on top of applying and removing because you're too mouthy and slow. Your unprofessionalism affects us all, Sonny."

Draya removed the cape from Helen and patted her on the shoulder. "You're done, Helen."

Helen stood and looked in the mirror. Her mystical, ocean-inspired creature transformation was completed with gills, rhinestones, and tiny bite marks.

Finally, Draya looked at Sonny and not her work. "When are you going to learn?"

Sonny's eyes widened. "I'll learn when your ass learns to leave the donuts alone." Helen turned from the mirror. The costume designers ended their inventory search, and the Huntsman's chin hit his chest.

"Are you serious?" Helen questioned, her words seasoned with disgust.

Reese infused herself. "That's uncalled for, Sonny. I can't believe you went there."

Each set of eyes radiated sweltering heat meant to set Sonny in flames.

"*That's* all you got?" Draya challenged.

"Jetson, this is where makeup is done. Budget is small; however, we make pretty good with what we have." Jeanie's voice entered the room before she had.

Staff members reverted to their duties once the curtain was pulled back and her physical presence was made known. However, before the anti-Sonny campaign ended, Draya and Sonny gave each other the "fuck you" glare.

Draya turned her back on the room to clean her workspace. Jeanie made her rounds around the small room, individually introducing the strong jawline, curly-haired, bronze-colored man named Jetson.

"Jetson, this is Reese, our lead costume designer. Her taste for design is fresh and original—the very thing fantasy films have been lacking these last few years. Her creativity is unmatched. Reese, this is Jetson, Phillip's nephew."

Reese shook his hand.

"That's all I get, Jeanie? No snazzy introduction? Man, I gotta step up my game in this business."

Jeanie joined in on Jetson's laughter.

Reese pointed at him. "The nephew in film school back in LA?"

Jetson rubbed his hands together. "My uncle's been talking about me. Good things, I assume, since you haven't confused me with the nephew who's in rehab back in L.A."

The three grinned.

"What else has my uncle mentioned about me?"

"Good things. Like you're who's going to change Hollywood for the better, and the very reason he's even doing movies of this small magnitude. Says you put him in his place when you said, and I quote, *'just because you're in Hollywood don't mean you have to get Hollywood. So give back to the up-and-comings and mentor,'*" Reese recounted.

Jetson rubbed the back of his neck and half-smiled.

"Damn, I didn't expect the world to know what I said."

"I'm glad we do," Jeanie slightly screamed. "We now know who to thank for this opportunity. Phillip working on this project gives us all a good look and makes dreams come true. Thank you, Jetson."

Reese nodded in agreement. The color red blossomed in Jetson's cheeks. He turned away from the women and faced the makeup stations. "Yes, now, *that's* where the magic happens." His hands clapped once. "Please take me to Wonderland." Then without waiting for Jeanie to lead, he rushed over to a slow-working Sonny.

Jeanie approached Sonny and the Huntsman. She cleared her throat and gave Sonny's work a quick once-over.

The introduction between Jetson and Gary, who played the film's Huntsman, carried on for some time. Jeanie fed the conversation. She hoped for some reason—any reason—Sonny would disappear, and no introduction would be needed.

Jetson was still engaged in a conversation three minutes later. So, Jeanie took the opportunity to whisper in Sonny's ear.

"Behave and fuckin' finish this up already. It's only a couple of gashes and shit." She rolled her eyes soon after Jetson turned toward Sonny.

Hand extended, Jetson introduced himself. "Jetson Cobbs."

Sonny placed the handles of the two tools he used in his mouth, freeing his hands for Jetson's handshake.

"Jetson, here we have Sonny, one of our two artists. He does lots of smaller pieces, such as wounds along with beauty makeup." Jeanie forced a closed-mouth smile.

Sonny shook Jetson's hand. His smile stretched twice its size.

"Jeanie's being modest. My talent surpasses what she's describing. Makeup-wise, this film is not challenging; therefore, my services are limited. However, they are locked and loaded when needed." His blue bang fell forward. Sonny pushed it back in place, a delightful smile staining his face.

Both sides of Jetson's mouth slouched while he nodded. "Motivation, the backbone of every film, is what my uncle always told me growing up. So, keep that drive, Sonny. I'm sure I'll need talent when I finally work on my first film."

"Speaking of talent," Jeanie led Jetson away, her right hand on his shoulder and left hand leading the way, "Draya is the real thing. Best decision made here, makeup-wise. We've gone through two artists before getting lucky and landing her. She does it all."

"Nope, I don't do beauty." Draya's back remained turned, her energy still off from the confrontation with Sonny.

"Why is that?" Hands stuffed in the pockets of his jeans, Jetson stepped close behind Draya.

Draya shut her makeup case and locked it. "It's not realistic. It's too pretty. I'm not a pretty type of woman." She bent down and slid her case underneath her station's bottom shelf, her rear-end grazing Jetson's crotch on the way down. Draya looked behind her. Her eyes traveled up Jetson's body until she hit his face. He smiled at her, following her gaze.

"Oh shit. I mean, I'm sorry." He stepped back. "I have a little hearing problem, so I had to get close to ensure I heard you." Jetson touched his left ear. "I'm sorry for invading your space." Without her permission, the corners of Draya's mouth turned upward. Right before teeth showed and lips parted, she wiggled her mouth around and dropped off the oncoming hint of flattery. Stone-faced, she focused on her station's leftover jewels.

"It's OK," she replied, her voice void of any emotion. One by one, she dropped cobalt blue stones into a pill organizer-turned-accessory organizer. "No harm done." Finally, she paused and set her sights on the man-made creature in the room. "Helen," Draya called out, "why don't you come and meet Mr. Cobbs."

"Oh yes, Helen, come, meet Jetson," Jeanie encouraged.

The organizer contained no more than eight stones before Draya looked into the mirror and saw him returning her stare. Flutters the size of butterfly wings erupted inside her stomach. Draya jammed her hand inside the pocket of her slacks, grabbed a slab of skin, and pinched herself. She twisted and turned the fat. Her fingers swam inside her skin, piercing pain and erasing all positive and womanly feelings making their way to the surface.

"Nice to meet you, Helen."

Inside the mirror, Draya watched Jetson shake Helen's hand. They engaged in small talk just as he had with everyone else. When he laughed, his teeth made an appearance, big and white. Perfectly cared for teeth that never missed a dentist appointment. Teeth she imagined her tongue gliding over if given a chance.

Eyes closed, Draya dug into her skin with more aggression, then pulled forcefully. Finally, she opened her eyes, her reflection looking her way. She searched her station for a tissue to wipe away the dripping tears. She confiscated a napkin from inside a drawer and held it up to her face in midair. Her hand froze, and she stood there. For seconds, the napkin was forced to wait to do its job because, at that moment, watching Jetson watch her through the mirror was much more fun.

Chapter 5

"I'm telling ya, nobody's gonna want your fat ass." Segel jammed hot sauce-saturated chitlins in his mouth. Before he swallowed, he stuffed some bisque inside his mouth too. "You can diet all you want. That shit never works. Either the weight comes back, or you're left with stretch marks. Lifelong reminders that your ass is really a fat bitch in a skinny bitch body and don't no man want a used-to-be fat bitch."

The fork he used to point Draya's way turned downward and stabbed into the red-centered steak.

"That's not true. I wouldn't be here if someone didn't want your sumo wrestler ass."

"Ha-ha, very funny. I'm a man. Shit's different for men."

Draya slumped down in her chair and folded her arms. "I'm not eating that shit," she mumbled.

"Yes, the fuck you are. You know how much this shit costs? Food ain't cheap, so your big ass gonna eat this shit, and you gonna like this shit."

He mixed his mac and cheese into his mashed potatoes and did some mumbling to himself. "Young, fast tail tryin'a tell me what she gonna eat, bull-fuckin'-shit."

Draya waited for her father to stuff more of his six-course, fatty meal into his mouth.

"How the hell am I fast when you just said no one wants a fat girl?" She shook her head. "And food wouldn't be so expensive if you stopped eating everything you buy in one sitting and let shit sit in the fridge for some time."

Segel held his hand up and sped up his chewing. Then two swallows later, he held up one finger. "Wait, now, hold on, now," he managed to let out but not before a piece of chitlin flew out of his mouth and landed inside the pitcher of fruit punch.

Draya leaned over to the side and swallowed the vomit that crept up her throat. Then when it was safe, she sat up again and fanned herself with her hand.

"I ain't never said a motherfucker wouldn't fuck a big bitch. I said don't none want a big bitch. There's a difference. These little 15-year-old fuckers out there dying to get their little dick wet by a big bitch or skinny bitch. Don't matter. And you, you a big bitch with low self-esteem, so they coming for your ass."

Draya slammed both hands on the table and pushed herself up. "I don't have low self-esteem.

I wouldn't be fat if it weren't for you. For years, you stuffed this shit down my throat. You had me thinking eating like this was normal. This shit is poison." In one swift movement, she cleared the table of her mountain-high plate of food, utensils, and the fruit punch he had contaminated. *"I looked at the photos of me when I was little. I wasn't meant to be big. You made me this way."*

"You done lost your damn mind, girl." Segel wiped his hands on the pants of his overalls and stood from the table. *"Hell naw,"* he hollered after seeing perfectly good food wasted on the floor. He stumped one of his giant boots and trained his sausage finger at the mess. *"You gonna eat that shit. I don't give a damn. You gonna eat that shit. There's people here in Mississippi that would die for this food, and you gonna throw it on the floor? Hell naw."*

"You're a farmer, Segel. You grow food. It gets no better than that. Yet, we eat like this? Why?" Draya's eyes watered, although nothing fell.

"We got corn on the table. What you talking 'bout?"

Draya slapped the sides of her head with her palms, her breathing irregular and painful with every breath. Then hand on her chest, she sat down and took several deep, slow breaths.

She abandoned screaming and spoke slow and calm. *"Just tell me why you did this to me.*

What good does this do for me to have high blood pressure and cholesterol?" Tears fell. "I don't want to get diabetes."

Segel cleared his throat; however, he didn't utter a word.

"I can't lose weight without the proper diet, and you refuse to supply me with that. Why? Please, tell me why."

Wake up . . . Wake up, beautiful. It's time to get up.

Wet-cheeked Draya opened her eyes. Her phone alarm called her beautiful and continuously told her it was time to get up. Things were a blur when she turned the lamp on and turned off her alarm. Quiet and alone, the dream she was pulled from replayed in her mind and added more tears to her already damp T-shirt.

The back of her hands wiped her face clean and got rid of the blurriness obstructing her vision. *Don't do it.* Opening the drawer to her nightstand, she went for the king-size chocolate bar amongst the gummy bears and bags of chips. When she read the note beside it, she paused. *You don't need those. Throw them out.* Draya picked up the chocolate bar and turned it over. *Throw me away,* the small Post-It demanded, and like every other time, Draya left them alone but didn't throw them away, leaving herself in limbo yet again.

The time on the cable box read five a.m. Draya repositioned her bonnet and threw her legs over the side of the bed. Then instead of dragging herself into the shower to begin her day, she just sat there.

Nobody's gonna want your fat ass. I ain't never said a motherfucker wouldn't fuck a big bitch. I said don't none want a big bitch. There's a difference.

Draya slapped her hands down on her thighs and rubbed. The friction created a burning sensation. She watched the color of her skin and the stretch marks turn red. The sight of the numerous lines forced her to rub harder to eliminate all evidence of who she was forced to become.

You can diet all you want. That shit never works. Either the weight comes back, or you're left with stretch marks, lifelong reminders that your ass is really fat.

After several more rubs, Draya's skin began to peel. Fighting the pain, she continued with the friction, the heels of her feet digging into the bamboo rug. Finally, when the marks didn't vanish but instead appeared clearer in their rosy hue, Draya stood to her feet, grabbed her phone, and headed for the bathroom. The need for a mental escape intensified. Taped on the bathroom mirror, she read off motivational quotes courtesy of the internet.

The beauty you're looking for is right in front of you.

You survived your past for a reason. Keep going.

Be kind to yourself. You deserve love.

She touched them with every quote she read, a slight feeling of contentment settling within her. After mouthing the last quote, she revisited the past once again. *You a big bitch with low self-esteem.* Draya reread all the positive quotes despite her mental being a battleground for her thoughts to duke it out in. The demeaning voices in her head spoke loud and fast, emphasizing words such as *pig, lonely, disgusting,* and *worthless*. The game of mental Ping-Pong caused Draya to break out in a sweat.

She squatted down with her phone still in hand. She tugged and pulled at her hair, the desperate need for a distraction imperative. It took some time for her to stand on her feet. Finally, Draya looked at herself in the mirror and roared, "Fuck it."

She snatched open the medicine cabinet and reached for the bag of Twizzlers next to the rubbing alcohol. "Don't do it" was written in bold red letters on a lined piece of paper taped to the candy.

Nobody's gonna want your fat ass.

"Fuck." With the arm of a pitcher, Draya threw the candy across the room. It slapped against the baby blue shower tiles and slid down into the tub.

Draya flopped down on the toilet. The lid wiggled before the center of her rump sank in some. Stuck in the middle of both her hands like cold cuts in between bread, Draya clutched her phone. After three minutes, she stopped contemplating whether to contact the only person incapable of passing judgment and made the call.

She waited the designated ten minutes for a return call. The five minutes it took for Draya's phone to ring while negative thoughts stomped through her mind were torturous. Then finally, the constant ringing ended, and a familiar voice filled the line.

"Draya, is everything OK?"

Draya could hear Dr. Vanity's slippers walk across hardwood floors and the office door's squeaking sounds when she entered her place of business.

"I had the dream again."

"I see." Dr. Vanity momentarily paused. "Did you see it through?"

Draya leaned back until her head met the wall and continuously banged it against the baby blue tiles. Her dreads blocked any pain from occurring, so she slammed her head harder and faster. Slow and steady heavy throbbing kicked in and escalated the more she banged. Finally, when her eyes saw specks of white before her, her pain threshold was met. *There we go,* she thought.

"Draya?"

"No. My alarm went off."

This time, when her head hit the wall, she accidentally bit down on her tongue.

The click of a pen's head filled the phone. There was no doubt in Draya's mind that it was the same gold-plated engraved pen Dr. Vanity faithfully used during their sessions.

"If your alarm hadn't gone off, do you think you would have gotten his answer?" Draya's toes curled. "I don't know. Maybe."

"Humph," Dr. Vanity let out.

"You don't believe me?"

"I don't believe you believe that answer."

Draya parted her legs and leaned forward. Her shoulders caved in. "Then what do you think? What do you believe?"

"Do you *really* want to know because if you're using this question only to deflect, you're wasting our time and a co-pay?"

"Tell me."

"OK." A slight cough came through the phone. After Dr. Vanity cleared her throat, she asked to be excused. "Now, in my opinion, you wouldn't have seen it through. You're not ready to face your past." She paused, leaving an opening for Draya to speak if she wished. "You've known the answer for years, but you won't allow yourself to relive those moments by repeating his words. Not even in your dreams, and because of that, forgive me, but I believe you're tormenting yourself."

"*Excuse* me?" Draya moved her phone from one ear to the other.

"Burying your emotions and not dealing with them does nothing but keep them alive, so you act out in self-destructive ways to release the pain. You'd do anything to avoid your demons instead of conjuring up them."

Draya's mouth opened, her truth. Then triggering discomfort, she swallowed her past and replaced it with a lie. "Interesting concept but ridiculously far from the truth."

"Draya, you've been a patient of mine for three years now, and you managed to admit you're selling yourself in our second session. Yet, you have never told me your father's answer, the key to turning your life around. What does *that* tell you?"

"You should let sleeping dogs lie."

"No, Draya, it says you'd rather sacrifice yourself, your happiness, and your health instead of taking the necessary steps to heal. Now, *that* scares me. Your coping mechanisms scare me."

Draya had never heard her doctor speak with such passion, concern, and fear.

"You shouldn't be. If you ask me, you're reaching. Thank you for your observation, but it's time I go, Dr. V. See you during my regular scheduled time?"

Dr. Vanity's failure to immediately respond had Draya question what she wanted to say but wouldn't.

"Draya," she finally said, "did something recently change or happen in your life?"

Draya leaned inside the shower and turned on the hot water. "What?"

"Has anything . . . new happened?"

"Why?" Draya stood erect, her focus on her reflection.

"I've been following the timing. This dream seems to pop up, and it's always when something big in your life transpires. For example, when you took on camming, major shifts you take in life or feel deeply about seem to bring on this dream. I'm trying to connect why."

"Nothing's happened."

"Are you sure?" Dr. Vanity pushed.

Draya turned away from the mirror and sat back down on the toilet seat. She scratched her head and felt the lump behind it.

"I'm working on the set of a fantasy film. The director's nephew came by yesterday." She stopped talking. If she stopped breathing, held her breath, and listened carefully, she'd hear Dr. Vanity's erratic breathing. "If I didn't know better, if I didn't know who I am, I'd think . . ." Draya licked her lips.

"You'd think what?" Dr. Vanity pressed. "You'd think what?" she asked for the second time. However, this time, she asked more slowly, each word more pronounced and clearly spoken.

"I'd think he was interested," Draya rattled off. "But that's only if I truly lost my mind and couldn't differentiate reality from fiction. I know the truth."

Dr. Vanity's dog barked uncontrollably, his barking so loud that Draya thought he was on three-way with her and his owner. Dr. Vanity shooed him away and demanded he shut up.

"Let's say you've lost your mind, and you're somewhere off planet Earth. How would that make you feel if you thought he was interested, or even just flirting because he found you attractive?"

"Again, you're reaching, Dr. V." Draya leaned her head back, but no violence was initiated this time.

"I am. I most certainly am."

Draya chuckled. "OK, I'll play along. I've lost my mind. I'm just out there, right?"

"You're in no-man's-land," the doctor established.

"I'd feel—"

I did you a favor. You can never want to be wanted if you know you never will be. No one will ever want you, and if you think they do, you're wrong.

"I gotta go. Have a good day, Dr. V. I'm sorry for the wake-up call."

"Wait! What's going on? It's a hypothetical question. I'm asking purely hypothetically."

"Dress it up how you want, Doc. I won't allow you to fuck with my mind to the point where I think for even half a second that I'll ever be desired. I know where I stand. So stop trying to move me."

"Draya, *listen* to me," Dr. Vanity pleaded. "You're traumatized, damn near brainwashed, but if you just try what I'm trying to show you, you will—"

"Cut the shit." Draya's head shook the bun out of her hair bow. "I'm not in therapy for you to feed me what *you* think I need to eat. I'm in therapy because I'm a lonely bitch trying to have someone to talk to other than my john, who's my fuckin' best friend." Draya's bottom lip twitched. "I know who I am and where I stand. Stop trying to undo that; stop trying to . . ." she hesitated. "Stop trying to sell me an unattainable dream that hurts more than what my father told me."

"Draya, I would nev—"

"Have a good day, Dr. V, and with your next patient, try not to push so hard. Not everyone can hold on to the cliff." With that, Draya hung up.

Her head hurt, and an aching in her chest was so intense that the only time she could recall such an agonizing feeling dated back to her teen years.

The bathroom filled with steam, her personal and sweat-worthy sauna. Draya moved to wipe the mirror clean. However, as soon as she attempted, she reneged. Her triple chin, bubble cheeks, and massive neck were nothing acceptable for anyone to see, let alone stomach—herself included. Then the intrusive sound of her phone ringing kicked into her mind. The sight of Dr. Vanity's name flashing across the screen accompanied by a photo of her slim, well-proportioned face and toned, thin arms hidden underneath her blouse was a body image she didn't need to be thrown at her. Draya declined the call, and when it rang again, sent her to voicemail.

She opened her medicine cabinet—her world of self-destruction. Still hearing the phone ring, she grabbed the Twizzlers. Opening the package, she tossed her self-help note into the toilet and ate her kryptonite. When finished, she went for whatever else edible thing the cabinet contained. Wrappers on the floor and her skin peppered with sweat, she stepped inside the shower fully clothed. The Triple X T-shirt, double D bra, and Triple X panties covered whatever skin it could.

Draya hugged herself, the heated water cutting into her skin and her tears slashing into her soul.

Chapter 6

The excessive skin crowding her arms, stomach, neck, and ass jiggled with each fast foot-pounding step. Its side-to-side movement weighed Draya down and added time to her tardiness.

Draya adjusted the falling straps of her backpack securely on her right shoulder and shuddered when Jeanie stepped in her path, arms crossed, and her resting bitch face on ten. Draya kept moving, speaking only when bypassing her. "I'm sorry, I'm sorry, something came up. I got the schedule. I'm on it." Draya turned the corner to the makeup room straight ahead.

Jeanie caught up with Draya and pulled her aside by the arm, her Mohawk ponytail swaying recklessly.

"I'm not gonna ride you about being late. You're one of the few that actually gives a shit about their job and this film. I respect that, but the schedules changed, and our asses are against the wall." Jeanie snatched a sheet of paper from the trusty folder she was never seen without and handed it to Draya.

Draya scanned over the itinerary. "You kidding me? I'm the *only* makeup artist? Where's Sonny?" She slapped the paper against her hip.

"Little fucker's claiming food poisoning."

Draya rolled her eyes.

"Listen, I know you feel fucked right now."

"You don't say."

"But I know you got this. The scene we're shooting today does not include our most intricate creatures." Jeanie touched her earpiece. "Give me two minutes." She focused back on Draya. "You'll have someone helping you." Her thin lips, plastered with black lipstick, broke into a smile. Her cheeks lifted upward, and the piercing acting as a dimple sank in.

"Why didn't you lead with that? I'm good then." She crumbled up the itinerary and continued on her way.

"Draya, let me first tell you who it is." Again, Jeanie rushed to play catch-up. "Damn, for a big girl, she can move," she whispered.

Too far ahead to hear Jeanie call out to her, Draya reached the makeup room within seconds. Actresses sat in both her and Sonny's chairs, the fairy in Sonny's chair with makeup that appeared almost complete.

"Ladies, I do apologize for you waiting! Now, let's get things going." She dropped her backpack at her station, unpacked the supplies she brought from home, and gave the actress in Sonny's seat a thorough once-over. "You look good. This stand-in artist knows what they're doing."

Rubbing hand sanitizer on her hands, Draya waved them around for instant drying and lifted the fairy's head by the chin. "Clean and well detailed. More color blending needs to happen to give the illusion of decaying from the previous fire scene." She turned the actress's head to the side. "They forgot to apply the fairy ears."

"He's getting to that after he comes from the bathroom," the fairy chimed in. "I didn't know the boss's nephew did makeup."

Draya let her go. "Excuse me?"

"Phillip's nephew, what's his name?"

"Jetson," the petite actress occupying Draya's chair answered. "I can never forget a piece of eye candy's name. Humph, brother's a cutie."

A sudden feeling of nausea accompanied by a touch of light-headedness hit Draya.

Fuck.

"I didn't know he did makeup either, and I didn't know he'd be here today," Draya admitted.

The petite actress smiled before saying, "A surprise I can't say I'm mad at."

The curtain opened, and without Draya looking at who owned the black leather and suede high-top sneakers, her heart fluttered.

"Hey, Draya, nice seeing you again."

Draya took herself over to her station, where she opened her makeup box and emptied it of its necessities. When she put out the gelatin, she wished she had it in her to look into the face that belonged to the upbeat, respectful voice.

She faked frantically searching for something in her box. "Good morning, Mr. Cobbs."

"Mr. Cobbs? Oh, man. Please, don't place me in the last name category. First names are much more . . ."

"Personal?" Miss Petite filled in.

Her legs crossed and eyes batted uncontrollably just as she eased her glitter-coated nail into her mouth.

Jetson snapped his fingers. "Exactly. Addressing one another personally by first names makes the working environment a lot less tense. I'm hoping we'll make everyone forget my uncle's the director. I want to be treated like everyone else."

The fairy spun around to face Jetson. "How long will you be visiting us, Jetson?"

"For the next month. School's out, so why not stick around and get to the core of experiencing how the business is run?"

The feeling Draya always got when someone stared at her overwhelmed her nerves. Therefore, she dug deeper inside the makeup box.

"We didn't know you were a makeup artist," Fairy expressed. "Is that what you'll be doing when you enter the movie biz?"

Jetson grabbed the thin, bristle brush he had used previously. "I know the basics when it comes to SFX. As a kid, I was fascinated with horror makeup and wanted to learn more about it, so I did, but to call myself an artist is overdoing it. I don't have the talent or credentials to uphold the title." Jetson continued working where he left off on the fairy's chin. "Only the talented and gifted deserve the title. You know, people like Draya."

Draya stopped fiddling with her supplies, and her toes curled in her sneakers. Although she wanted to, she couldn't ignore a compliment, Draya was many things, but classless in a work environment was never one of them.

"Thank you. You're too kind, but anyone can do this job. It's really not a big thing," she shrugged off.

"Yeah, right!" Jetson's fairy objected. "This shit looks hard. I can barely apply eyeliner properly, and you think I can turn a human into a dragon? Nope. I'm leaving that to the gifted."

Contributing to the laughter in the room relieved some of Draya's nerves and helped her fall back into her talent wholeheartedly. After that, getting to work on her firefly fairy came naturally.

"Thanks, but seriously, if you practice hard enough and dedicate yourself to the craft, it comes easily." Draya handed the actress medical-grade adhesive. "Do me a favor and make sure there's nothing in this glue you're allergic to."

Reading the label, Miss Petite nodded and handed the jar back. "We're all good."

Carefully, Draya applied the prosthetic piece to her actress's face. Once secure and in place, her journey of coloring and detailing took place.

The time Draya and Jetson worked on their girls, conversation flowed effortlessly. The ongoing laughter and personal story sharing gave Draya a sense of belonging. Homeschooled from junior high through high school, she was robbed of practicing and bettering her social skills and building friendships.

"Jetson, you working mighty slow over there. Tinsley should have been done." Draya added more detail to Miss Petite's forehead.

Miss Petite raised her hand and said, "I ain't want to say anything, but yeah, even I know you need to put a little pep in your step, bruh."

Jetson lowered the tattered brush he used on her ears. "Y'all coming for ya boy? I told y'all earlier, I'm no artist."

"Oh, wait a minute. Did college boy just get hood? Where did your professional talk go?" Miss Petite questioned.

In union, Draya and Tinsley said, "I was thinking the same thing." Then the ladies laughed in unity.

Jetson placed his creativity back onto the fairy's warped ear. "See what happens when you get a little personal, call someone by their first name, and give a backseat to their status?"

Jetson cut his eyes to Draya, a swift move she caught.

"I hear you, brother. Point made," Miss Petite voiced.

Jetson moved on over to the right ear. "Man, y'all the only Black people here today, so if y'all didn't put your professional guards down, how was I supposed to survive not being 100 percent me? You know you can't fully let yourself go around white people. They always trying to see if you're one of the good ones."

Miss Petite held up her finger. "Draya, give me one second, just one second." She hopped out of her seat and approached Jetson. "Brother, you gotta give me a pound on that one. You're speaking the truth."

An enlightened brother with a touch of hood. So . . . damn . . . Draya wiped her hands on her jeans. A surge of pleasure raided her body, and a thin layer of sweat covered her skin. *Sexy.*

Miss Petite piggybacked off Jetson's comment on her way back to Draya's station. "White people always give off this vibe that you have to prove yourself while in their presence." Then using the arms of the chair, she pulled her small, short body into the seat. "When in reality, we don't have shit to prove. Our people's résumés speak for themselves."

Draya plucked a Kleenex out of its box and dapped her upper lip before wiping her forehead dry.

"I want to go to Africa one day, where we were kings and queens, and just soak up all my history. Y'all know what I mean?" Tinsley folded her hands in her lap and gazed out into nowhere.

"I know *exactly* what you mean," Miss Petite nodded.

"Me too," Jetson confirmed. "Going back to the motherland has always been a part of my life plan."

It wasn't until silence caved inside the room did Draya acknowledge she had checked out from the conversation and was obsessed with ridding herself of sweat. She rewound to the last thing she remembered.

"That's why I keep to myself. I can't stand"—Draya put up quotation marks using her fingers—"trying to be figured out. Especially by people who can't respect me, let alone fathom my pain."

"I hear that," Miss Petite cosigned.

"African American women are the least protected. Never will I allow my woman to go disrespected and suffer while with me. Not happening. Black women are queens for a reason."

The room stood still. The only movement was Miss Petite frantically fanning herself with her hand.

"OK, then. Jetson, do you have an older brother?" Tinsley half-jokingly, half-seriously asked.

"No, but you're done. Queen Draya, mind doing me the honors and looking over my work? You know, help a brother out?"

"Umph, he called you Queen Draya," Miss Petite said loud enough for only Draya's ears to catch.

Draya gave her a look and made her way to where Tinsley's face awaited. After several minutes of examination, Draya determined that she was more satisfied with Jetson's work than she had been earlier.

"This is really good. You've even fixed things I noticed earlier needing altering." She couldn't hold back. She smiled, and she smiled hard. "Very good."

Arms crossed, Jetson carried a Kool-Aid smile across his face. "I try to do my thing." Draya giggled and laid her hand softly on his arm. Then noticing him looking down at her touch, she quickly removed her hand and took a step back, an awkward smile on her face. "Good job." Then she gave him her back.

Idiot, she mouthed.

Jeanie poked her head in. "Jetson, Phillip would like to see you on set when you have a moment." In true Jeanie fashion, as quickly as she appeared, she disappeared.

"Excuse me, ladies."

Immediately after Jetson's exit, Draya exhaled.

"Giiiirrrl, he wantsss you," Miss Petite swerved around in her chair.

"What?" Draya played dumb.

"You heard me. This entire time, he was throwing hints like no one's business." She slapped the arm of the chair while squealing with glee.

Draya approached Miss Petite in a hurry. She grabbed her brush and leaned down to her. Miss Petite leaned as far back as she could. "Admit it. You want him too."

"He's not interested in me, Phoenix. Now, please come forward."

"Why? Because you're a big girl?"

Rolling her eyes and huffing, Draya responded, "Just big?"

"Big, obese, large, heavy, whatever you want to call it. He wants you and all the weight that comes with you."

"Draya?"

Draya gave Tinsley her attention.

"He should have been finished with my makeup. He told me that it would only be half an hour more before you showed up. Then you walk in, and a half hour turns into an hour and a half. Doesn't sound like a coincidence to me."

"I told you," Phoenix shouted.

Tinsley stood and stretched. Her shoulders dropped just before she planted her hand on

Draya's shoulder and headed for the cameras. "Send me an invite to the wedding."

Standing back in front of a now properly positioned Phoenix, Draya tried to continue applying color. However, when the brush was inches from Phoenix's face, she stopped. She felt a quick thumping in her chest and her ears. *Breathe, breathe.* She swallowed, shook her hand holding the brush, and tried again. This time, the bristles made contact and swept the lid of Phoenix's eyelid from left to right.

Not having Phoenix stare at her or have the silence ruined with words, Draya's anxiety began crumbling. Finally, her airwaves opened, and the screaming voices in her head turned to whispers. Things were now bearable.

However, her paradise was shattered when Phoenix told her in a matter-of-fact tone, "There are men out there who like big girls. So, get used to it and get yours."

Chapter 7

Nipple pasties and cut-up jean shorts with the crotch exposed were the only things covering Draya in front of the camera that handed her over to anyone who subscribed and entered her chat room. It was Wednesday night, and on this day of the week, Draya connected to her audience on a deeper level that surpassed sex and made communication an actual priority.

On her bed, rocking back and forth, Draya asked, "Truth or truth?" she waited for the irritating notification jingles to go off and announce the presence of her viewers who hid behind computers and voiced their perverted thoughts through keys on a keyboard.

CUM4Me: Truth
ILoveBigGirlz: Truth
RIDEORRIDEDICK: Truth
TheseBottomLips: Truth and nothing but the truth.

***

The notification chimes went off faster and faster. Draya could imagine all of the gifs displaying the word *Truth*. She sat up, her legs clasped closed and feet planted on the shag carpet. In search of comfort, she moved from side to side. Unfortunately, the motion was futile since all that was achieved was her daisy duke jean shorts riding up the crack of her ass where they made a home for themselves.

She ignored her jean-textured thong and caught sight of her Peepers.com ranking, #50.

RealAllDay: It's nothing like the truth.

Draya crossed one leg over the other and folded her hands together.

"Why do you all like big girls? Excluding you fetich-having freaks, why do you like big girls?"

This was a loaded question. She knew this. Knew that in the internet world, nothing was off-limits, and things could go anywhere real fast.

Although true, this small nagging piece inside of her begged her to inquire. Yearning for even just the smallest crumb of hope, of acceptance, Draya laid her eyes on the screen, her planted leg slightly shaking as a thunderstorm of answers scrolled through her chat room.

DeliciousAtHeart: I'm respected by them.

ILoveBigGirlz: I'm a big girl. To not love big girls is to hate myself, and I love myself!

WestSide: Them girls good in bed! Lady in the streets, freak in the sheets. I only bring home the big girls to meet my mama #100.

Harvey01: My first love had meat on her bones. Never gone back to boneless since.

Fast and furious, the replies kept coming. Not one negative opinion in the batch. Draya read as many as she could as fast as she could. The sounds of coins hitting her account were loud and demanding. The payment raised her ranking three slots.

"TrueNut, you never ever been with a woman under 230 pounds?"

Anxiously waiting on a reply, Draya captured stories from others.

KissMe: Large women have more class. They're dignified and can hold their own mentally. The world's always after them, so they have tough skin.

GoBlackDontGoBack: My mama was a big woman, my aunty a big woman, my grandma, and my sister. I'm not breaking the streak by bringing home a stick.

A stick emoji sat at the end of the comment.

RideThis: I just do.
TrueNut: Never have, never will.

"Wow," Draya let out. "Are you guys serious or just fuckin' with me? There are a lot of pro-fat girls in here. Y'all not bullshitting me, are you?" she chuckled—forced with amusement, however, poisoned at the core.

PhatRichard: Why are you so surprised?
RideThis: You do know your target audience is plus-size lovers, right? Whether or not physically, we love a big girl.
ILoveBigGirlz: <---------------- the name says it all.
ChocolateThunderstorm: I'm 53, too old to sit around and lie about shit.

Draya shrugged while rolling her eyes. "I'm just saying it's shocking that you all love you some big girls. Have you really taken a look at us? We're disgusting looking. Am I right?"

SpankMe: Did she really just say that?

HorneyRabbit: Self-hate much?

HersheyKiss: What the fuck?

CowBoyTony: You OK? You PMSing or something?

ILOVEBIGGIRLZ: Bitch! I ain't fuckin' disgusting! Don't put your dislike for yourself on me!

TasteJustLikeCandy: I disagree 100%. Really hoping you're saying this to rank.

Draya's face scrunched up. "I hate myself because I know my weight's disgusting. That's not self-hate. That's honesty. I love myself because I accept myself and am honest with myself. All you guys are doing is trying not to hurt feelings by being politically correct and pacifying the unhealthy."

The room of forty members instantly evolved to seventy. As quickly as attendees increased, so did the pro-big-girl posts. There was no understanding of Draya's mind-set. There was no proper communication if she was not smothering herself with body-loving comments.

***

TinyJinney: OOOOKKKK, this whole conversation has me lost. How can you love yourself but think you're unattractive? Make it make sense.

Scarface: Reword it, big mama. Reword it quick! Lol!

SlipperyWhenWet: There's no loving yourself if you don't like yourself.

Draya stood. "So, according to you all, if a person doesn't like their nose, gets butt implants, or a boob job, then that's self-hate? If they don't think they are perfect looking in every way, they hate themselves?"

KissDownThere: No! They're changing that one thing, not downing themselves like you.

9inch: Yup! That's that Hollywood shit.

BigButtBrenda: Nope! Called making adjustments. Which is obvious you should do some since you don't like how you look.

Contagious: You got us there. I got work done, and I love myself.

BlueBalls: Damn, y'all acting like she talked about y'all mama. If old girl don't like how she looks, that's her business. So what's with all the shaming? I bet y'all chicks in here got brooms on ur damn eyes acting as eyelashes. Should I say you hate yourself nonsense?

CarryOn:@BlueBalls, not brooms. Lmao.

The responses were mixed. An array of people's attitudes shifted when Draya gave her examples; however, a number still stuck with the belief she was body-shaming herself.

"See, this is why Wednesday night is the best night. You motherfuckers can't help but force your opinions, even when you're told what it really is." Draya laughed. Her face reddened, and her ears got hot. "The nerve of you fuckers."

Coins rang out, and her ranking jumped another five spots.

JumpMyBones: Love yourself, girl, bc we do.

Hearts were posted after the comment.

Bones: Wish I looked like you. #NoBodyShaming.
GlitterandDiamonds: Love the skin you're in.
OGPimp: If you think you're disgusting, why are you on here? Obviously, you just want attention

"If I wanted attention, I'd do this." Draya opened her legs, her crotchless shorts revealing her vagina. "Now, fuck you and pay me."

Sounds of a cash register going off indicated Draya gained heavy payments of $100 or more from those who paid. She was now sitting at the thirty-fifth spot.

"Oh shit, y'all liked that?" She stood and jumped up and down, her hands clapping together frantically and offbeat.

DirtyOldMan: Show me more!
DrugHead: Now, that's more like it!

"Ranking 35! Hell yeaaaah." For the first time that night, Draya smiled. She removed one pasty, then danced to the sounds of cash registers and coins exploding.

FaceDownAssUp: #NoBodyShaming #JustLove.
ILoveBigGirlz: #TeamLoveUrSelf bitch or die! Fuck your dirty pussy!

The more *love yourself* and *stop body-shaming* comments were posted, the more Draya danced. She took turns shaking her ass and titties directly inside one of the cameras. Her dreadlocks fell from out of her bun and danced with her.

***

JunkNTrunk: Go, Casey! Go, Casey! Fuck these haters, boo!

WestSide: You jiggling, baby!

FuckOff: I bet bitch got daddy issues.

XXLPornStar: #TeamLypo

BigBucksBigDick: Have some pride, baby girl. Love yourself regardless of how you look.

Draya turned around. Her hips swayed from left to right, and her locs blocked her face. Then seductively, she pushed them aside and faced the comment written by BigBucksBigDick. Her hips grew stiff, and her feet sank into the ground just in time for her mind to fly back to the past.

Lying in bed in a hospital gown, Draya watched and listened to the two detectives outside her room located across from the elevator talk about her and her case. Not long ago, the two stood at her bedside, attempting to question her. Then upon their departure, the door remained open. A front-row seat to their conversation, Draya occasionally shook her head over their loud voices and failure to detect someone watching them.

"She's not talking. She doesn't even seem to be physically hearing us." The bedroom-eyed, Hispanic female scratched her forehead, then

locked her finger inside the belt loop below her badge.

"She's in shock. The hospital's rape counselor is due to meet with her real soon. So I say we go grab a bite to eat, come back, and see where we are then."

The female officer nodded at her partner, whose hair and mustache contained strands of gray. "All right. Let's give it a try." She rubbed her eyes and pushed herself up from off the wall. "But answer me this, does questioning rape victims ever get easy?"

He opened his mouth to answer; however, she put her hand up. "Feel free to lie to me."

He patted her on the back while waiting for the elevator. "You're new on the force. I'd be doing you a disservice if I told you what you wanted to hear."

He used his knuckle to ring for the elevator once more. Immediately, the two doors opened, and a short, stumpy woman whose dreadlocks were held in place with a Tam cap walked out, her phone to her ear. She stepped to the side of the doors and ended her call.

"I'll call you back. I'm on my way to a patient now. Love you too. So long."

Both officers looked at each other. Finally, the veteran of the two nodded in the direction of the phone carrier.

"I know what you want to do. Go ahead. I'll be downstairs."

"I won't be long." The female detective stepped in front of the round woman and spoke just as she slid her phone inside her jeans pocket. "Excuse me. Are you going to meet with a patient named Draya Ruckers?"

She looked the rookie over before asking, "And you are?"

"My apologies. I'm Detective Morales." She opened her coat and flashed her badge. "I'm working on the Ruckers case."

"Oh, lead with that next time, honey. I'm Burnett, the rape counselor, and, yes, I'm heading to meet with Ms. Ruckers right now.

"My partner and I just came from seeing her. She's in shock and not speaking. All we know is she was found in a cornfield not far from her family's farm by a group of teens. She was found naked from the waist down and repeating the words"—Detective Morales took her phone from her back pocket and looked at her notes—"I have no pride."

"Bastard."

"I agree. Listen, here's my card. If you get her to talk, please call me ASAP."

She gave her card to Burnett, who took it between her two fingers.

"Rookie?"

"Six months on the force."

"Can tell. You're anxious—a piece of advice. Have patience. These types of situations can require time."

"And that's the problem. No rapist should have a second longer out of jail."

Burnett breathed out heavily. "If I get something, I'll call."

She tucked the card into her purse. Then before stepping inside Draya's hospital room, she bowed her head. "Father, please guide me and work through me to help this child. Amen."

Standing in front of Room 543, Burnett knocked. Had she looked inside, she would have seen Draya staring right at her. After seconds of being answered with silence, she let herself in. The first thing she caught wind of was Draya's heavy, red eyes.

Burnett walked over and stood beside Draya. "Draya, my name is Doris Burnett. I'm a counselor. Doctors thought you might want to talk."

Draya kept her eyes trained on the door. "As you can see, I'm fairly old, so I need to sit. Is that okay with you?"

Nothing.

Burnett picked up the chair tucked in the corner and set it next to Draya. She looked over Draya more technically this time. She took visual notes of her uneven hair, the finger marks around her neck, and what looked to be a bite mark on her earlobe.

"They believe you were raped. Doctors and the police, that is, but I've never been one to believe information entirely unless I got it from the horse's mouth. So, if you can perhaps move your fingers or blink your eyes several times, then I know they're telling the truth."

Nothing.

"I get it. I get it. The last thing you want to do is talk to some stranger, let alone some chunky counselor at that." Burnett was not looking directly at Draya, but she firmly believed she moved her arm slightly. "I get it. So, I will try to make myself less of a stranger to you by putting us both on the same playing field."

Burnett coughed in her hand. "It's not fair that I want to know about your traumatic situation, and you don't know shit about me. Oh, goodness, I'm sorry. Never could speak clean for long. Anyway, I was raped. Twice, and by the same person at the age of 18. No, I didn't know him—never saw the animal in my life. However, he managed to rape me for the second time six months after the initial attack. I was short and chubby back then, so he viewed me as easy prey. Knife to my throat, he told me, 'You're despicable. Look at you. You're a pig. Have you no shame? Have you no self-love?'"

Draya looked at her, her bottom lip trembling as she pushed herself up. Burnett saw her and kept talking.

"The entire time he violated, he called me every filthy name in the book. I have to tell you the truth. None of those names bothered me. None even really stuck out, but him constantly asking and telling me that I lacked pride, for some reason, carved itself into my mind."

"He told me that," Draya said, her voice hoarse and low.

Burnett turned her body a little more in Draya's direction. "Told you what?"

"Said I had no pride because of my size." Draya erased the falling tears with the back of her hand. "Said the sight of me sickened him and that I didn't deserve to live. Said because of that, I had to be punished."

"Do you know who did this?"

"Yeah." Tears welled in her eyes. "This homeless man who hangs around the market. I see him whenever I go into town."

Burnett leaned in closer to Draya. "Did you go into town today? Did he follow you home?"

Lips rolled into her mouth as Draya lifted her head and nodded furiously. The tears her eyes held teeter-tottered at the rim. Then losing the battle of containing water, she dropped her head forward and felt the coolness ripple down her cheeks.

"I saw him watching me, but I paid it no mind. I was focused on getting my dad's stuff. Whenever I went into town, I was always on the clock." She wiped her nose with her palm. Burnett reached inside her purse and handed her a small pack of tissue.

"I never cross through the cornfield. Never. But I was late and didn't want to get in trouble, so I took the shortcut. I don't think I was there for thirty seconds when he grabbed me from behind. First, he called me a fat, nasty bitch. Then he turned me around and started to choke me." Draya's last sentence clogged her throat. She touched where his fingers left marks behind on her neck.

"He choked me so badly, I was scared I'd black out and hit my head on the ground, so I got down on my knees. He looked down at me and told me to repeat after him and say I had no pride, and when I didn't because he was still choking me, he let me go. That's when he screamed for me to say it. So, I did but saying it once wasn't enough. He made me repeat it twenty times. I know it was twenty because I counted. When I finished, he started to hit me and told me I had made him sick. 'All fat bitches must die,' he yelled, and then he bit my ear. I couldn't stop crying. I kept begging him to stop." Draya used a new tissue to blow her nose.

"When I begged him to let me go, he'd tell me not until I received my punishment." Draya clutched the tissue she held and slammed her fist into the side of the bed. She bit down on her lip so brutally that she drew blood. "He ripped my pants off! When I tried kicking him off, he punched me in the stomach." Draya covered her face with her hands. Then although muffled, she continued speaking.

"The last thing I remember was screaming for help, screaming 'no,' and then everything going black. When I woke up, my hair lay next to me. His bum ass cut my hair." Draya cried out in agony. The pain she let out shook her body and chattered her teeth. "The one thing I like about myself, he took away." Draya fell into Burnett, and she did nothing but embrace her.

"You're going to be OK. Do you hear me? You're going to be OK. You're going to tell the police everything you told me. Give them a description of that sack of shit, and they're gonna throw the book at him." Burnett licked away the tears heavy on her top lip. "You're going to continue seeing me, and we will talk this thing out, you hear? We're gonna kick this demon the hell out of your life."

"You promise?" Draya's cheek rested on Burnett's shoulder, her eyes as red as a stop sign.

"I promise. I got you."

Chapter 8

Draya returned to reality to an empty chat and leftover post asking if she was OK. What was wrong with her? Had she lost it? She pushed one of her locs out of her face.

After taking a deep breath, she moved on to cut off the cameras and television. Then slowly and while cracking her knuckles, she approached the bedroom closet that she pretended didn't hold mementos. Draya turned the knob with such shaky nerves that she could've taken on the lead role in a horror film. Without looking, she opened the door.

Smells of the past triggered memories that lay dormant in her mind. She pushed herself inside the closet. Her fingers tapped on the door frame, and she coached herself with her breathing exercises. *Breathe in deeply, breathe out deeply, breathe in deeply, breathe out deeply.* Her arms and legs shook, ridding her limbs of whatever fear and nerves sat within. The step she took inside the condensed space brought her in front of the perfumes and scented candles that were given to her.

However, she never again used them once they became sentimental. Fighting the urge to remove lids from the jars she wanted to jam her nose into, she reprogrammed her mind-set and reached for the top shelf. The tips of her fingers tapped around the wood above her head until her middle finger grazed the opening of a small box.

Adding height to her frame, she stood on her tiptoes. Then with both hands above her head, she removed the box from its shelf. Outside the closet door, Draya sat on the carpet Indian style, where she opened the sneaker box and absorbed her past again. She emptied the small package of printed photos and flipped through each picture as if seeing it for the first time. Burnett and Detective Morales smiled at her from the fall parade, museums, and parks.

Although the happiness in those photos was given birth years earlier, it still filled Draya with peace today. The last photo in the stack was her mentor's engagement announcement. Draya spotted the faint penmanship written behind the announcement through Morales's powder-blue blouse.

Without flipping it over, Draya read aloud the message she had held in her heart for over ten years.

"Your strength and your fight to rid the world of hate inspired us to rid ourselves of fear. Thank

you for showing us it's okay to be you and never forget to tell the truth and shame the devil. #self-loveisthebestlove."

The tears tumbled down her cheeks, which she didn't bother cleaning. She placed the announcement beside her and dug into the bottom of the box. Discolored, however, still readable, Draya unfolded the front page of two Kansas newspapers.

Homeless Psycho Insanity Plea Lands Him in the Looney Bin

Draya's teeth clamped down on her bottom lip, and her hands shook, the restraint practiced against crumbling the article. She placed the headline next to the announcement, then carefully opened the second battered and ripped article.

Rapist Declared "Cured" Released from Mental Institution after One Year

That article, like the first, took a seat next to the announcement. The rubber band-secured stacks of letters confined in envelopes were given no attention other than a swift glance. Those memories were needed for another time. This time was needed to shame the devil.

Beneath the envelopes, she randomly pulled out a photo of herself as a child. Young Draya. Skinny Draya. She tucked it into her back pocket. On her knees, Draya grabbed her phone from her bed. The phone rang once before Willard answered.

"Draya, tonight's episode was . . . interesting."

"Are you still logged into Peepers?" she quickly asked.

"Yes. Many of your viewers are now in Housewife Katie's room. She's cooking with nothing on but an apron."

"Spread the word and tell everyone you know of who was in my room tonight I have an announcement to make. Shit just got real."

"What are you going—"

Draya hung up. The fewer questions asked and communication transpired regarding her second Wednesday night appearance, the more likely she'd get through it how she envisioned it.

"Lights, camera, action," she whispered.

All the equipment and necessities needed for a well-functioning camming platform were back up and running. In front of the camera, stone-faced, Draya held on to the articles and announcement just below her hip. She watched as familiar screen names dropped in.

RealAllDay: You good?
KissMeDownThere: Surprised you're back.

Draya waited for the room to grow.
Romeo: Back for more humiliation? Damn, you got balls.

***

The number of attendees surpassed the highest number she had reached earlier that day. *Perfect,* she thought.

"Welcome back, everyone, and to answer a few of your questions and thoughts, no, I haven't lost my mind. I just had a moment, but I'm back." Draya paused, the comments appearing by the loads. "It's Wednesday night. Truth night. However, I haven't been truthful tonight, haven't followed my own rules of purging what's holding me down, and worse, breaking me down. Instead, I've done the opposite, but now, I'm ready to reverse that and do my part."

FaceDownAssUp: My heart's beating fast. What are you about to say?
TongueBandit: Bring it on.

Draya held up the newspaper article where her rapist's face stained the front cover. She pointed at it, then at the headline declaring his insanity.

"When I was a teen, I was raped by a homeless man in my town. He told me during the attack how disgusting I was and that I had no pride because I," Draya's fingers mimicked air quotes, "allowed myself to be fat." She laughed. "Now, *that's* the funniest thing I've ever heard because up until I was 10, I looked like this." Draya pulled the photo of little Draya from her pocket and showed it to the camera. She was petite and grinning from ear to ear. Her two front missing teeth were the highlight of the photo.

Emojis of bulging eyes and GIFs of celebrities continuously shaking their heads filled the chat.

Draya pushed the photo closer to the camera. "Look closely. It's me. I didn't gain weight until my mother left my father and me, and my father, who, mind you, was heavyset himself, pushed his unhealthy eating habits on me. There were never any fruits, vegetables, or even bottled water in our house. It was the house of fried foods, junk foods, soda, and every sugary drink and candy created. I was homeschooled. So that way of eating was normal to me. Then the weight started coming on while my doctor constantly voiced her concern."

Comments were coming in. However, Draya ignored them and kept on with her confession.

"I tried to lose weight, to get healthier, but when you're a kid and under the thumb of a controlling father who'd rather starve you instead of giving you vegetables, that's pretty hard to do. Did I mention him supplying me with healthy food alternatives would have been easy as fuck, since he was a farmer?"

***

BigRig: Fuck out offffffffff here. That's some shit right there. Smiley faces with enlarged eyes and opened mouths raced down the screen.

"I didn't like how I looked. So, I tried exercising, eating that garbage food in portions, and telling myself every day in the mirror that I was beautiful and would get past this. Some days were better than others, but the bad always stuck around longer. It's hard to keep positive when you had no friends and no mother to help uplift you, guide you, and fight against the daily comments." Draya dropped the photo of herself. "But I kept fighting. Fighting my father, the world who'd stare and whisper whenever I was out. I kept fighting the negativity because you are what you think, right?"

Draya looked around. The closet holding the good and bad of her life, the door slightly ajar, stared at her. "Then I got raped, and instead of my dad showing support and wanting to crack the skull of that sick fuck, he tells me it's *my* fault because I'm so fat." Draya pushed out air.

"But regardless of the bull, I managed to gain two mentors who became my best friends." She looked down at the announcement, then slowly held it up for her viewers. "My counselor and the detective assigned to my case became my guardian angels. They told me every day I was pretty, smart, and loved. They became the moms and womanly figures I needed. That was the first time I believed I was decent looking."

One of the viewers wrote in caps.

FiftyShadesofFreaky: WAIT A MINUTE. DID THAT ARTICLE SAY YOUR RAPIST WAS DECLARED INSANE? THE BASTARD DIDN'T GO TO JAIL?

Draya scratched the corner of her mouth. "The bastard didn't go to jail. His public defender pleaded insanity, and what do you know? The fucker goes right into a mental institution, surrounded by his kind. They basically sent that fucker home."

Romeo: Well . . . Some people are sick and deserve to be in there.

DrugHead: I agree with psychos getting help, but that's if they're really psycho. But for some reason, I'm getting the feeling your rapist should have got the book thrown at him.

StreetWalker: I don't believe in the insanity plea. Motherfuckers know what they are doing. That

bitch ass consciously thought to force his dick in
you!

The debate over whether the insanity plea was
actually a real and logical thing swarmed the chat.
So, Draya moved on to the next article. She said
nothing, only held it up. The comments slowed . . .
and then sped up again.

Bones: They let him out after a year?
PeepersFan: Cured! Yeah, right. #nojustice
#bullshit
Romeo: Maybe he was cured. We're not doctors.
Jugs: @Romeo, there's no cure for being a rap-
ist! I was raped several times by different people,
so I know! They're all monsters!
DiamondCuchey: @Romeo, shut the fuck up.
You sound stupid.

"They say after undergoing intensive psychiatric
therapy and administrating medicine, he'd shown
improvement beyond measure. A great front-page
cover, right? But the truth would have read better.
How does this sound, ladies and gents? '*Looney
Bin Runs Out of Beds, Patients Are Being Released
and Declared Cured.*'"

Draya pulled out the engagement announce-ment. "The news of his release and the police investigation for the truth sent me into a deep depression. Then two months later, he raped again, and again, they sentenced him to a mental institution. A different one this time. Wayyyy better, right?" Draya screamed sarcastically before rubbing her eyes.

"For once, my town didn't view me as the fat girl but the girl deserving of justice. The world had finally turned a blind eye to my physical, but it was too late. His voice telling me how ugly I was held my mind hostage. So, when she," Draya pointed at Morales, "was assigned to transport him to the facility, she made sure they'd never release him again."

Sword&Jewels: I heard about that case! They gave the cop the chair for murder!

"Bingo," Draya voiced.
The chat room roared in chatter.

JumpMyBones: This is sad as hell but real as shit. Wednesdays are the truth.

PEater: Y'all talking about the gay cop? Didn't her fiancée commit suicide after she was given the needle?

Romeo: How do we know you're telling the truth?

TongueBandit: Want me to kiss it and make it all go away?

"Yes," Draya said once loudly for all to hear. "Detective Morales was given the needle, and only five hours after her death, her fiancée, Doris Burnett, my counselor, committed suicide. The two women I loved because they loved me are dead. Why am I telling you all this? Because you're right. I don't love myself. Self-love does not exist in a world where you're told on a daily that you're unworthy of love, and when you finally start seeing the sunshine after the storm, you get shit on by family, the government, and your friends. It's hard to love what destroyed your life and the lives of others. It's hard to accept this," Draya looked down at herself. "When this," she pointed at her head, "can't seem to move on."

Draya stepped backward, and when the back of her heels hit her bed, she sat down. The back of her hand wiped the corners of her eyes. A few times, she closed her eyelids and inhaled long and hard. "So, for you losers out there who want to shout self-love, why don't you learn the story behind the person before you start judging? Educate yourselves."

SexSells: Then why be on this site? Why make yourself seen?

"Don't you get it? I don't like myself."

In the middle of a flurry of questions mixed with the noise of coins and cash registers ringing out, Draya shut down the chat. Once the screen turned black, and the room grew silent, her leg shook, and her heart tripled in beats. The eyes from her past staring at her from different textured papers raised the hair on her arms. She dropped them. The words and photos burned her fingertips. Her phone went off. A picture of Willard's dick underneath his name filled the cell phone's screen. The ignored rings went to voicemail, then, shortly after, a text came through.

Are you OK? That episode was heart-wrenching. So sad I almost didn't jerk off.

Draya turned off her phone and tossed it on the floor. The electronic tumbled on the photos and

articles she wished to disconnect from. She looked
at the walls. Each slowly inched forward, closing in
on all the space her lungs craved. She opened her
legs and placed her head in between. There, she
counted each of her deep breaths. "I got to get out
of here."

Removing herself from her calming position
and abruptly cutting off her breathing tactics
triggered her to feel light-headed. Her hand on
her forehead, Draya's feet took control and led
her downstairs to the coat closet. The black trench
coat and knee-high boots . . . The first items seen
following opening the closet door.

The long coat and boots paired with gloves and
a scarf covered Draya's next-to-nothing outfit.
The outer gear played as her only line of defense
against the winter's chill. Applying an additional
layer of lipstick and eye mascara brought about
the desire for Draya to shift her hair over her left
shoulder. The mirror hanging on the back of the
closet acted as her assistant. She tightened the
coat's belt as best she could and tried positioning
her breasts to the best of her ability without the
help of a bra. From the pocket, Draya kept her
black marble beaded bracelet. She snatched it out
and slapped it on her wrist. Now, content with
what the mirror showed, she went out into the
world she didn't like and never liked her.

Chapter 9

Ruby's Crystals was New York's proclaimed next big hotel entertainment atmosphere to hit since the pandemic ended two years before. Its huge building is fixated with marble flooring and walls, aromatherapy-scented fog traveling throughout the halls. Exotic-themed restaurants and lounges acted as venues for small concerts and listening parties. The culture and class it supplied every visitor and event were invisible elsewhere. The respect never varied from person to person. This establishment was a neutral welcoming ground for all walks of life who passed screening and paid a fee to conduct business, legal or illegal. RC's was a peaceful, nonjudgment zone and a place for all to indulge sexually and financially on Wednesday nights.

Draya sat at the hookah lounge bar, the top three buttons on her coat undone, allowing a preview of her cleavage sprinkled with fruit-scented perfume. Glow fish in the bar's counter circled her coaster. Occasionally, she tapped the glass, causing their immediate dispersal.

"Looking good tonight, Casey. You do something different?"

Skylar set the heart-shaped shot glass down in front of Draya, laced with an ecstasy-dipped cherry, just how she liked it. Draya downed the brown liquor not one minute from it leaving the bartender's hand. She held her head back, the effects from both drinks she kicked back finally showing themselves. Her eyes fluttered when she let her head up.

"Mascara."

"I like, I like."

"Yeah, so do I," Draya mumbled.

"Hello, miss, can I trouble you for some bourbon?" Behind Draya's neighboring seat, a cowboy-hat-skinny-jeans-wearing white man stood tapping the back of the barstool. The recurring taps pulled Draya's sight his way. Finally, catching her stare, the gator-boot-wearing man tipped his hat to her.

"Evening, ma'am. How are you enjoying yourself?"

Draya didn't know if the smile plastered on her face came about due to the stranger's accent, southern manners, or because he called her ma'am.

Yeah, it's all of the above, she thought.

"I'm doing well, and yourself?"

"Better than I expected. I'm here on business and wasn't quite sure how I'd take a liking to this here New York, but after setting my sights of this here beauty, I am impressed." Arms outstretched, he nodded while looking around.

Skylar set down his glass. Then he pulled out his money clip from his back pocket and relieved himself of a fifty. "Go on and buy yourself something pretty," Mr. Texas instructed just as he slipped the tip to Skylar.

"I most certainly will." Skylar pushed the bill deep inside the right cup of her bra.

"What line of work are you in?" Draya motioned for another drink. She gave Skylar a wag of her finger, indicating to withhold the X.

"Good old oil."

"Oil? Well, aren't you a big fish?"

"Yes, ma'am, I believe I am." He flashed his top and bottom row of teeth stained with a light hue of yellow.

"I like a big fish," Draya admitted. "A nice, country big fish."

Her seat turned fully in his direction. Her leg crossed over the other, cutting in between the opening of her coat and showcasing her coochie-cutter shorts.

Cowboy stole a glimpse of her marble bracelet. "Well, you don't say. No fairy tales were told when I was informed of tonight's available entertainment, now, was it?"

"Not one bit, Big Rig. Now, are we going fishing or what?"

Skylar set Draya's drink in her open hand that rested on the bar. "Cowboy, if you're really looking for a rattlesnake to tickle your fancy, this one here is the one for you." Skylar winked at him.

Looking from Skylar to Draya, a mischievous grin covered his lips. "You don't say."

Draya kicked back her drink, then stretched her leg out until the tip of her boot poked the cowboy's groin. In one swift gulp, he annihilated his bourbon and held his hand out for Draya to take.

"You, my dear, have just earned yourself some time with Texas's best."

Hand in hand, Draya stood to her feet. She closed the space between them, and her breasts pushed into his chest. "Well, prove it then, Cowboy."

"Follow me." Mr. Texas dropped her hand and turned away.

"Hold on now," Draya called out.

She waved him over when he looked her way.

Draya took the two full shot glasses from Skylar's hands and held one out to Mr. Texas. "Let's drink to the magic we're about to make."

He smiled, rushed over, and together, they took the drink.

"Yummy, now, let's get." Then as quickly as before, Mr. Texas took off for the exit.

"You remembered the roofie, right?"

Skylar nodded. "Just like always."

"Good. You'll get your cut when I'm done. Shouldn't be long."

Both women shared a laugh.

"I believe it. I highly doubt everything's bigger in Texas."

By the time Draya caught up with Mr. Texas, he was standing at the elevator, his fingers gliding over the bills sticking out from the money clip.

"Well well well, Cowboy, what do you have there?"

He held the knot inches from Draya's face. "All yours if you play your cards right, little lady."

"Oh, sir, I do believe you have given me the vapors." She used her hand to fan herself and chuckled.

He stepped close. His long, thin nose grazed her cheek. "I'm about to give you a lot more," he whispered. She lay her head on his shoulder temporarily and giggled.

"I'd like that, Mr. Texas. I'd like that a lot."

The glass elevator doors opened. The two stepped inside, hand in hand. *"Good evening, and welcome to Ruby's Crystals. Tell me, what floor are we traveling to?"* Mr. Texas notified the voice-activated elevator of their destination, then put his full attention on Draya. He tucked one of her dreads behind her ear where it belonged.

"Please take this with no disrespect whatsoever, but I have never been with a Black woman before."

His green eyes looked into hers. It was almost invasive how deep he gazed into her.

"That's OK. There's a first for everything, wouldn't you agree?"

He gently pushed her into the corner of the elevator. Privacy was nonexistent within the four glass walls. However, the corner they adorned acted as their little hideaway.

"I do, and I dare admit, I always dreamed of bedding a woman of your caliber."

"Caliber?"

"Yes. Such beauty and voluptuous physique, I find." He rubbed his hand down her arm to her hip. His nose inside her cleavage, he inhaled. "Intoxicating." With one hand, he dug inside her hair and, with the other, lifted her head to see her chin. Her cheeks reddening, she looked away.

"You don't have to woo me. You've already proven you can afford me."

He turned her face to his. Mr. Texas's eyebrows caved in. "Regardless of whether you were a working girl, I would have still approached you. What you are, how you look, I've always yearned to indulge in by any means necessary."

He dove into her. His lips meshed with hers. Kissing johns was a no-no for Draya. The only one she dared to lip-lock with was Willard, and although she felt comfortable with him, it still took effort. Mr. Texas's tongue's movements and hands exploring her body from her hair down to her thighs disintegrated all discomfort and written-in-stone rules she set when entering the sex for money business. The bumps and jitters running across Draya's skin pulled Mr. Texas away from the kiss.

"Relax." He kissed her nose, then blew it, the smell of cinnamon seeping inside her nostrils.

"You have reached your destination. Have a good evening, and thank you for choosing Ruby's Crystals as your home away from home."

Before they left the elevator, Mr. Texas cleaned away the lipstick residue cramped in the corner of Draya's mouth. Then taking her hand, he led her out from the glass walls into the hallway. Walking down the hall, Draya fixated on the sight of her hand intertwined with another's. The personal, romantic gesture she had only experienced through movies and couples she bypassed on the street. The intimacy she was now encountering had never previously visited her. Before talking herself out of it, she rubbed his knuckle with the tip of her finger. The emotion ignited inside of her felt nice.

"My room is just after this corner."

Draya looked at his black hair sticking out from underneath his hat and smiled. "I can't wait."

They turned the corner, and just as Draya peeked around Mr. Texas and down the hall, she saw Jetson walking their way. She pulled her hand

out of Mr. Texas's grasp and raced back around
the corner. Hand over her chest, she felt her heart
beating erratically. She stood in the middle of the
hall debating what to do. Several feet away from
her, she caught sight of the stairwell. She slid
inside and hugged the side of the door.

Fuck fuck fuck. She toyed with the bracelet.
Then noticing her behavior, she took it off and
stuffed it into her pocket. *Did he see me? He
couldn't have. Mr. Texas blocked me.* She peeked
through the small glass window, and Jetson came
into view, walking by the stairwell. Although no
longer in sight, Draya heard his footsteps pause on
the marble floors.

"No one's here, man. Give her a minute. I'm
sure she'll come back. Probably forgot something,"
Jetson shouted.

Fucccckkkk. Draya pulled away from the window and slapped her forehead with the palm of her
hand.

"My man, she's right here," Jetson called out a
little louder.

Quickly, she looked back out just to see Mr.
Texas jog down the hall. The light in his eyes and
the teeth-revealing smile disappeared when he
turned and looked down the hallway. Draya slowly
opened the door and peeked her head out. Next to
the elevator stood Jetson and a woman. Mr. Texas
headed their way.

"Thank you, sir," Mr. Texas told Jetson. "But this lady here isn't my lady friend I'm looking for."

Draya slid back inside the stairwell. The curvy woman passed the small window not long after.

"Sorry about that. I'm sure she'll show up," Draya heard Jetson tell Mr. Texas.

"Good evening, and welcome to Ruby's Crystals. Tell me, what floor are we traveling to?" the elevator asked.

"This is me," Jetson announced. "Have a good night."

"You too, sir." Mr. Texas turned his back and took the first few steps toward his room.

Draya crept out of the stairwell and, when she could, placed her hand on his shoulder.

Mr. Texas spun around. "Where on God's green earth did you go?" He wrapped his arms around her. He stepped back when she didn't respond and waited for her to speak. Still without a word uttered, he looked down at her naked wrist.

"You knew him."

Draya covered her mouth with her hand and nodded her head.

"Rest assured, he didn't see you." Both his hands sat on Draya's shoulders, his thumbs rubbing into her skin.

She dropped her hand. "Are you sure?"

"Sure as a groundhog on Groundhog's Day."

She laughed. "You're so country."

"That is a fact. Now—" Mr. Texas's eyes closed and quickly reopened. His shoulders dropped, and he let out a yawn. "My apologies. Now, as we were." Again, he took Draya's hand. Slow and unbalanced, he fought to walk.

Draya took the lead. "Don't worry, sweet pee. I got you. I'll lead the way."

Chapter 10

Four a.m. the following day

Skylar pounded on the door with three loud bangs.

"Ole girl's not about to gyp me out of my cut. Probably gathering up her shit right now, preparing to dip. No no no, I'm going to get mines before Cowboy Sam comes looking for her ass and his money."

She banged three more times.

Skylar crossed her arms and looked around. Then whistling a low tune, she counted down from thirty to one.

"3, 2, 1, oh, fuck this." She dropped her arms, cocked her foot back, and swung forward when the door opened . . . and she kicked Mr. Texas in the knee.

"What the fuck?"

Skylar's eyes blew up into balloons and both her hands flew over her mouth. She bit down on her lower lip before holding both hands out in front of her.

"I am *so* sorry! What are you doing up? I mean, I'm sorry to disturb you so early. I got no response when knocking, so I was going to try to kick the door in. But oh no, are you bruised?" Skylar bent down and looked at the damage. Although his knee was bright red and thin pieces of skin had peeled off, all she thought was, *I should have added more. Motherfucker should still be on his ass.*

Hunched over, Mr. Texas repeatedly rubbed his knee. Curses mumbled from underneath his breath.

"I'm sorry. I can get you some ice." Skylar ran her hand down her bald head.

Two groans left Mr. Texas's mouth before throwing his hand up and telling her no. Then finally, he stood up and got a look at who kicked him for absolutely no reason.

He squinted. "You're that hookah lounge bartender."

Draya pushed past Mr. Texas. The long cotton robe revealed nothing but wet hands and feet. She held together the towel wrapped around her head.

"Please tell me I left my keys at the bar. I've been calling the front desk all morning looking for them." She batted her eyes and curled up her top lip.

Hugging the corner of the doorjamb, Mr. Texas constantly rubbed his knee. "Ethan, honey, head on inside." She looked down at his leg. "You may want to tend to that knee. Looks like a knot coming in."

"I suppose you're right." Ethan rubbed it some more. "You have a good day." He waited for Skylar to fill in the blank.

"You can call me Tiny. Again, I'm so sorry."

"It's quite OK. Accidents do happen." With that, Ethan limped from the room.

Draya gave him some time to drag himself inside the suite. Then before she could explain why she hadn't met up with Skylar and handed over her share of the lick, Skylar started and led the conversation. She stepped closer to Draya and lowered her voice.

"I promise I drugged that motherfucker, but I didn't add enough for him to be up this early and that alert. It's all my fault. Fuck, were you able to get anything?" The wrinkles under Skylar's eyes deepened with her explanation. Her pale ivory skin glowed a raspberry red.

Inside, Draya smiled. She looked behind her and stepped farther into the hall. "What the fuck do you think? All that happened was he got a little drowsy and drifted off to sleep from time to time. He woke up each time I tried looking through his shit. I had to do a lot of dick sucking not to look suspect. Did you change up and use some new shit or something?" The lies leaked from Draya's mouth as quickly as ice cream melted on a summer day.

"Yeah."

Draya threw her free hand in the air and turned around in one full circle. The few acting classes she took for two summers were finally put to good use. "You dumb fuckin' ass. Now, I bet your ass thought I screwed you over, so you came here ready to collect, didn't you?" Draya raised her voice just a little.

Skylar scratched her elbow. "Maybe."

"Oh, bullshit, I see right through you. Listen, you'll get your cut. I'll put you in on what I'll make just by giving him companionship and a few blow jobs."

"Wait a minute. You can still fuck him, Casey. There's still time."

"No, the fuck there isn't. Fucker's feeling guilty for cheating on his wife, so he pushed up his last meeting and changed his flight so that he'd head on home early."

"Fuck." Skylar punched her thigh. "All right, fine. I'm doing a double, so when he checks out, come to the lounge."

Hard-faced, Draya closed the door. She searched the suite for Ethan and found him in the bedroom icing his knee.

Draya sat next to him on the couch. "You OK?"

"Nothing some frozen H20 can't fix." He patted her knee. "I'm sorry about last night. I guess I can't hold my liquor as well as you Big Apple folks."

Draya forced out a smile. "It's all right. I'm happy I was here to take care of you." "Did you at least order some room service or something while I was passed out? I just hate to think you sat here bored without a lick to do."

"It's OK, Ethan, really. You're a nice guy. That's not common, so for me to have stood by your side all night really was my pleasure."

"Now, Casey, I do believe *you're* now giving me the vapors." Their foreheads touched while sharing a laugh.

"I should be going." Draya stood, then sat back down on top of Ethan.

"Hold on now, little lady."

"Little?"

Ethan rolled his eyes. "You still have a job to do. There's a stack of money over on that dresser waiting to be collected."

"Yes, honey. I know. That money has been staring at me all night."

"Then go and get it, sweet pea."

Draya disrobed and let go of the towel holding up her hair. Ethan paused their intimacy.

"Darling, did that nice bartender return your keys?"

"Yes, she did. Why?"

"Good. I don't want to forget now, but on that dresser is an additional two thousand for my foolishness last night. So, hand that girl on over three hundred out of the eight thousand for her good deed and not a penny more, you hear? The rest is yours."

Draya clasped his face between her hands. "I promise you, Big Rig, not a penny more."

"That's my girl."

Chapter 11

Parked inside the studio's lot, Draya took the key out of the ignition, lay her head back, and closed her eyes. Rest was nonexistent for her last night. What Ethan had gone through surpassed simply passing out. What was slipped in his drink caused him to vomit profusely and struck him with chills before the peacefulness of sleep subdued him.

Never had Draya witnessed a mark react to the drug as badly as Ethan. His reaction was ideally an easy, fast way to get whatever of value a john had, whatever of value there was to cut Skylar in and then get out. First, they'd have to have the security tapes erased by the hotel. Draya's dirty deeds were easy to follow through on when all her johns took on the face of Steward. Then there was Ethan, who Steward's face didn't fit, and she knew that had she met him under different circumstances, they both would have written a story with a possibility of a beautiful ending. So, as a thank-you for treating her and making her feel like a woman in the movies, she treated him as Ethan and not Steward.

Physically beat, Draya lowered her overhead visor and took a look at how apparent the damage was. Beneath her eyes, she'd collected heavy, dark bags. Her lips had chapped, and her cheeks were ashy. She rolled her eyes.

"Oh, fuck it. They're just going to have to take me as I am today."

She pulled out a pair of dark shades from the armrest and slid them over her eyes. Then eyes watering and nose tingling, she mumbled, "You got to be shittin' me." Her hand's next destination landed inside her backpack and wrapped around a bottle of nasal spray.

"Allergies during the winter . . . Just what I need today."

The spray brought instant relief. Then her phone vibrated and delivered a text. Ethan, the screen read. *There's no reason for me even to check this message. You shouldn't even have my number. I just gave it to you because I didn't know how to say no.* Draya pushed her finger under her glasses and rubbed her eyes. Then without another logical thought, she opened the message.

I'm boarding. Heading on back to good old Texas. So tell me, will we meet again?

***

Draya's thumbs hovered over the keyboard. She shifted to every angle possible. Her chest poked out and fought to hold in place the pieces of her heart falling into her stomach.

Her thumbs wrote out the words. No, followed by, I'm sorry. Then her thumb on top of the circle picture of a paper plane taking off, she read his message once more. Then she erased her response and replaced it with the saying, Maybe in another lifetime. Her lashless eyelids batted, reeling back in the waterworks. She deleted those words and wrote again minus the word no, I'm sorry. Then she sent it.

Ethan's wrinkled, colorless skin, shiny black hair she pictured full and thick when in his twenties. Piano fingernails, she was sure, were filed and clear coated shown in her mind's eye. Punching the three vertical dots opposite his name, Draya hit the block button. Both hands choking her phone, she leaned her head against the tip of the phone protruding from between her fingers and let out a strained, glass-cutting scream. She let it all out, along with feet stomping and dashboard slapping.

Draya ripped the falling shades off her face and threw them and her phone on the passenger's seat.

"If only things were different," she whimpered.

"If only I didn't look for confirmation from the world, I'd be happy," was the last thing that left her mouth before the *should've, could've, would've* wrapped Draya in a sheet of peace and rocked her to sleep.

Tap! Tap! Tap!

Draya's body jerked forward. Bug-eyed, she used the collar of her shirt to wipe away the drool smudged on the side of her mouth. She looked from side to side before turning around and seeing Jeanie outside her window. The clock showed twenty minutes had passed from when she was expected at work.

"Dammit!" She grabbed all her belongings from the passenger seat and rushed out of the vehicle. Sunglasses in hand, she jammed them on her face while struggling to juggle all her items and walk at the same time.

She pushed Jeanie, the slight skin-to-skin contact knocking her phone from her hand and onto the floor, where cracking sounds rang out. Draya slammed her feet on the concrete when she stopped in place.

"Jeanie, tell me that *wasn't* my phone."

Jeanie picked up the screen-shattered phone frozen on the cartoon cat giving the middle finger screen saver. The camera lens was destroyed, now pieces on the ground. Jeanie handed it over.

"I'm sorry for your loss."

The lighthearted smile awkwardly sitting on her face agitated Draya even more. She took her damaged electronics, pumped her arm back as much as her arm allowed, and chucked it. The endorphins released freed Draya of reality, failures, sadness, and aggravation.

There was no telling what was on the other side of the gate Draya's phone flew over.

Still looking in the direction her phone had gone, Draya loudly admitted. "Damn, that felt good."

"OOOOK. Not sure what that was about, but can we get inside now? Everyone seems to be running late today, and we have three girls in there looking like humans instead of forest creatures."

"I'm on it." Draya went straight for the back door.

Passing by the set and all the equipment had Draya contemplating picking up all the high-tech things and trashing the place. Launching her cell phone got her wanting to make her job her personal rage room. Crew members and actors waved as she passed by. Her lack of sleep made her head hurt just by smiling. The bright lights made her wish she could run into the nearest cave. Outside the makeup room, Draya heard Sonny's condescending, flamboyant voice. She rolled her eyes and sucked her teeth.

"This bitch. Not today, not motherfuckin' today." Draya pushed aside the curtain. Once inside, she added a little pep in her step and a smudge of perkiness in her tone. "Good morning, all."

The one actress in Sonny's chair and the two waiting on the side all spoke in unison, "Morning."

Sonny looked over his shoulder. Eyeglasses on the bridge of his nose, he looked Draya up and down and let out a hard sounding, "Humph."

"Welcome back, Sonny. Glad you're feeling better."

"Yeah, well, you know, gotta make sure I stay off the stroll." He popped his hip out and got back to painting. Then suddenly, he stopped, brush in hand, and pointed at Draya. "Because had I resorted to the ho stroll, I wouldn't be doing"—he turned the brush on his actress—"this here *full* prosthetic look that you kindly pointed out I *don't* do." Sonny's vicious eye batting action brought attention to his fluffy, one-inch lashes.

Draya hung her ski jacket on the coat hanger, waved over one of the actresses, then took herself over to Sonny's small working area, where she planted herself in front of him, arms crossed.

"Sonny, we both said things that day, and even though I was trying to help you . . ."

He huffed.

Draya shifted her weight to her left leg and repeated a little louder and harder, "Even though I was *trying* to help you," she brought her tone back down to its initial volume, "I apologize if I offended you. From now on, you do you, and I'll do me. No advice or comments needed about anything."

Sonny looked her in the eye, snapped his neck to the side, and asked his actress how she was doing.

Draya slightly lowered her head and covered her forehead with her hand. Then chuckling, she said for all to hear, "I tried."

Two hours later, the room was still drowned in a lake of silence. The only constant sounds heard were bristles dipped in paint and slabbed on skin. Draya sat on her stool, popped the cap off a water bottle, and moistened her desert-dry throat.

"Pamela, you're finally done." Draya secured the H2O between her thighs before leaning back against the wall and closing her eyes.

"I'm taking a break," she announced.

"Enjoy. You deserve it." Pamela slid out of her seat and crossed the room to the door.

The woman whose face Sonny worked on hollered out for her comrade to stop. "We have some time before our scene. Let's run our lines together."

"Sounds like a plan," Pamela cosigned.

"Jackie, keep quiet and turn to your left," Sonny demanded.

"One more thing, Sonny. How much longer?"

Sonny dapped her chin with brown. "When I say so." He bent down and added more detail to her jawline.

"Really, Sonny, I want to estimate how far in the script we can get before we're on."

Sonny slammed the brush down on the vanity. Then his finger pointing at her, he snapped, "Bitch, I *said* when I say so!"

He rolled his eyes and grabbed a thinner brush. As he reached for her, Jackie pulled away. Draya opened her eyes.

"Don't call me out of my name. What's wrong with you?" Jackie used her toes to push her chair back and away from Sonny.

"Girl, stop. It's a term of endearment. You should know that. Your people use it all the time." Sonny stepped closer to her.

She pushed herself farther back. "*My people? What kind of racist crap are you spewing?*"

Slowly, Draya sat up.

"Damn, bitch, you ain't never been called a bitch before by one of your hip-hop friends? What, you a bougie bitch or something?"

Out loud, Jackie said to herself, "Here we go again with the bitches." She stood up and pushed her chair under the vanity with a curled lip and wrinkled forehead. The mirror rumbled, and drawers popped open as supplies rolled onto the floor.

"Call me a bitch again, Sonny, and I'm going to rip that raggedy patch of hair you call a bang from off your head, you fuckin' bigot."

Jetson pushed through the curtain and rushed straight into the battlefield. "What's going on? We can hear shouting from the set."

"I'm sorry, Jetson, but I will no longer work in an environment where he's around. You get rid of this mediocre makeup artist, or I'm done. Your uncle can get someone else to act as the leading lady. That is, if anyone is *willing* to take on a part for a movie people are already predicting will be a flop. No job is worth me taking disrespect from a racist." Jackie shot Sonny a look that would have turned him to stone if she had been a mythological creature.

"Racist? What the hell was said?" Jetson glared at Sonny.

"Some people are just a little sensitive. I am no racist." Sonny put on a smile and put his hand on Jetson's shoulder.

Jetson shoved his hand off. "What was said?"

Sonny's cheeks sank in, and his lips poked out. "I may have mentioned her having hip-hop friends. There's nothing racist about that."

"It's ignorant," Jetson spat. Then tight-jawed, he turned to Draya. "Draya, were you present during this entire situation?"

"Yeeeppp."

"As a neutral party, is that all he said?"

Sonny threw up both hands and blocked Draya and Jetson's view of each other, "Hold on now, Draya has nothing to do with this."

"Sonny, step aside. I'm speaking with Draya."

Sonny gave Jetson his back. His cheeks sank in, and lips poked out. Then he reminded Draya, "No comments needed, remember."

"Sonny, step aside," Jetson demanded with an increased amount of bass added to his voice.

Sonny took one giant step over to the right.

"Draya, I'm sorry to have to bring you into this, but I need the truth from someone who has nothing to lose or gain from this."

I'll learn when your ass learns to leave the donuts alone.

Draya smiled, the dimples in her cheeks as deep as a coffin. "No, that's not all. He continuously called her a bitch and referred to Black people as *'you people.'*"

"You bitch!" Sonny snarled. "You fat fuckin' bitch."

"Hey! Show some respect," Jetson found himself invading Sonny's space. Deeply, he inhaled. "Jackie has a point. Mediocre artists aren't needed here, and since you have a problem with African Americans and women, let me help you get away from working with a couple of them. Your services are no longer needed. Have a good day." Jetson stepped away, his broad shoulders demanding distance.

"Oh no, you ain't nobody. You're just the boss's nephew. So go on with your whole 'your services are no longer needed' speech. You have no clout here."

"Then *I'll* tell you. Your services are no longer needed. You have a good day, Mr. Huang." Phillip Cobbs stood in the doorway.

Jeanie and other crew members peeked in from behind him.

Sonny immediately started packing his things. He unnecessarily banged and slammed items down. Every time he looked up and around him, Jetson was there shooting laser beams at him from his glare. Finally, he stood erect after collecting his things and zipping up his leather jacket.

"Good day, Mr. Cobbs." He glided past Jetson. While holding the curtain open with one hand and without granting the decency of facing her, Sonny said, "I tried to be nice, but now you're going to regret not staying true to your word, Draya. Believe it, honey."

"Is that a threat?"

"It's good, Jetson. I'm sure it's not. Sonny knows. I warned him."

Sonny straightened the strap on his shoulder. "You sure did. Now, remember that I did too."

After Sonny's spectacle, the day seemed to bombard Draya with extra work whenever she found herself taking a breath lasting for more than two seconds. Once the day ended, she felt more run-down than when she first entered the building. As much as her soul yearned to get home, her feet could hardly lift from the pavement. She took baby steps to her car and contemplated lying down right in the middle of the lot several times. Finally, Draya took out her keys on the verge of opening her doors as footsteps approached her from behind.

"Draya," Jetson called out.

She covered her keys with her fist. "I want to thank you for putting Sonny in his place. I appreciate it." She gave him a half smile.

"If you really want to thank me, tell me why you ran from me last night."

Draya's hand tightened around her keys. The tips poked at her skin. "Excuse me?" "Ruby's Crystals. You saw me in the hall and booked it. Why?"

"Jetson, I've never been to Ruby's. I can't afford that place. I'm sorry you thought I'd do something like that instead of speaking." She scratched her nose. "Today's been a lot. I need to get home. See you tomorrow?"

When Jetson remained tight-lipped, she waved and went for the car door.

"So, this what we're doing?"

Draya chirped her car doors open. The headlights assisted the streetlights in killing off the darkness. "Huh? Yeah, it's not fancy, but it gets me around. Good night."

Jetson reached around Draya and closed the driver's door as soon as she opened it.

"I know you don't have a problem telling the truth because you did it in there. So, do me a favor and do it out here."

Draya turned around. The closeness took her back to when they first met. However, this time when Jetson noticed the privacy invasion, he didn't move.

"I keep my personal life and my work life separate in every which way, shape, and form."

"Are you keeping areas of your life separate or hiding that you're seeing Ethan Singleton?"

"How do you know his name?"

"He's loaded. Everyone knows his name."

Draya tried creating some room between them by flipping up the collar of her jacket.

"I'm not seeing him." She hit her hip with her knuckles. She wasn't aware that Jetson had caught a glimpse of her nervous twitches. "It was a one-night stand thing. Us big girls need love too, ya know." Her smile was not enough to trigger her dimples. However, it was strong enough to offset the sadness in her eyes.

Jetson pushed into her. She still took part in the games they'd been playing even until they now became mundane. What now took precedence was getting to know the woman behind the pretty face and makeup coverups. Seeing her with Ethan confirmed that whatever he felt for this stranger needed to be explored before it disappeared and was stolen before being tested.

Jetson would never say it verbally, but jealousy pulsated through him when he saw Ethan dedicated to finding her, knocking him off his pedestal. His stubborn cockiness in assuming she'd come his way could cost him.

He forced her hands open, her car keys and makeup box crashing to the ground. Jetson intertwined his fingers with hers, and against the car, in a calm, gracefully lit parking lot, he stole several kisses.

After what felt like kiss number one hundred, he held the back of her head. Then forehead to forehead, he kissed her nose.

"Stop running from me," he whispered.

Draya thought a failure to respond would follow his comment, but her lips moved to her surprise and against her nature.

"I don't know how," she admitted. "Feelings scare me. *You* scare me."

"Then prepare to be frightened because this is happening."

Draya's heart raced. The blood in her veins pumped hard and fiercely.

"All you have to do is say yes," he promoted.

No one will ever want you. You have no pride. How much for a blow job? It's Wednesday night, y'all. Let's speak the truth. You're a fetish, a bet. You're nothing.

She thought of it all. She thought of every reason to say no. The reasons that always made her say no, want less, and accept nothing. She pulled her hands from his, and he took them back.

"Say yes," he repeated. "Unless someone is preventing you from doing so."

The voice inside her, the small, timid voice always shot down and shut up for wanting what she had been poisoned to believe was out of reach, found his comment amusing. How could someone else have prevented her from getting close to him when her mind had secured that position? As much as she fully wanted to blame her depression and past for rejecting Ethan, she couldn't. Seeing Jetson at Ruby's confirmed what Draya was running from. She couldn't fend off forever. For years, she tried fighting off the need for love and a human connection, tried fighting nature. A battle you can't win. And now that voice was screaming for affection uncontrollably from someone she couldn't get away from and wanted her as much as she wanted him.

"I'm not a bet," she confessed. "I'm not a fetish. I'm not . . ." she held on to the word and hawked it up before she lost her nerve, "skinny."

"I know. Now, say yes."
Tell the truth and shame the devil.
"I'm fucked up, really fucked up."
"Good," he said. "You're not boring."

Chapter 12

Draya, it's been a week and no Peepers episodes. Text me back. I have two guys willing to pay out the ass for you. Where are you? Are you okay?

The last thing you ask is if I'm okay instead of it being the first. Good job, Willard. Draya rolled her eyes. `

"Give me get your hand."

Draya clicked her phone's screen off and took Jetson's hand into hers.

"You ever been with a big girl?" Draya almost didn't recognize the sound of her own voice. She sounded upbeat and perky with a pinch of giddy.

"Nope. Wasted my time with the scrawny types. The ones with no curves and shit, the model type."

"You don't sound proud of it."

He turned a corner with one hand on the steering wheel and the other holding Draya's hand.

"I was a follower. From high school up until college, I was attracted to the type of girls my friends were attracted to. When your family's a part of Black Hollywood, you grow up around the elite and form a distorted belief of what beauty is."

"Who else besides Phillip is in the business?"

Jetson threw on the right signal. "Ever heard of Hendricks Cobbs?"

Draya's phone vibrated. She turned the screen over.

"Wasn't he the showrunner for the TV series *Blueprint, The President's Rook, Midnight Rain,* and a few sitcoms? Wait a minute."

"My pops."

"Get the fuck out of here. How did I not piece that together?"

Jetson pulled into the lot of Centra. Young men wearing peacoats on top of three-button vests, slacks, and pointy leather shoes opened doors and got in and out of vehicles just as pricey as Jetson's.

A couple of inches more, and Draya's face would have pressed against the tinted window.

"Jetson, why are we here?"

"We're having dinner."

A parking valet with slick hair gelled back into a thin ponytail plagued with an ultrathin unibrow opened Jetson's door. His skinny cornrows-wearing coworker jogged to the passenger's side and opened Draya's door. Draya slapped the overhead flap open and quickly gave her face a once-over.

With the tip of her finger, she removed the excess lipstick from off the corners of her mouth, used the same finger to rub over her eyebrows, and tucked in one of the dreads collected inside her high ponytail. The valet held his hand out. Her thigh-high burgundy suede boots hit the asphalt just as her ring-decorated hand fell into his.

"Good evening, and welcome to Centra." His tall frame made his voice sound galaxies away.

Draya looked up and nodded. The smile she deliberated giving canceled when the giant's eyes slowly enlarged.

"Are you okay?" she questioned, taking her hand back.

"Yes, everything's fine." He laid on a weak, strained smile. "The entrance is to your right. Please, enjoy your meal."

It took a second for Draya to answer. She searched him up and down for the truth to spill out somewhere but sadly came up empty. "Thank you . . ."

On the sidewalk, Jetson helped Draya over the block of ice stuck to the sewer drain. She pulled him aside just as he tried leading her into the restaurant.

Under the golden-lit naked tree, she huffed. "I can't go in there," she complained as loudly and silently as possible.

"Why?"

"Look at me! This is a four-star restaurant, and you want me to step in there wearing a turtleneck, jeans, and boots? Hell, I'm sure they won't even *allow* me in there like this."

"You're getting in. You're with me, and you look fine." Then with his hand on her lower back, he gently pushed her toward the building.

Typical fuckin' man.

"You had me over here thinking we're going to Outback," she continued protesting, her feet moving faster with Jetson's guidance.

"You look fine. Our seats are in the cut. We oversee the entire restaurant where only a select few can see us. We have reservations. I'm sorry, but I wanted *you* tonight. Not the Hollywood glammed-up shit. Just you." His finger pointed into her chest.

"I'm going to be so out of place." She held back tears.

Jetson noticed the emotions covering her face and took her over to a stone bench connected to the restaurant. "You'd be out of place if you were dressed up, and I couldn't recognize you. You don't need all that extra shit." He kissed her.

Draya spoke in the middle of their kiss. "Just because I'm a big girl doesn't mean I don't clean up nice."

Jetson pulled away and rubbed the sides of his temple. "Your weight has nothing to do with

this. Everything is *not* about your weight, Draya."
Aggravation was highlighted in his words. Then
feeling annoyance emerge, he paused. "Don't take
this the wrong way, but are you self-conscious
about your weight because you're unhappy with it,
or has someone got into your head about it, like an
ex or something?"

One week into their relationship and Jetson
was already trying to peel away the layers of her
existence.

Draya folded her arms to fight off winter and to
contain herself. "Whatever." She got up.

Jetson grabbed her wrist and directed her back
down next to him.

"I'm serious. Why is your weight such a touchy
subject?"

Draya gawked at the empty, frozen coy pond.
"I've never had a boyfriend. Kansas guys aren't
big on big girls, so when I moved here, I didn't try
dating. Why set myself up for rejection, ya know?"
She kicked her leg in and out.

Jetson gripped her thigh, slowing her nervous
movement. "I'm your first boyfriend?"

This was the moment Draya discovered Jetson
carried dimples. She blushed.

"Shut up," she joked.

"I promise you if your weight ever becomes
a problem, I'll tell you—no dropping hints and
keeping secrets. I'm going to be everything you

deserve. Just," he used his thumb to wipe away the tear gliding down Draya's cheek, "give me a chance to show it without you jumping to conclusions."

Draya allowed herself to spit out a few tears and melt into Jetson's arms. As exhausting as love was, it was also liberating.

Hand in hand, the two approached the hostess, who couldn't have been one hundred and twenty pounds soaking wet. Acknowledging her arrival, the overly thin woman lit up like the trees outside the restaurant.

"Leslie, good to see you," Jetson greeted.

Leslie dipped her head to the side, her blond hair falling over her bony shoulder. "Jetson . . . Long time no see." She tapped a pen against her pink lips.

"Yeah, I know. I've been a little busy this visit." He tightened his hold on Draya. New to this game of tit for tat between the same sex, Draya gave it a whirl. She straightened her back and cocked her head to the side, her ropelike hair surpassing her shoulder. Leslie followed the length of her hair, which led to the couple's cupped hands.

"I see." She took the pen from her lips. "Very nice, anywho. Let me show you to your table."

Walking inside the dining room felt like a game of Pac-Man. Dodging and avoiding every table bypassed so her hips wouldn't knock over wineglasses and purses hanging behind chairs became a job. Leslie weaved in and out of aisles effortlessly. Draya looked over her shoulder at Jetson, curious about whether he observed her battle with the table and chairs. When he caught her eye, he gave a pretend kiss.

No lies were told when Jetson said their seats overlooked Centra. The two sat tucked in a corner inside a widened circular booth with silk drapes tumbling at the sides on a slightly elevated stage. They gawked at each other from underneath the spotlight and fiddled with each other's fingers. There was no waiting for the waitress to appear and take their orders and even less of a wait for their appetizers. The two fed each other. Draya swallowed her second jalapeño popper cheese ball when Jetson excused himself to the restroom, leaving her to enjoy the view. Scanning the room's starch-white patrons, she took a sip of her wine. *And here I am, thinking I'd stand out because of my clothes.*

She took another sip. Appreciating the shimmery floors and golden-tip tabletops, Draya's sight landed on specs of color three tables to the left. A group of elderly men surrounded by bottles of wine and shot glasses on and around their plates conversed in small groups.

It's like a miniature United Nations of the old.

"More wine?" the waitress questioned.

Draya held out her glass. "Thank you."

The oldest of the batch, his olive-skinned face full of gray and wrinkled skin overlapping his collared shirt, made eye contact with Draya. He politely smiled and nodded, then revisited his conversation. He shared a few words with his friends before looking back over at Draya. His face contorted, and he nudged the stumpy Middle Eastern man beside him. It didn't take long for the men surrounding the old-timer to dump all their attention on Draya.

"What the fuck are they looking at?"

The Middle Eastern man held his phone up for those across from him to see. He pointed in Draya's direction, then at the phone.

Shit. Those old farts know me from somewhere. Draya reached for her phone, and a new text from Willard was displayed.

Draya, let me know if you're okay or I'm coming over tonight. Where are you? LadyJogs is bashing you and taking viewers.

From the corner of her eye, she saw the entire table staring her way. She texted Willard back.

I'm fine. Is there anyone talking about me on Peepers?

Draya looked across the restaurant in search of Jetson. *Man, I hope he's taking a shit. He's been gone for a while.* Her leg jumped while watching those small brutal dots move next to Willard's name, confirmation that he was typing back. She had to submit a complaint to Peepers. It made no sense that camgirls couldn't disable their chats and must go live when signed in. They should be able to appear without notice to viewers. *Come on, Willard. Hurry the fuck up.*

There's a public chat dedicated to you. Men are saying they're at the same restaurant as you and that you look even better in person!

The entire table had their heads in their phones.

Draya, is this you?

Willard sent a photo. It wasn't clear who it was. The distance was too far. However, the burgundy sweater and high dreaded ponytail were noticeable.

They're saying you're at some restaurant called Centra?

***

"Casey?"

Draya jumped, her phone dropping on the table.

"Casey, it's me." The balding, tanned Italian slapped his hands against his double-breasted suit. "CumDaddy. I watch all of your shows." He tried to take a seat.

"Whoa, I'm sorry, but you have the wrong person." Draya changed her voice.

She made it deeper, raspy, with inspiration taken from smokers worldwide.

"You, you look so much like someone on," he leaned down to Draya's level and, in a hushed tone, told her, "a website I frequent."

"I don't know what you're talking about."

Draya watched Jetson bypass Centa's second replica of the table they occupied a few feet away.

"I have no idea what you're talking about, but I'm highly offended by the implication that I'm some-some porn star." Draya breathed heavenly, her hand on her chest.

"No, no, I don't mean to—"

"Listen, please, leave me be. My boyfriend is returning from the restroom, and I'd like us to eat in peace."

Looking behind him, he caught sight of Jetson heading their way. He looked once more at his phone and back at Draya. "It's just so uncanny."

Jetson made it to the table when their unwelcomed guest made his exit, his head stuck in his phone.

"I miss something?" Jetson slid inside the booth and watched the stranger take his seat amongst his peers. "Why was Grandfather Time at our table?"

"Mistaken identity." She sipped the red wine, licked her lips, and decided to test the water. "He thought I was some camgirl."

"What's that?" He folded the bottom of his sleeves and picked off the remaining poppers.

Draya took another sip of her drink. Then, noticing only a few sips left, she flagged down their waitress and pointed to her glass.

"It's people who are watched over the internet. Think of it as reality TV on the internet."

"I know what you're talking about." He indulged in his rum. "That's some good shit right there."

"What do you think about that?"

"About what?"

"Camming. People getting paid to entertain over the net."

He grinned. "If it's adult entertainment, and you were on it, I'd watch every day." He leaned back, giving him a better view of her backside. His eyes wandered up and made their way to her breasts.

"Really?" she asked. Innocence drenched in the question.

He spoke directly into her ear, his lips grazing it. "You're pissed you're not more dressed up, but I think you look sexy as fuck." Then from underneath the table, he grabbed her hand and placed it on his growing package.

"Let's leave."

Draya's mental reverted to a juvenile state of mind. Her pulse raced, palms moistened, and a wave of shyness whisked by. "We can't leave. Our food hasn't come yet."

"We'll take it to go. I want you now." He unzipped his pants, and the pulsating monster slithered out of the split and pushed at her hand.

Playing along, she grabbed it, then immediately dropped it. She balled up her lips and grabbed at her throat, her soap opera reenactments strong.

"Jetson, is that all you?" She couldn't close her open mouth.

He put her hand back on it. "Leave with me and find out."

It didn't take long for Draya to snatch her purse and jacket and stand from the table. "I'll get the car. You pay the bill and get the food."

There was no waiting for an agreement.

Draya dashed for the exit. Needing to slow her pace when bypassing tables was a buzz kill.

"I have to fuckin' lose weight," she mumbled.

Avoiding eye contact with the table housing her viewers, she slid by as gracefully and swiftly as possible. Head held high, she almost made it without the comments and gazes when she heard one man say . . .

"It has to be her. Looks just like her."

"Well, you know what they say," another chimed in. "Everyone has a twin."

Chapter 13

Draya didn't miss her home. Didn't miss the gloominess, darkness, or isolation it provided. She hadn't seen her place in the week she'd been seeing Jetson other than to grab her belongings. His place was different. It supplied an entirely different aura. He had colors, rich colors, bright lights, and many frames preserving the happiness captured. His Brooklyn town house defined what it was to be happy and accomplish goals set forth. The environment alone sucked out her misery and planted seeds of hope that she could be at peace and enriched with surroundings of positivity within her own space one day.

Jetson held her naked body from behind, his nose occasionally breathing in the mango honey scent spewing from her hair.

"I like you here."

"I like me here too." Draya looked at his luggage neatly posted against the closet doors. "What will happen to us when you go back to L.A.?"

Jetson squeezed her. His feeling alone took her breath away and rejuvenated her all at once.

"I've been thinking a lot about that. And there are only two things that make sense."

Draya slightly looked over her shoulder. "Break up or stay together?"

"Yeah, that," he sarcastically spat out. "Either I move here, or you move to L.A."

The knots already unpacked inside of Draya's gut suddenly tightened. Those very options hit her mind daily. However, to even voice the possibility of it after only dating for a week would come across as desperate.

"That's moving fast, don't you think?"

"We've already been moving fast. You've damn near moved in after day one of us seeing each other. We work together, and still, I'm not tired of you."

"Yet."

"Nah, I don't see that happening." He kissed the back of her head.

Within those seconds of silence, Draya thought deeper about the idea. *Move to L.A.* The thought was disappointing, not because she would abandon everything and everyone in New York, but because there was no one or anything to abandon. Draya had nothing. No real friends or career she could proudly boast about. Yes, she was an SFX makeup designer, but the movie she worked on wasn't in the big leagues. It had potential only because of Phillip, but that was about it, and Willard, a freak without friends, was just like her.

"You know what? As sad as fuck as this may sound, I have nothing or no one here to stay for. Hell, even if I were still in Kansas and my parents were around, I'd still have no reason to stay."

"Turn around."

Draya did as she was asked.

"What's the story with your parents, the full story? You told me when they divorced, you never saw your mother again and that your father stayed in Kansas until he died, but that's about it. There has to be more to them."

Where's your waterbed when you need it? Draya wanted to drown. She wanted the world to open and suck her in.

"I don't feel like getting into that now."

"I get it, but if we're talking about moving in together, shouldn't we start the process of getting to know each other? I feel like I know nothing about your past."

He's right. Tell the truth and shame the devil. Draya lay on her back. If she would reveal information, she couldn't do it while looking him in the face. Had he shown any expression of disgust or judgment, it would break her. She couldn't go through another breakage when his presence made her feel she was being rebuilt.

"I'm self-conscious about my weight because I was made to be. I was made to believe I was ugly, unwanted, and unworthy because I was fat. I was told on a daily by my father that no man would want me and no person would respect me. Then when I was 15, I was raped, and my attacker made it known I disgusted him because I allowed myself to look the way I had."

Jetson sat up. The words leaving her mouth were too real, heartbreaking, and unbelievable. She wanted to look at him, to take a break and allow him to voice his thoughts and questions, but she didn't. If she were opening Pandora's box, she had to do it fast, so she did. Before she lost the nerve, she told him the entire truth and story regarding her rape. Although tough, she left nothing out and pushed through the emotions when speaking about Taylor and Doris.

"Hold, hold, hold up. Are you serious?" the details strangled Jetson's heart and made him ache.

"Those women, they-they," Draya's voice cracked, "were the two who led me on the path to love myself. They were helping me eat right and exercise. After a month of their support, I lost twenty pounds. They were doing everything I needed my father to do but hadn't."

"You asked your father to help you lose weight?"

"Yes. He was the one responsible for putting it on me."

Draya could see Jetson open and close his mouth from the corner of her eye, internally deliberating what to say.

"Then they were the big ones. My mother hated herself for it, so she got her shit together and lost over 100 pounds. I guess she started feeling herself because she picked up, filed for divorce, and disappeared. That fucked up my father, so he took his pain out on me." Draya went on to explain how her father killed her health and self-esteem.

After laying on him the details, she stopped talking. Her knotted stomach tightened around itself so much that she almost vomited. Then finally, after taking a few deep breaths, she spoke again.

"One day, I asked him why he was doing this to me, and he told me. He finally fucking told me." Draya used the cotton sheet to dap at the corner of her eyes. "He told me, 'Your ass will never leave me like your mother did. You'll never have the opportunity to be more or do more. Skinny bitches are evil, and I'll be damned if you'll ever be a skinny bitch.'"

The years of bottling up the truth and leaving her father's work untouched and undone came seeping out through her eyes and soul. She tried to continue talking, but her voice was lost, and her throat closed. Her shoulders jumped up and down as she hid her face in embarrassment.

Jetson pulled her into him. Her breasts smashed against his stomach, and her tears lubricated him. She hollered, her only way of letting out her voice. She screamed while her balled fist banged into the bed.

Sobbing while trying to catch her breath, Draya stuttered, "How could-how could he-he do that to me?" She pushed her face deeper into him. "When my friend died, you know what he told me? The same day I found out?"

Jetson didn't respond. He only listened.

"He told me she offed herself to get away from my fat ass, and now he's the only one left who can stomach me." She huffed. "That was the day I fell off the wagon, ate everything in sight, and put back on double the weight I'd lost. Since then, I stopped caring about my health just enough to stay alive. So, unless you tell me I can't bring my art with me to L.A., there's nothing I'd be leaving behind." Draya pulled out of Jetson's hold, turned around, and plucked a tissue from the nightstand's tissue box.

Back turned to Jetson, she dried off her face. Then dabbing her cheeks, she told the end of her life story.

"My father died of a heart attack. Go figure. I went back out to Kansas, cremated him, and spread his ashes over his farm, the only thing he did and knew how to care for properly."

"Have you ever tried looking for your mother?" Jetson's hand rubbed the center of her back.

"I never even thought of it. What woman, let alone a mother, would leave her family because she shed some weight and got a new ass and pair of breasts? She left her daughter to fend for herself because her husband sure didn't. Her never returning or even calling let me know everything I needed to know. I don't need to reach out."

"Have you noticed no one mentions *my* mother? All the documentaries and speeches made at galas and birthday parties, and no one mentions *my* mother?"

Draya pulled another tissue. She held it and thought. She'd done a lot of research on people in the film industry when deciding on doing makeup, and Jetson was right. No one ever mentioned his mother.

She sniffed, then wiped her nose. "I noticed that. What happened to your mother?" She sat up and leaned against the headboard. She took Jetson's hand, and he too used the board for support.

"My mother was a child star. A big fuckin' deal from age 5 until 21. She was so booked that it became overkill. She played almost every movie that required a child or teen role." Jetson dropped his head and smiled. That made Draya smile.

"I have all her movies. As a teenager, I memorized all her lines for all her roles. Anyway, she hit a dry streak at 22. A surplus of new blood hit, and everyone wanted a new face. My mom was put on ice, and that's when she met my dad, who was a writer and on the come up."

Draya made a face. "Your mother's Grace Hill? When you Google your dad, there are a couple of pictures of him with an actress named Grace Hill. She was young and stunning."

"Yup. That's her. The relationship started as a publicity stunt. Although slowing down, she was still known and on the fast track. My dad was still not fully known, so they thought to join forces, and how my dad tells it," Jetson changed his voice, "give the people something to talk about." Draya lay her head on his shoulder.

"After two weeks of them *seeing each other*, they both got what they wanted. My mom was getting booked again. This time for the roles of mistresses, and my father was working Black Hollywood's top scripts. I don't know when or how, but the fake relationship became real, and she was pregnant with me. Fast-forward two years later, and she left us for Hollywood's new heartthrob. At the time, he was able to give her more publicity than my father could, so she left."

Draya looked into his face. Since she met him, a light always glowed inside his eyes. That light brightened when he mentioned memorizing all his mother's roles, but now, she noticed that light had dimmed.

"Let me guess, you never saw her again?"

"I did. My father and uncle took me to an awards show where my uncle was the recipient of two awards. After the show, my mother approached me. New lips, high cheekbones, and Botox. A fucking walking Barbie. I was so happy to see her. I was 10 years old then, so I ran into her arms. When she let me go, she asked me before saying anything else, 'Is your uncle still married to Aunt Karen?' She didn't give a shit about me or my father, only her next meal ticket. After that, I saw her only in gossip magazines. I wanted to hate her so fucking bad, but my mother's a beautiful woman, which makes it hard to hate someone."

"Do you think that's why you dated a certain type of woman? Did they all resemble your mother in some way?"

Jetson nodded. "I think so. When you really think about it, they were all skinny, dark-skinned, and all fancy, even when shopping at the supermarket. I say I was following my friends, but that's not the truth. Maybe psychologically, in some sick sort of way, I was searching for my mother."

"It's not sick; it's human." Draya had a burning question to ask. One she was scared to ask but had to know. "Is there anything about *me* that reminds you of your mom?"

She hoped he didn't notice her holding her breath.

"Nope, which is exactly why I think I like you so much. There was a fast-revolving door of women who've come and gone, all because they were too much like her. They looked like her, talked like her, held secrets like her, and as expected, hurt me like her."

Draya tensed up. "Secrets?"

"My mom was married when she met my father. Yeah, it was fake in the beginning, but they were still fucking."

"Wow. So secrets are a deal breaker for you?" She quickly tried cleaning up the question. "I mean because you mentioned your exes being like her in that way."

"Hell yeah. Isn't it for you?" He looked at her, his face scrutinizing her.

"Depends on what it is. Depends on the situation."

Jetson scratched his bare chest. "I used to think that way, but there is no small secret when it comes to hiding things from people you claim you love and who you trust."

"Sounds a little close minded," she admitted.

Over the sheets, he rubbed her knee. "Only to those with something to hide."

It became the battle of the stare. A good old Western stare down.

"Is there anything *I* should know? Speak now or forever hold your peace." He gave a half smile. A conscious, forced smile.

Without breaking eye contact, she told him, "Not at all."

The stern intensity his eyes held vanished as quickly as it appeared.

"Good, now back to us discussing moving in together."

Chapter 14

"Where have you been all my life?" Willard landed face down on the bed in his birthday suit, sweaty and breathing off-key. His ashy ass was up in the air and available for a second. When he caught his breath, he slowly crawled to the top of the bed, where he flipped on his back, legs wide.

"Here and there, wherever there's money, honey."

"There's more of that green for you if you're up for round two in thirty minutes," Willard beamed.

"Thirty minutes?"

"Thirty minutes," he repeated. "Scout's honor." He threw up three fingers, grabbed his pants from the floor, and snatched his phone out of the pocket. He set the alarm for the agreed-upon time, then showcased it. "See. I shall not tell a lie. Now, in the meantime, sit with me and keep me company." Willard patted the space next to him.

"All right, but only because you have such a cute ass."

He waltzed over to the opposite side of Willard's bed and flopped down. Then he wiggled around until he found comfort.

Willard slid closer to his paid companion and tossed his arm around him.

He pulled away, his colored bang swaying from side to side. "Oh, dollface, cuddling's extra."

"I'm good for it." Willard pulled him in and under his arm. He lay his head on Willard's shoulder and wrapped his arm around his stomach.

"There we go, nice and comfy," Willard boasted.

He held his phone out in front of his face and logged on to Peepers. Then he scrolled down the profiles of all the camgirls he followed and looked for who was logged on.

"What's that?"

Willard answered without looking at his playmate, "Peepers. It's a camming site. I'm a VIP member." Willard flashed his yellow choppers.

"Really? So that stuff's real, huh?"

"As real as it gets. I call it reality porn. There's something for everybody." He tapped on Betty Big Boobs' profile. "You see Betty here? She specializes in getting titty fucked and motor-boated." He clicked on one of her past shows where Betty was getting motorboated in the shower. Her jumping up and down fast, then slowly, increased her ratings. "They get paid? How?"

"When you subscribe, you attach your credit cards or bank account. It's just like shopping. You see what you like, and you pay. Only difference is you decide on payment. The better their pay, the higher they rank."

"Ummm, they got anything up there for the boys?" Willard's playmate inquired.

"Of course, I just don't visit those rooms. Too many people know me on here. Don't need them knowing I dabble in extracurricular activities."

"Umph," Playmate huffed. He moved over a little.

Willard ignored the judgment and agitation covering his playmate's tone.

"Here you have Tongue Twister Abby. I think the name says it all." Willard winked.

His playmate looked everywhere except at the phone. Instead, he focused on the closet door dangling from one hinge, the leftover two-day-old burger and fries that attracted flies, the paper plate pushed in the corner on the far end of the bedroom, and the slabs of brown paint on the eggshell walls. Totally uninterested in heterosexual sexual antics, he'd rather look at the mess he was paid to screw in.

"Okay, okay, 3-Way Karen has a few shows where she's in a three-way with two men, and there are a few scenes where it's just the men. Here, look."

"Thank you," Playmate smiled and looped his arm with Willard's.

Willard scrolled through the profiles.

"Wait wait wait. Go back down. Oh no, no, is she wearing a latex dress? Damn shame. All right, keep going."

Playmate found amusement in judging the girls off their profile pictures. A fashion guru in his own right, he played a fashion critic and took joy in the bashing.

"Zoom in, daddy. Oh no, she's the worst. Do you see her toes leaning over the front of her shoes? I can't. I'm done."

"Princess, are you going to judge every girl we pass?"

"If she's a hot mess. Now, keep scrolling."

Willard bypassed three women without interruption. By the seventh profile, he was ordered to stop.

"Hold on. Zoom all the way in on that one." He pointed at the photo of an overweight woman dressed in a sheer bra and matching thong and closely examined it.

"Pretty, right? She's my friend. I mean, my *real* friend, not that social media shit." Then slowly, Playmate asked, "Can you go into her profile?"

"Sure, her real name is Draya. Cool as fuck. We're good friends. We fuck around every now and then, but we're not in a relationship."

Now inside the world of Casey, Playmate asked Willard to go through her pictures.

"You met her off this site?"

"No. She's a pay-for-play girl like you." He formed his lips in a kissing motion. "I was at a bachelor party a couple of years ago, and we ordered a few girls to come in and shake up the place, but that was back in the day. She doesn't do parties anymore."

"She's been doing this for years?"

"Prostituting? Yeah. Camming only for about a year."

"She does this stuff for a living or sporadically? You never know, I may want to try out this camming shit. Bitch can never have too much money."

"Oh, she's in this to win. Girl's a pro, so I'm shocked she's been under the radar for some time now. Hasn't done a show or taken on clients I was sending her way. I don't know what's gotten into her."

Playmate placed his hand behind Willard's head and rubbed. "Darling, you mind letting me see your phone. I want to get a good look at Draya, pretty thing she is. She's the only one I have not one bad thing to say about."

"Here you go." Willard handed over his phone.

"Thank you, puddin'." Playmate pecked him on the cheek. He took the phone and looked through all twenty photos posted on the profile page. Each one provocative and seminude. "Dollface, show me where to go to see one of her shows."

Willard's hand was under the faded sheets. His hand moved up and down. "On the top, the top on the right," he panted.

"Thank you, puddin'. Now, don't get too comfortable over there. I won't be too long."

Willard's hand moved faster, and his breathing labored. "Hurry."

Playmate clicked on the green button with a small video camera imprinted on it. The page it directed him to was called The Vault. Inside contained at least fifty videos. The first video he watched involved Draya pleasuring herself. The camera started from her face. It recorded her facial expressions for five minutes before moving down to her womanhood.

This really is that bitch.

The camera was so close you'd think she was filming herself. Then suddenly, something shot out at the camera and wet the screen, the ending the show.

Oh, bitch is a squirter. What a talent.

He returned to the video inventory and tapped on a video dated October 31, 2022. There, Draya's entire physique was covered in body paint. She used her time on the screen slowly peeling the paint from her skin.

Willard's legs grew stiff. "Sonny, hurry up. I can't hold it much longer."

"Hold it, dollface, hold it. If you end the party, and I have to stay longer. I'll have to charge you double for the clients I miss!"

"I'll try," Willard whimpered, his hand moving faster.

Sonny scrolled down to the last video in Draya's vault. The date read almost a week and a half ago. He clicked it. Draya's voice was loud and clear.

"Welcome back, everyone, and to answer a few of your questions and thoughts, no, I haven't lost my mind. I just had a moment, but I'm back. It's Wednesday night. Truth night. However, I haven't been truthful tonight, haven't followed my own rules on purging what's holding me down, and worse, breaking me down. Instead, I've done the opposite, but now, I'm ready to reverse that and do my part."

"Sonny!"

"I'm coming, dammit!"

"Please don't say that word," Willard pouted.

Sonny fast-forwarded a few times, getting the overall gist of her speech without missing every little thing.

Why am I telling you all this? Because you're right. I don't love myself.

Willard's legs buckled, and he moaned in a state of pleasure, which sent him to a world of ecstasy. Then having lost his breath and his chest heaving in and out, he managed to say, "Sonny, I did it again."

Sonny dropped the phone on the bed. "You love pissing me off, don't you? Love paying extra just to get me to stay longer, huh?"

"Yes," Willard nodded.

"You know what, Will?"

Panting, he responded, "What?"

"Today's your lucky day because I'm throwing you a freebie."

"Really?" Willard beamed, an overgrown, troubled child.

"Yes, you just gave me the ammo I need to demolish one big bitch."

"Huh?"

Sonny went in for a kiss.

"Wait. Let me clean myself off first." Willard grabbed the dingy, stained washcloth he used to wash up that morning.

Sonny snatched it from his hand and hurled it across the room.

"I like leftovers, baby. I was always taught never to let my food go to waste." Sonny dived in Willard's lap, Draya's pained, battered voice echoing inside his head.

Dumb bitch. I knew you weren't perfect.

Chapter 15

"You have to tell him."

Sitting on the couch in Jetson's town house, staring at the muted cooking channel, Draya regretted telling Dr. Vanity about Jetson and him needing transparency.

"This man clearly has trust and abandonment issues, and you not coming clean can jeopardize your and his relationship and his healing process. How is he ever supposed to grow when he keeps getting beat down by every woman he gives a chance to?"

Draya turned the television up. She watched as the chef added eggs, onions, and bacon topped with an array of seasoning in a skillet.

"Draya, are you listening to me?"

She muted the station. "Yeah, I'm listening to you."

"So, what are you going to do then? You're in the man's house as we speak, and you two seem to be doing more than contemplating moving in together. Much more. I won't be surprised if I speak to you next week, and you're poolside in his L.A. home."

Draya got up from the couch and walked over to Jetson's trophy case. That man had partaken in every sport under the sun and came out triumphant.

"Do you understand what he doesn't know about me isn't something as common as me having a boyfriend on the side or pretending I want to move in with him when I really don't? You can see my ass live and in color anytime for a nine-dollar ninety-nine-cent monthly subscription. I'm sure those men who recognized me at Centra's were loaded. Can you only imagine which of Jetson's peers saw me?"

"I understand where you're coming from—" Dr. Vanity tried to interject.

"No, Dr. Vanity, you don't. I'm a fucking camgirl and, on top of that, a prostitute. That type of shit doesn't make a woman a housewife."

Draya went quiet, trying to figure out how to possibly get the psychologist to understand a portion of where she was coming from if not much. But then again, while she went on the hunt for words, she questioned whether a 50-year-old, attractive Caucasian woman whose first career venture was modeling lingerie and had two living, doting parents who renewed their vows every other year could truly understand.

"I have nothing. I've had nothing damn near all my life, and now it seems the curse has finally been lifted, and I can walk amongst the loved and happy. I'm not giving up that."

"Even if it cost you eternal love?"

The question lingered in the air. Then on the crystal-clear glass, Draya placed her finger over Jetson's face in one of his team pictures and rubbed it.

"It won't cost me if I keep quiet."

"Draya."

"No, Dr. Vanity, my mind is made up. Next subject. I have many issues you can lecture me on. Leave this one alone." Draya waved her hands around, the pods in her ear not moving an inch.

"Draya, listen to me. Answer me this, and the issue's a goner."

"What?" Draya leaned on the frame of the balcony doors.

"I know it's early, and maybe it's too soon to know. But I've always believed that someone can fall for someone as fast as a few days if the two spirits connect and they're truly meant to be. Do you love this man? Or at the very least care deeply for him?"

Draya's head tapped gently against the door frame several times before answering.

"I love this man. I'm in love with this man, in awe, infatuated, and have puppy love. I'm in lust.

I'm in every and anything possible for a woman to feel for a man in a romantic way, and I don't think it's because he's my first love. It just feels so right." Her eyes closed, and hand slid down her neck.

"Then why start things out like this? Why, when he's given you the opportunity to come clean and has done nothing but be truthful, give you respect, and the love you prayed for? Why be another liar and replica of his mother? Why not be better?"

Draya's hands wrapped around her throat and applied pressure. She squeezed until her hand plunged inside her skin and disrupted her breathing. Finally, she squeezed out the truth she kept repeating once more.

"Because I don't trust it will matter. I don't trust my honesty or his love for me would be enough to accept this." Draya's bottom lip quivered. "I can't lose someone else, Dr. Vanity. I don't think I can survive it. But I'll do right from now on. No more camming, no more prostituting. I'll jump on the straight and narrow. I'll become who he thinks I am."

"You say you can't lose him, but, honey, you already have if you're going against one of the most important things he needs from you, which is honesty."

Draya released her neck. Although free of the physical punishment, her mental stepped in and had her still believe, still feel her neck was on the verge of choking the life out of her. She struggled to speak.

"That's your thoughts."

"That's a fact," Dr. Vanity threw back.

"Everything will be fine. I have what I need now. Like you told me, this camming, hooker shit resulted from chasing what I've wanted—love and acceptance. I have that now. I'm cured."

"Ms. Ruckers, you're *not* cured. You're doing nothing except what you've been doing, and that's living with the pain and not coming at it head-on. You bury things. You bury your mother, you bury your weight, and now you're burying how you self-medicated to survive your past. You want to get rid of it all for good? Come clean and not just to Jetson but to yourself. The truth shall set you free. You know what they say . . . Tell the truth and shame the devil."

The imaginary hand tightening around her neck released.

"Well, Draya. I wish you luck with your decision, and I really hope you make the best one. Are we still on for next week?"

Dry and harsh, Draya managed to say, "No, I don't think so."

"Then how about the following week?"

"Not looking good either."

Dr. Vanity pressed on with the hope she tried keeping alive. "And the next?"

"I'm sorry, but no."

"D, you here?"

Jetson walked through his home. Ever since he met Draya and she started staying over, it became a habit to call out to her whenever arriving home. He liked the gesture, liked the corniness of trying to mimic TV families. The dining room table's centerpiece played as a porcelain vase with different shades of green and gold trim holding two dozen pink peonies. They were the first flowers he'd purchased for Draya. The first flower to give her the gift of peace.

Jetson learned when he walked in on her watching a Netflix gardening show that she had a thing for the smell of flowers. She believed it stimulated the positivity in her and uplifted her spirit. It was a pleasure she mainly partook in during the spring and summer months when she could walk in the parks, sit on a bench next to a lake or a garden, and just be. There was no number named for the times she visited the botanical gardens. Draya did not discriminate. She loved all the botanical gardens New York had to offer, even those geared toward children.

So, Jetson promised twice a week during the spring and summer months and three times during the fall and winter that she'd have colorful bouquets wherever she laid her head. They'd be a variety of flowers used to give off several scents for Draya to inhale and soothe her soul. Whatever was needed to conquer the demons her parents left her with, he'd do.

He looked over the flower petals and their stems, spending hours researching how to care for the different breeds of flowers he tended to shower upon Draya. He constantly joked and referred to himself as the flower doctor.

"Looking good, Ivy." Then holding on to a bouquet of marigolds, Jetson scooped up the vase in his other arm and went for the kitchen. "Ivy, this is Ginger. Ginger, Ivy."

"Ginger?" Draya appeared from around the corner. "You're naming the flowers without me? I know you said talking to plants and stuff is a good thing, but now you're just taking over my girls." Draya flashed her dimples.

"Come on, look at her. She has Ginger written all over her."

Draya relieved Jetson of Ginger and followed him into the kitchen. He emptied the vase's contents, replaced it with fresh water, and set Ivy beside it. "Do me a favor. There's a lime-green and blue vase in the second cabinet to the right. Put it on the island next to Ginger."

"You don't want me to put her in water?"

"Not yet. I'm trimming her stems after I finish with Ivy's."

Draya stretched her arm up to the cabinet. The tips of her fingers managed to open it on the first try. Inside sat five brightly colored decorative vases. "What happened to all your sports mugs?" She separated the requested vase from its tribe and placed Ginger inside her new home.

"I moved them in the cabinet under the vases. Research shows color stimulates the brain and puts people in a better space. That's why people recommend painting classroom walls in color versus the mundane white. So, I got a few bright-colored vases." Jetson moved from one side of the kitchen to the other. He slid open the kitchen drawer declared the junk drawer and pulled out florist scissors. Leaning against the sink, Draya watched Jetson intensely work on the new and old bouquets.

"Man, I feel dumb as well. I never knew you're not supposed to put flowers near windows where there's bright light."

"Really? I never knew that. Isn't it supposed to help them?"

"If I understand it right, we're treating them how we'd treat plants, and that's where we fuck up. We cut flowers and sell them because they're at their best, the top of their game, to place them next to the heat. But unfortunately, the light will only speed up the death process."

"Really?"

"True story." Jetson slowly and carefully nipped at Ivy.

"What else have you learned?" The sound of excitement radiating through Jetson's voice gave her life meaning and purity.

"You know how flowers come with flower food?"

"Yeah."

"It's not for show or some marketing scheme. It actually helps them last longer. I always thought it was bull, but nah, it's true, and when we run out, we can make our own. It's easy."

"That I knew." Draya tilted her head to the side, taking in the view of what she'd gained.

"I forgot to tell you when you want your flowers in the kitchen, don't put them next to fruit or vegetables."

Draya grinned. "Is that way you moved the bowl of fruit from the dining room table?"

"Yeah, they give off harmful gases to flowers."

"Tell me about that," she encouraged.

She listened to him break down the process nature set forth when it came to fruits such as apples and bananas giving off gas known as ethylene. Step by step, he explained it all, and Draya just listened. The flower and plant research instilled in him made her feel she had finally found her purpose in life. She had made him happy. A rich, handsome man, who had nothing to ask for or wanted, learned something new from a broken, overweight woman searching for herself.

"The gas is not harmful toward humans. It—"

I can't tell him. Look at how happy he is. I made that happen. I don't see positive marks left by his exes on him. So why would I want to mess this all up?

"I think I want to take some horticultural classes. They have some available at the botanical gardens I might sign up for. If I like it, I'll take it more seriously when I go back to L.A. and get a degree in it or something. You never know. A brother might have the green thumb and can fire his gardener and really put in some work. I can dedicate a spot in my backyard to your flower garden and have you sitting there drinking wine and chilling like Jody's moms in *Baby Boy*." He flashed his smile, that gorgeous smile.

Draya took her weight from the sink and batted away the tears on the verge of explosion. "You would do all of that for me?"

"That, and much more." He placed Ivy back inside her vase and moved on to Ginger.

"I told my friends about you. They act like they're happy for me, but I know they think I'm bat crazy for how deep I'm going into this relationship so soon."

"I can understand where they're coming from, but how does that make *you* feel?"

"Not a damn thing. I'm happy. I'm on the road to finally having the family I always wanted . . . A two-parent household where the mother isn't a clout-chasing ho, but instead, an honest, everyday woman with beauty to match. Do you know how hard that combination is to come by, how long I wanted this? My moms really fucked me up when it came to relationships, and now I got a shot at changing my family's failing relationship rate."

Draya was glad he kept his focus on Ginger. In fact, she'd have to thank Ginger later for coming around because had she not been there, Jetson may have caught the number of tears that collapsed out of her eyes onto the tiled floors.

Eyes still locked on Ginger, Jetson asked for confirmation. "Right?"

Draya sucked in the sobs attempting to crawl out of her mouth. "Right."

Chapter 16

Tea light candle glimmers of fire sprinkled throughout the three-floor town house escorted Draya from the front door through the second floor's library and sitting room, past the bedroom, and up to the glass-covered rooftop. Tall patio heaters radiating heat transformed the winter season to spring-glowed yellow. White hydrangeas with one red rose in the middle of each batch filled every empty space the rattan sectional sofas, coffee tables, and the sunk-in pool did not fill. Large, circular LED floating pool lights transitioned from the color white to red every thirty seconds. In front of the pool stood a round glass table set with a pair of metallic gold candlesticks. Dinner plates and oversized goblets sat next to pure, gold silverware. On a plate, a card labeled with her name on the inside read . . .

Turn Around

Hands stuffed inside his gray slacks, folded bottom offsetting the black loafers, Jetson closed in the space separating him from Draya.

"Welcome home."

"What is all of this?"

"We're having dinner. Have a seat."

Draya was gently led away by an elderly man dressed in a black and silver butler's uniform from behind. His long-wrinkled fingers held on to her arm and whisked her over to her seat.

"Where'd you come from?"

"A great man never tells his secrets," Jetson answered.

Draya looked around the rooftop. She'd visited it many times; however, its romantic makeover made it a first-time experience. Jetson sat down. The two undone top buttons on the polka-dot, black, long sleeve dress shirt he sported pulled Draya into a constant ring of improper thoughts.

"I wanted to do something special for you tonight. Wanted you to come over from work and be at ease. Did I do good?"

"You did more than good."

The change of color from the pool's LED lights reflected off the glasses Jetson only wore when home. Draya became lost in the smell of the flowers and the peacefulness the flames burning from the candles demanded. Waitresses she recalled seeing that night at Centra presented their table with hors d'oeuvres and chilled champagne. The ongoing acts of class and surprises drove Draya to finish her glass in one gulp. Her need for liquor *was to calm her so that she'd avoid making stupid comments.*

"*I'm dying to know, have you decided yet?*" *Jetson's voice was always smooth. There was always an enjoyable hint of smooth jazz whenever he opened his mouth. Yet, it was more like honey dripping off his plump lips tonight.*

"*What decision?*"

"*About moving?*"

Now's the time.

"*Before I tell you, there's something you need to know.*"

The waitresses came and removed the untouched food. Quickly, it was replaced with two salad bowls.

I was going to eat that.

"*Tell me. I want to know whatever it is you have to say.*"

Must he always say the right thing?

Aware of the champagne Jetson hadn't touched, she pointed at it and asked, "May I?"

"*Go ahead.*"

The laugh that came out harbored nothing but stress and fear. "A little liquid courage," she tried to joke. However, when the joke fell flat and Jetson remained straight-faced, she spoke in a hurry and without breathing.

"*I'm a prostitute and work on a camming website called Peepers. Since being with you, I've* given it all up, but I still wanted you to know. So please, don't leave me."

"Draya, what are you saying? I understood nothing you just said."

On cue, both waitresses came out, removed the salads, and filled their goblets to the very top. Draya's overflowed and dripped down the table's leg.

Eyes closed, she talked slowly. "When we met, I slept with men for money and was on a camming site called Peepers."

Jetson said nothing, and neither did he move. Draya jumped from her seat and raced over to him. On her knees, her hands grabbed hold of his pants. Fast-talking again, she explained. "I'm done. It's all over. It's in the past—in the past forever, never to resurface."

Jetson pried her hands from his clothes and stood.

"Where are you going? Where are you going?"

From her position down on the ground, the red light glimmering from his glasses made his eyes appear to be holding flames. She got up from her knees, and Jetson held his arm out, pushing her aside.

"Jetson, please say something." She filled in the space he created.

"Move," he roared.

Draya staggered backward, her arm raised in front of her face. Her feet kept moving until she bumped into the sectional, and her heavy mass fell into the seat.

"Fuck." Jetson flipped over the table.

One of the glass legs banged into the ground and broke, the rest of the table sinking inside the pool.

The waitresses and butler reappeared and removed the once-beautiful dinner items needed for a successful night. In seconds, they gathered the silverware, candlesticks, and broken glass from the ground. After ridding the rooftop of its mess, they all jumped into the pool to pull out the table.

Draya approached Jetson from a distance. The fire in his eyes still burned.

"I'm sorry," she cried. "I'm so sorry I didn't tell you before, but I'm telling you now."

"You fucking slut! You're far worse than my mother. You have no pride, no morals! No self-respect!"

"Jetson, please! Just hear what I have to say!" She moved in and grabbed his hand. He pulled away, raised his hand high, and with all the anger built from years of disappointment, used the back of his hand to strike her on the right side of her face. Draya crashed to the ground and rolled into the pool, sinking deeper and deeper

inside the chlorinated water. She watched as the serving staff continued trying to remove the table from the water. The pool became endless, and the staff got tinier the longer Draya sank and the harder she cried.

Draya's feet kicked the bedsheets off her, and in a flurry, she sat up and tried to gain control over the coughing fit railroading her chest. Repeatedly, she banged her fist into her chest and didn't stop until she was knee down in front of the porcelain and pushing up last night's dinner. Catching her breath, she sat on the bathroom floor, not bothering to clean the vomit residue coating the corners of her mouth. After minutes of collecting herself, she used the bottom of her shirt to clear her face. Then with light feet, she reentered the bedroom Jetson allowed her to share with him. She could see where his sweat pasted the fabric through the white sleeveless shirt covering his chest. Without getting too close to where he lay, Draya avoided the floor's hot spot areas where, if she stepped there, the wood creaked like a haunted house. She stretched over to the dresser and ripped her phone off the charger.

Retreating downstairs and into Jetson's guest room, she sat on the armless cushioned chair and waited for the other line to pick up.

"Hello?"

"Dr. Vanity, it's me, Draya."

Draya prepared herself for Dr. Vanity to put her on a temporary hold so she'd slide out of her side of the bed, leaving her husband in a peaceful sleep, but she didn't.

"Are we having second thoughts?"

I can't stand when she's right. "Yes. I can't do it. I can't hide it from him. If I don't tell him, it will eat me alive. I feel like I'm drowning with every minute he doesn't know."

"Guilt has a way of doing that," she whispered. "Telling someone something as big as what you have to say is not easy, but it's worth it. You're doing the right thing, Draya. I'm proud of you."

Then why doesn't it feel like that? Why does it feel like I'm setting myself up for heartbreak?

"I just don't know what I'll do if he leaves me. I feel like I'll start from point A all over again, and I don't think I have it in me to do it. How many people must I lose before I get it right?"

"Don't think of it as losing him. Think of it as finding yourself. You must conquer this demon. It's taken over far too much of your life for too long. It's time for the showdown. Regardless of whether he stays with you, you'll have won your life back, and that's something to be celebrated, not mourned."

A wooden desk sat inside the room next to the wide double windows equipped with a range of stationery. From out of the large bottom drawer, something stuck out from underneath. Draya's curiosity won her over as she strode across the room, the phone clasped to her ear and Dr. Vanity explaining the significance of her findings in greater detail and getting to know herself. She snatched the paper out to not rip it. Its plain white side read *The last time I saw her*. Draya turned the glossed paper over. It was a photo of Jetson as a kid and his mother. They were fancy and dapper looking for the event they attended that evening. Celebrity ceremonies were a time to get out and show out, pose for the cameras, and give your beauty pageant award-winning toothpaste commercial smile. Unluckily for Jetson, that was a time for heartbreak and shattered dreams of a mother he yearned for. There was sorrow in little Jetson's windows to the soul.

Damn you, Grace. You ruined him for us all.

"Do you understand what I'm saying, Draya?"

"Yes, I hear you." Draya didn't put the photo back how she found it. Instead, she wrapped it in a piece of paper and set it on the top shelf of the room's coat closet.

"So, when do you plan on telling him. Have you given it any thought?" Dr. Vanity probed.

"Yes, as a matter of fact, I have. I'm going to do it tomorrow night, over dinner. I have to get this off my chest sooner than later."

"Sooner than later is always a winner," she agreed.

"Yeah, but just in case, be on the lookout for my call. I'm sure I'll need some talking to."

"Always," Dr. Vanity honestly replied. "Call me anytime."

Chapter 17

The Next Morning

The pleasurable shooting feeling of an orgasm robbed Draya of her sleep and brought her to the morning, moaning and pushing Jetson's head farther inside her wet box. Back arched, she pumped her stuff into his face. When her orgasm wore down, she tried to escape his thunder tongue. She pulled away, only for him to retaliate and pull her closer to him. The overwhelming charge of pleasure sent her kicking and slamming her hands down on the bed. Draya went back and forth between begging Jetson to stop and begging him to continue. Kisses on her second pair of lips brought her back to sanity and the world she spent most of her life taking abuse from. Jetson crawled from under the blankets, his tongue licking Draya's pleasure from his lips.

"Good morning."

Damn, I'm going to miss that. "Good morning."
She sat up and kissed him intensely. Their lovemaking mouths began with checkered kisses and
developed into hard, saliva-leaking mouthfucking.

"Damn, girl, and here I am thinking I would be
the one who laid it down this morning."

"Trust me, you did."

He went for one last kiss. "I call first dibs on the
shower," he said in-between pecks. Draya pushed
him away.

"No!"

Jetson stood up and jumped off the bed. He
sprinted for the bedroom's bathroom, which had
the best shower in the house.

Draya kicked her feet in the air. "You cheater!
You used sex as a weapon!" Her legs crashed on
the bed, and she lay spread eagle. "Damn, what
time is it?" With the palms of both her hands,
she rubbed her eyes and let out a semi fulfilling
yawn. Oversized and displayed on her smartphone
screen, 5:02 a.m. glowed in white against the
charcoal-black background.

Draya, what's going on? Where have you been?

Willard had been texting and calling Draya more
and more with every day that passed, and she'd
failed to update Peepers with a new show.

You're ranking is horrible. You have to get back in there.

Fuck, how the hell am I going to tell him I'm done with this shit? How am I going to tell him that I'm done with him? Yes, Willard was an odd, offbeat, nerdy, annoying kid at school that no one wanted anything to do with. Their friendship was uncommon and, from the outside looking in, disturbing, but it was theirs. Willard kept her socially available and one step above falling entirely into the darkness of life. *Maybe there is someone I'm leaving behind.*

Good morning, Willard. I'm sorry you haven't heard much from me.

Willard responded immediately.

Where have you been? Sonya the Nut Cracker and DeepThroat Chrissy are cleaning house. What's the plan?

Water pounding against the shower walls and tub screamed from the bathroom, and so did Jetson's off-key singing.

Willard, I'm done with Peepers. I'm done with sleeping with men for money. I'm done with it all.

I really wish I had taken the time to figure out how I'd tell him all of this. He deserves that, at least.

? What? Why?

Jetson had just hit a broken high note from Chaka Khan's "Ain't Nobody."

I'm moving. It is not who I am or want to be anymore.

Draya sent that message before writing the hard part of their conversation. Part of her wished Jetson would end his encore and give her a reason not to text.

I want to thank you, Willard. Thank you for being my weird but nonjudgmental friend. I'm going to miss you.

There go those dots. Little sons of bitches cause major anxiety.

Where are you going? I can come with. It's cool. You don't have to sell yourself or cam anymore. We can find something else for you to do. What are you into?

Draya became misty-eyed.

I'm sorry, Will, but I won't be alone where I'm going. Now, you take care of yourself, and again, thank you.

Draya felt a pinch in her heart when she sent her final text. Before he could write back that would have her consider keeping him in her life, she blocked his number. The ball to letting go of her past had started, and it had to continue. She signed into Peepers and went straight for her profile. Inside, she scrolled down to the end of the page where the bottom *Cancel Camgirl Services* stared back at her. Draya had visited that button many times in the past. She'd go to it and read it over and over. Her finger had even hovered over it a few times, threatening to press down, but she never found the will or reason to hit it. Jetson's one-man concert concluded shortly after the shower, which acted as his background singers who had also gone quiet.

Her finger over the button, messages appeared, spamming her page.

Raw: Where you been, sexy?
CornbreadGrown: Welcome Back!

Oh fuck, I forgot this shit immediately records when you sign in.

Message after message bombarded Draya's screen. So many hits they had blocked the cancelation button. She went on a message-canceling spree, canceling every greeting that blocked her magic button.

"Stop fucking writing me," she spat into the camera.

The bathroom door opened. "Babe, I forgot to tell you something." Jetson made his way over to Draya, his chest still damp with water beads and a black cotton towel wrapped around his waist.

Two more messages popped up, and Draya slapped her finger against the small x on the corner of the box.

"I spoke with my uncle and *if* . . ." Jetson emphasized.

Draya deleted the last message, and now the cancelation button came into view. Jetson had made it to the opposite side of the king-sized bed and strolled over to his side, his feet sinking into the carpet and leaving behind wet footprints. Draya slammed her finger down on the cancellation button. Automatically, a confirmation message appeared.

Are You Sure You Want to Stop Entertaining for Peepers?

     Yes   No

Jetson stood next to her. "*If*," he again emphasized, "you decide to move to L.A., my uncle has a job for you."

Face still on the phone, Draya didn't reply.

"What are you looking at?"

"Huh?"

"I asked what you're looking at." Jetson bent down.

Draya flung herself to the other side of the bed, her fingers moving quickly as she clicked yes, exited the site, then pulled up her gallery where the last picture was taken of Jetson's junk and left it on the screen. He straddled her. When he started to tickle her, she rolled on her back, and he took the phone out of her hand.

"You fuckin' freak. You ain't get enough?"

"Never," she shouted.

He tickled her some more, then got up and removed his towel. Walking over to the closet, he continued with what he was saying.

"My uncle's taking on a new business in L.A., so you're guaranteed a job in SFX if you come with me."

"You serious?"

"As a heart attack." Jetson removed a sweater and jeans from their hangers. "That is, if you'll move in with me."

"Why do you keep mentioning me moving in with you and not the other way around?" Draya playfully folded her arms across her chest.

Putting on his pants, Jetson answered her question. "Because you told me there's nothing here for you. Out in L.A., I have more, which means we can make better lives for ourselves." Buttoning his pants, he asked, "Are you coming?"

If we're still together after tonight.

"Yup, only if you'll still have me in the morning," she recited, the truth concealed inside every word.

"Then that means you're coming. Welcome to L.A., baby."

***

Leaving with Jetson in the morning meant always getting to work at least twenty minutes early. His discipline and early-morning routines took a lot for someone as unorganized and slow moving as Draya to adapt to initially. However, she received benefits when joining Jetson in his morning workouts and meditation. She gained more energy, felt clear minded, and her anxiety dipped lower than ever before. That was when she wasn't thinking about losing him to her degrading lifestyle choices.

The first in the designated makeup room, Draya took the time to examine her supplies and inventory what needed to be replaced or bought. The silence covering the room gave her mind the unwanted opportunity to wander and fall on the conversation she'd later face.

Draya tried foreseeing the anger, pain, and confusion Jetson would exhibit. She conjured up all probable reactions to the news of her dirty deeds. There, she envisioned him walking out on her, not one word spoken. Then there were the acts of destruction. He'd demolish any and everything around not to touch her, and then came the cursing—the out-of-the-name calling, berating, and threats. Not a thing was off the table and unconsidered. When it comes to the heart, everything goes dark.

"Draya, glad you're in early. Come on out on set. Phillip has an announcement to make. We're catching everyone as they trickle in." Jeanie dipped back out, the voices in her headset navigating her around the building.

"Lights, camera, action," Draya said out loud.

Most of the crew stood around the set patiently awaiting the arrival of two actresses and one cameraman. Draya sat off to the side in one of the oversized throne chairs used when introducing the king and queen of the forest land. Small conversations were held throughout the room, some lighthearted, some entertaining. However, there was only one Draya repeatedly played in different variations in her head. She made it to her fourth scenario when Phoenix, Jackie, and the cameraman all dropped in together. Jeanie rushed them over once everyone was in attendance. Then she flopped down inside the royal seat next to Draya, huffing.

"They don't pay me enough for this shit," she said only loud enough for Draya to hear.

Coffee cup in hand, Phillip walked over from the table of refreshments to the center of the set where everyone could see him. The spotlight above his head beamed down on him just as he stood and looked around the room.

He looked up, chuckling. "A bit much, don't you think?"

The set laughed. Everyone looked up at George above all their heads, giving a thumbs-up.

"I want to start by thanking you all for taking on this project before I even came aboard. The long hours and low pay and budget here are not something people would normally chase after, but we're here and trying to make the best of it. I can only imagine since my coming on set, many of you hope I can transform what naysayers are calling a flop into a moneymaking machine that will catapult all of your careers. I get it. I feel you. I was once where you are now, hoping what you're hoping, needing what you're needing."

Every cast member nodded.

"But let's go back to the naysayers, the haters. They claim that it'll be a flop because this film is low budget and cast with amateur faces—an embarrassment to not only the industry but to your résumés. Now, let me tell you what I have a problem with. I have a problem with associating myself with a project and not bringing some . . ." He looked around, his fingers snapping. "What's the word you kids use? Doctors give you blood thinners for it."

The room erupted in laughter only made possible when pushed up deep from within the core. "Clout!" they all answered.

"Yes, that's it. Clout. I have a problem with taking on a project and not ensuring everyone is involved.

I don't walk away without at least gaining some sort of clout. I don't do that crab in a barrel shit. If I win, you win. If I eat, you eat. Y'all get me?"

Phillip was now slapping his chest; his eyeglasses dribbled down a little. He pushed them up before they hugged the tip of his nose.

"Hell yeah," a man's voice shouted.

The energy the room possessed before Phillip's arrival doubled in positivity and roared with confidence.

"Can I guarantee this film will be a hit and rake in a shitload of cash the first week? No, I can't, but I can have the reason you took on this project be the reason you gained some clout."

"How so?" Phoenix inquired.

Phillip pointed at her. "I'm expanding my catalog. I'm venturing into television. I want to swim with my brother in the world of sitcoms, and I want all of you to bring it to life."

Faces scrunched up. Some looked around, while others stayed fixated on Phillip.

"I'm doing a fantasy television series. Think of a modern-day version of Shakespeare's *A Midsummer Night's Dream* with you all front and center and the heads of whatever it is you were hired here to do."

Eyes bulged out, voices mumbled, and hands clapped.

"Wait wait wait," Phoenix spoke over the growing applause and voices. "So, are you saying, if we were the leading lady in this film, we'd be the star of your show?"

"That's *exactly* what I'm saying. If you're not the star, you will have enough camera time throughout the series to be seen. Mark my words."

Before it got more out of control with joy and relief, Jetson shouted from behind one of the cameras, "Mr. Cobbs, does that mean wardrobe, makeup artist, cameramen—any and everyone will have a role in your show?"

"Boy, you ain't gonna make it in this business if you're not listening." Phillip, joined by several crew members, chuckled. "To answer your question, yes. No one is exempt. Make sure this is something you all can do. All expenses are paid, so get y'all shit together because we're filming in Los Angeles next."

Crazed screams and foot stomping trumped all the previous excitement raiding the set.

"We're going to Hollywood! We're going to Hollywood!" Tinsley and Phoenix gave the room eighties dance moves.

Their throwbacks got almost everyone out of their seats and joined in on different dance moves—some from the eighties, some from the nineties, and some from the early two thousand.

Phoenix threw up her hands. "We in there like swimwear, y'all!"

"We sure are."

Moving his hips from side to side, his arms straight in the air, Sonny danced in the direction of the set, his blond-dyed bang flapping in the wind.

"What is *he* doing here? Where's security?" Jackie demanded.

Jetson abandoned his act of make pretend cameraman and jogged toward Sonny.

"Stand down, y'all. He's here for his check."

"Check? The work he produced should have been free," Phoenix jabbed.

Sonny cocked his head to the side.

"Oh yes, I heard, Sonny. No more club hopping with me." Phoenix sat down and crossed her legs.

"What Jetson said. I'm here to collect." Both of Sonny's hands held on to a manila folder. Then standing in place, he swung it from left to right.

"I'll be back with your check." Jetson went for the back office tucked in the shadows of the first floor.

"So, you all miss me? Bored with Draya's work yet?"

The set fell silent, and glares diverted elsewhere.

Phillip walked out of the spotlight. "Sonny, let's not do this. Why don't you wait here and keep to yourself? Jetson will be back shortly."

"I could do that."

Phillip smiled and faced his crew. "Like I was saying—"

"But I won't," Sonny revealed.

Disrupted, Phillip looked Sonny's way once more. A gush of irritation and tension changed the atmosphere. Everyone began to huff and puff.

"This motherfucker is toxic," Phoenix spewed.

Phillip walked over to Sonny. Then man to man, face to face, he asked him, "Now, why is that, Sonny?"

"Because of that bitch right there." Sonny pointed straight ahead at Draya. Once all eyes were on her, he began to fan himself with the folder. "Now, I may be a little politically incorrect in my speech from time to time, but little miss sunshine over there has some dirty little secrets I'm sure would rattle everyone's sensitive feathers in here."

Phillip asked him, "What are you talking about, Sonny? What is it that you need from us today—attention?"

Sonny flipped open the folder and thrust photos into Phillip's chest. He held them there until Phillip relieved him of the duty.

"I hope you like porn stars because you have one working for you."

Phillip pulled the stacks of photos off him and skimmed through them. They were of Draya's Peepers profile. He set his eyes on Draya and Willard in a collection of compromising positions.

"You should have thought twice about firing me. Is *this* who you want to be associated with your image, Mr. Cobbs?" Sonny tapped his lip with his newly applied manicured tip.

Draya shot up. "What are you showing him, Sonny? What the fuck are you showing him?" she hollered.

Having a clear view of Phillip doing nothing except scanning through photos of the unknown brought on her anxiety and pumped her heart in such a way that she knew her blood pressure had soared.

"You want to see, huh? I'll show you. Who else wants to see?" Sonny snatched the photos from Phillip's grasp and paraded around the room. He stuffed a picture into the hands of those who didn't willingly take one. Then approaching Draya, he waved two in front of her face. When she tried to grab them, he pulled them out of her reach.

"Say please," he taunted.

Jeanie snatched them out of his hands and handed them over to Draya. Draya took hold of the photos and, before she could talk herself out of it, followed behind everyone else and looked. She fought to maintain control of her bowels. She clutched the photos so intensely that her thumbs ripped through the pages, and her body broke out in a sweat storm.

"What the fuck are you doing, Sonny?"

Phillip raced over to his nephew, his hand held out in front of him so he could not take any additional steps. "Don't worry about it, son. Security is on its way." He put on a reassuring stance.

A deflection tactic Jetson learned his uncle adapted during his adolescent years. Jetson moved Phillip's hand aside. "What's everyone holding? What are they all looking at?" Jetson asked the easy questions when he really wanted to ask why Draya's skin had turned pale and her body trembled.

"You want a look-see too? Oh, I got you, Jetson."

Jeanie dove forward just a little more, trying to grab hold of Sonny's coat and drag him back.

"You made your point, Sonny—now leave."

With the last couple of photos in hand, Sonny extended his lanky arm out to Jetson and waited for him to take them. Jetson tossed Sonny's check on the floor and snatched the papers. It was minutes, a full two to three minutes before Jetson pulled away from the pictures and rejoined the group of people he'd met not too long ago. Draya had fallen to her knees, Jeanie down on the floor, rocking her back and forth.

Phoenix clapped her hands repeatedly while talking. "I don't give a fuck if this was proof of her fucking the president. You are fucked up, Sonny. Airing out her dirty laundry like that and with her man around. You need your ass beat, bitch."

"Draya and Jetson are together?" Tinsley asked.

Phoenix snapped, "Girl, *where* you been?"

"These real?" Jetson asked. Although they stood a great distance from one another, everyone knew who Jetson's question was directed at. "You cheating on me?"

Draya wiggled out of Jeanie's hold. Her tears and running mascara left their mark on the arm of her shirt.

"Never! Never! It was before we dated. I promise." Tears mixed with snot trailed down Draya's face that she didn't care to remove.

"You do porn?"

"I did camming." Her face fell in heartbreak. She bit down on her bottom lip and hugged herself tight before continuing. "And I slept with men for money." She dug her nails into her skin and took small steps forward. "I'm sorry. I was going to tell you."

"Don't come near me." Jetson crumbled the pictures and dropped them. "You know how I feel about secrets." His calm demeanor and ability to discuss his girlfriend's betrayal in the work environment with her pictures circulating the room brought discomfort to everyone who witnessed.

"We're gonna die. We're all gonna die. Only psychos are this calm. He's going to cut us into little pieces," Phoenix rambled.

Sonny stuffed the empty folder inside his man purse. "I didn't know you two were seeing each other, Jetson, but it's best you find out before things got serious."

"What did you say to me?"

Focused on Sonny, Draya took his shift of attention to come closer.

"It's best you—"

Jetson charged him. He latched on to his coat and repeatedly buried his face with punches. A busted lip, blood coated Jetson's knuckles and colored the tips of Sonny's hair. Finally, security pried Jetson off the scrawny man.

"I'm suing! You bastard! I'm going to drain you and your entire family dry!" Sonny's refusal to leave on his own led one of the guards to fling him over his shoulder, carrying him out. "Whoever acts as my witness, you'll get a cut of my winnings."

Draya took Jetson's battered hand into hers and examined it. "You okay? You okay? Is any of it your blood?"

Jetson pulled away. He pointed his bloodstained finger in her face. "Stay the fuck away from me. Whatever shit you have at my place, I'll leave at your front door."

He tried to turn away, but Draya pulled on his arm. "I was going to tell you! I was going to tell you."

Jetson spoke to the group of women standing off to the side, teary eyed.

"Get her," he told the women. "Someone get her the fuck now," he shouted.

Tinsley and Jackie rushed over. Jackie managed to break Draya's hold on Jetson, and the two tried leading her away.

"I'm sorry, I'm so sorry," Draya cried. She jumped up and down, wailing uncontrollably.

She pushed Tinsley away and ran Jetson's way when Phillip grabbed her. With the help of a guard, they held her in place. "This-don't do this. Don't do this. I'm sorry," she repeated.

His hand on the handle of the exit, Jetson froze. Thoughts of turning around, grabbing Draya by the hand, and leading her off set so they could talk stormed his mind.

"Leave, just fucking leave," he told himself.

He opened the door, and when the cold air nibbled at his face and his coatless body, he used the back of his hand to wipe away his falling tears and went home.

Chapter 18

Jeanie didn't know what to say when she pulled up in front of Draya's home. So much had already been said at the studio that there was a shortage of words. Her artist sat with her head leaned against the window, her face soaked in tears.

"I can stay overnight if you don't want to be alone, Draya, or you can come to my house."

Draya said nothing. She just rubbed her head into the window and minutes later mumbled, "I should have said something sooner."

"Do you really think it would have helped?"

Draya pinned her forehead to the glass. "It would have saved him the embarrassment of finding out in front of a room full of people."

Jeanie opened, then closed her mouth, selecting her choice of words carefully so as not to cut the faint of heart further. "Were you really going to tell him, or were you just telling yourself you were? You know how it goes. Sometimes, we make plans we never intended on keeping."

"I was going to tell him tonight."

Jeanie leaned back against her seat. "Cool, that counts for something."

"Well, not much." Draya didn't bother putting on her winter coat. Instead, she flung the car door open and dragged the coat out by its fur hood.

She allowed it to act as the city's street sweeper just after slamming the car door harder than she intended. Yet, instead of apologizing, she kept walking. *I said enough* I'm-sorries *for the day. She can take one of those.* Jeanie lowered the passenger's window. Her head dipped low as she called out to Draya.

"You need anything, D, let me know. The next few days at the studio makeup is light work, so Phillip suggested you take some days."

"I bet he did," she shot back without turning around.

Draya slipped her key inside the lock of the home that had grown to feel foreign. Had she had it her way, her next appearance would only have consisted of packing what items of little value she owned, then retreating. After that, she and Jetson would ride off into the L.A. sunlight, where they'd tan and live happily ever after. Instead, she dropped her things in front of her door and dragged herself inside the first-floor bathroom. The bottom of her dress pants, stained by snow residue, left a wet trail behind her. Feminine products stacked next to pain relief and allergy medicine populated the three short shelves built inside the mirrored medicine cabinet.

From the third shelf, Draya went for the eight-month-old tampon box used for nothing but to harbor small baggies containing a white powder she dabbled in when hard times called for it and misery demanded company. Grabbing hold of the sink's corner, she lowered herself to the floor. A couple of grunts followed by a few *motherfuckers* and *dammits* as Draya pinned her elbows on the cover of the toilet seat.

Two small baggies and a replacement hobby blade used for her art tumbled from the box and hit the seat. Draya emptied the baggies' contents, the tip of her battered nail cut into the substance creating jagged lines impossible for her nose to snort. So, she agreed to the terms required of abiding by the unsteady, rickety road ahead of her. Head down, she took out the first line of defense and moved on to row two in a hurry. She rubbed at her nose and treated the drug as a genie, wishing for the day to be nothing but a dream.

She attempted to stand to her feet, crossed her legs, and toppled over. Her shoulder slammed into the wall, and her body slid back down to the tiles. "Fuck." Both hands flat on the floor, ass in the air, she pushed herself up and went for the door. Massaging her shoulder blade pulsating in pain, she returned to the bathroom. *Fuck it. Might as well finish it all upstairs.* She scooped up the last baggie and slid the razor into her pocket.

Slowly, she climbed the steps to her bedroom, giving herself massages, bettering the aches and pain. Then in her short hallway, she heard the sounds of a cheering crowd. The high-energy roaring was a familiar sound. *Is that NBA 2K playing?*

Draya hurried to her room. Before entering, she peeked inside the slightly opened door when her phone went off. Without looking at the received message, she put her cell on vibrate and continued her quest to satisfy her curiosity. Willard lay on her bed, his hands folded behind his head without shoes or socks. At his feet, two figures whose faces were out of sight sat on the floor, aggressively pressing down on the game controllers. Draya pushed her room door open.

"Willard, what the fuck are you doing here?"

"Draya, welcome home."

Draya ignored her ex-friend's greeting and focused on the strange men using her PlayStation. "What the fuck is this? Who the fuck are they?"

"Finally, party's here." One of the men put down his controller.

When he turned to face Draya straight on, he gave her a clear view of the burned left side of his face and missing eye. In shock, Draya backed away and caught her breath.

"Willard, come here, in the hall." She created an even greater distance between her and One Eye.

As soon as Willard stepped inside the hallway with her, she shoved him in his bony chest. "Fuck do you think you're doing? You brought fuckin' johns to my house after I told you I'm done with that shit? Didn't I tell you not to use your key unless it was an emergency?" She got in his face. The spit that flew out of her mouth landed on his cheek.

"It *is* an emergency. Your text messages had me worried. You said you wouldn't be tricking anymore and moving. So, I came to check on you. Annnndddd, since I knew of guys in need of a good time, I thought, why not kill two birds with one stone?" He lowered his head and smiled.

"This shit ain't funny. Get them the hell out of my house."

"I waited two hours for your ass. I'm not going anywhere without getting mine," the bald man whose head was covered in tattoos voiced.

Without invitation, he joined in on their conversation.

"*Excuse* me? You need to get the fuck up out of my house."

After Draya's demand was made, her uninvited guest pressed his arm against her neck and slammed her into the wall, her windpipe now blocked.

"I'm not asking for much," he explained. "Only what your friend over here promised me." Draya scratched and pulled at his hands. With every struggle made, more pressure was applied. Then, wild-eyed and leering at her, he finally eased up on his hold.

Draya desperately drew in globs of air between her coughs. When things no longer looked cloudy, she spoke her truth, her voice low and rough. "I don't know what he told you, but I don't do that anymore."

"Well then, you're going to have to make an exception, now, aren't you?"

Swallowing hard, Draya pushed out Willard's name, her eyes telling him many things all in one stare.

"Just give them what they came for, Casey. Why are you being so difficult? Give them what they want, so we can go back to how things were before you tried changing it all." He stroked her tear-streaked cheek. "You can't just up and leave, Draya. You're my best friend." His voice cracked. He caressed her cheek harder, then whispered in her ear. "I killed for you. You owe me. There's no breaking up this comradery."

"If I'm your friend," Draya wrestled to say, "then please tell them to leave."

The stranger's hand inched up her shirt.

"Willard, please."

"No," Willard snapped.

The tattooed human Mack truck put one finger over her lips. "Shhhh. Now, you heard the man. Give me what I want because no one is going anywhere until you do."

He grabbed Draya by the shoulders and repeatedly slammed her head into the wall. His goal was for her to black out so that his sexual encounter would go without incident. By the second crash against the wall, Draya had slid her hand inside her pocket and pulled out the art blade. Tightly holding on to it as deep and fast as she could with three fingers, she jammed the razor into his Adam's apple. Then pulling it out, she repeated the process. Once Draya was finally released from his hold, she dropped her weapon and watched as his hands became occupied with pressing themselves against the blood-squirting wound. Blood seeping from between his fingers covered his hands like gloves. Not long after, he plummeted to the floor. Bodies shaking, Draya and Willard made eye contact.

"Rin!" Willard hollered. He never took his eyes off his old friend. "She killed Tat!"

Draya took off, her fear pushing her body and all it carried to race downstairs to the front door. Her hand met the doorknob.

"Turn the fuck around, don't scream, and don't say shit unless I tell you to," Rin ordered.

Draya froze but didn't turn around.

"Now!" Rin yelled.

The base and high-volume scream Rin gave off caused Draya's body to jump and her to turn around without hesitation, remaining where she stood. Willard hustled downstairs, his untied sneakers occupying his feet.

"Unlike Tat up there, I'm a gentleman," Rin expressed. "So, I'ma do like gentlemen do and give you two options. You do what the fuck I paid my man over here for you to do, and because of this volatile environment, I suggest throwing in a dick suck. Or I can lace your ass the fuck up for all these motherfuckin' inconveniences and you having the audacity of killing my boy up there." Gun aimed at her, Rin asked, "So, what's it gonna be?"

Both Draya's hands lay at her sides, balled into fists. Her arms and legs shook, and her lips trembled in an effort not to cry out. In control of her screams, yet out of control of all the tears removed from her eyes, she just let the waterworks do what they did. Flow.

"Do it," Willard encouraged. "Do what you're good at, Casey."

"My name's not Casey," she whispered.

"It's gonna be a dead girl if you don't pick what it's gonna be. Now, speak."

"I can't," she yelled out.

The pressure to respond and the pressure of letting go of who she was and remaining true to that, even if it meant giving up her life, increased the volume in her voice.

"You can't, or you won't?" Rin pried.

Tell the truth and shame the devil. "I won't."

"Too bad. I was looking forward to some big girl pussy." Instead, Rin shot at Draya's body four times, once in the head.

When she fell, her body twitched, and her eyes locked open.

In pursuit of the back door, Rin stuffed the gun in the back of his pants and beat the pavement with the bottom of his sneakers, leaving Willard, who stood over Draya's body, to mourn her with drops of tears.

"You should have given it up, Draya. You should have just given them what they wanted, what *I* wanted." He wiped away the snot beneath his nose. "But before you go, how about one for the road." He unzipped his pants, looked at the time, and promised himself to make it quick.

Detective Harper sat behind her desk, alternating between finishing up paperwork and keeping an eye out on a lead her old partner from Detroit believed she could help her out with. Head buried in papers, Harper's nose perked up, and she inhaled the foulest body order she had ever come across since her high school locker days. She searched for the offender subjecting them all to such funk and covered her nose when Willard sped past her. His coat and pants hung so drastically off him that it left Harper wondering if they had fallen from him once he pushed through the exit's double doors.

Detective Stony came out of the interrogation room and sat at his desk facing Harper. Hands folded in his lap, he lay his head back and closed his eyes.

"That bad?"

"That's fucking sad." Stony opened his eyes and sat up. "You saw that walking garbage pail that just left?"

"I didn't see him. I smelled him."

Stony leaned over, his pale elbows on his knees. "Dude's best friend was a prostitute. He brings a couple of johns back to her house to do what they do when things get out of hand, and a fucking scumbag by the name of Rin with a rap sheet as long as my arm shoots her four times. Smelly admitted that before Rin got to her, she took down the other dude, a local cokehead she stabbed in the neck."

"Rin?" Harper tapped herself on the side of her head with a pen. "Didn't we bring that fucker in for vandalism, but he was let go because two of our brilliant officers forgot to Mirandize him?"

Stony nodded. "This time, he's not going home. With Mr. Smelly as a witness and neighbors who saw Rin run out of the vic's back door after hearing gunshots, Rin's out of luck."

"What went wrong? Guys wouldn't pay?"

"Yup. Mr. Smelly claims his friend required money upfront, but Rin and his junkie friend weren't down for it. They tried to rape her."

"Damn shame. What kind of friend promotes you selling your body? I wouldn't want him as a friend. So, what did Mr. Funk do when they tried raping his friend?" Harper sat. She folded her hands on her desk.

"That's what makes it so sad. Nothing. Said he froze. Old man's been bringing her business for years and even fucking her from time to time. Before things went haywire, he admitted to having a go at her. We found traces of his semen."

Harper opened her hands. "How do we know he didn't play a bigger role in this than he's leading on?"

"Everything checks out. There's no proof that says otherwise. He cooperated when it came to leading us to Rin, and he even supplied pictures of her being a working girl on and off the net. Nothing suggests he was in or a part of the fallout."

"Humph," Harper let out. "Don't let the old, stinky man act fool you. I bet there's something there. You're just not looking close enough."

Stony shrugged.

A tall officer with glasses and dressed in uniform approached Stony. "There was evidence missed at the crime scene. The morgue took this off the body of that prostitute. Techs already got in the phone and said you should check out the text between our vic and her friend and the very last text between her and Jetson Cobbs. Explains why he was there." The officer handed over the bagged cell phone.

"Jetson Cobbs?" Harper questioned.

Stony took a deep breath. "Did I forget to mention Jetson Cobbs, family of Hollywood royalty, took the bullets fired at the vic from the other side of the door? He was at her doorstep when two bullets went through the door and struck him twice in the chest."

"Fuck!" Harper spat.

Stony took the phone out of its packaging. "Let's see what we have." Then with the phone already unlocked, he first navigated through the text between Draya and Willard. "Son of a bitch."

Harper stood up and walked around to Stony. "What?"

Stony opened the text between Draya and Jetson. "Shit just keeps getting worse." He passed the phone over to Harper. "The vic's friend's name is Willard."

Harper quickly read the text. "Bastard lied. She gave up prostituting and look. She even blocked him after telling him she was moving. Who says he didn't take the news hard about her leaving and set her up to get raped?"

Stony leaned back on his desk and crossed his arms. "Jetson was involved with the girl. Read the last text he sent her."

I can't do this. I can't walk away. I don't care what you did in the past. I'm coming over to see you now. We can make this work.

Harper pursed her lips together and shook her head. "He was going to her place to reconcile. Whatever was wrong, he wanted to make right."

"Poor kid died for love," Stony declared.

Red Flags

by

Niko Michelle

Chapter 1

I grunted and swatted at my junky bedside chest, accidentally knocking over my inhaler, a Kleenex box, and a bottle of lotion. "Tempo" by Lizzo played for the third time before I snatched up my cell phone and interrupted the song that served as my ringtone and big girl anthem.

"It's after two in the morning, and I have an exam, so somebody better be dead or on life support, or we finna have a serious problem," I groggily threatened my disconnected Siamese twin, Yara. We weren't twins for real, not even biologically related, but as much as we stayed glued together in our friendship, we should've shared an organ or been connected by a piece of skin. Something more than aura and similar-sounding names.

"It's worse than that, Redarra," Yara said, proving how much emptiness surrounded my threat. I would never intentionally hurt her or anyone. I'm all bark, no bite unless it has to do with food.

I smacked my teeth at her dramatics. "Girl, what can possibly be worse than death?"

"Taylor," she responded. Melancholy was never her, no matter what was going on. Somehow, it spoke for her in that one word.

My wooden gray-and-turquoise-striped DIY headboard smacked the wall, and the mattress springs cried assault as all 280 pounds of me jiggled and wiggled to roll from my stomach to my back and into a sloppy dismount. The tissue box flattened like a smashed pea underneath the weight of my wide-width size ten foot. My body type wasn't built for gymnast shit, but I made it to my feet and scored myself a solid four when I heard my boyfriend's name associated with "worse than death." With that performance, no one could tell me I wasn't training for the Olympics, but one specific to overweight, out-of-shape five-feet-two-inch girls like me.

The sheer white curtains hit the floor first, and then the blinds followed when I forcefully pulled them open to look out into the parking lot and at the apartment building perpendicular to mine. That's where Taylor lived. A hop, skip, and jump, and if I did more of those things, I wouldn't be panting like a thirsty dog.

No flashing emergency lights. No sirens. No rescue. Not even a gleam of light from campus security's weak Dollar Tree flashlights. It's not like the security in our complex was dependable anyway, and I didn't blame them. It was a paycheck, but I wouldn't willingly risk my life for a bunch of unruly college kids when the only form of protection was a can of mace and a plastic-looking club that I'd exchange for a pair of nun chucks any day. I'd bet my last dollar that the switch my grandma made me pick from the tree in her yard hurt worse than those low-budget security guard batons.

After practically busting through my window and exerting what little energy I had, I felt dizzy and in need of a damn oxygen tank, but I huffed and puffed and blew out, "What about Taylor? Is he hurt? Oh my God. Taylor's dead?" I cried all dramatically, immediately thinking the worst.

"Taylor's not dead," Yara yelled and abruptly paused. She lowered her voice like she didn't even want to hear what she was about to say. "But you might kill him when you see what I just saw," she hesitantly added.

My stomach twisted like a Rubik's Cube as my ears latched on to her statement like a suction cup. There was no hint of Yara's usual sometimes hard-to-understand Southern drawl. I'd grown used to her broken dialect, but, at times, I'd have to make her repeat herself. Not this time. Every word she spoke was clear but also hard to understand. Only because I still had no clue exactly what was going on with my man.

I was scared to ask for more details. I was the elephant, and Yara's words were the mouse.

"Redarra, slip on some shoes and get over here." Urgency jumped into her voice like a grasshopper.

"Is Taylor okay? Please just tell me that."

"Taylor is fine. He's in his apartment with . . ." Another pause.

"With whom?" I questioned as I slipped on my purple Crocs and tied the drawstring to my black sweatpants. "You saw him with another woman?" As soon as I asked that question, my throat felt like it was the home of a prolonged drought.

"I saw him with *someone*. Just . . . just please, get over here. *Now*. And please try not to freak out and lose it when you get here."

Still, I popped off question after question. "Saw him with someone like who? Doing what? Why would I freak out?" I prayed she'd answer at least one question. "Yara, what's going on? You have me scared."

"I'm sorry, Redarra. You wouldn't believe me if I told you. You have to see it with your own eyes. Please, hurry," she said and hung up before I could inquire further.

I hoped to God Yara was luring me to Taylor's apartment for some random overnight surprise party. Silly thought, maybe. However, there was nothing worth celebrating that I could think of. My birthday wasn't for another eight months, and no one in our meager little circle had one approaching. Nothing magnificent had happened lately. Well, I made the dean's list again, but it wasn't anything that I broadcasted. Nothing celebratory crossed my mind, so something fishy was going on.

I rushed out the door, not bothering to remove my pink satin bonnet. Taylor hated seeing me in it. My long, walnut-colored, type-one hair was hard to maintain with pizzazz or curls and constantly needed some sort of protective style. Plus, Georgia heat was envious of hair. Braids and wigs were my go-to. When I needed protection from protective styles or was in between salon visits, I'd sometimes flat iron my hair or brush it into a ponytail.

Though if a drop of oil from my natural hair touched my face, it would have been Pimple City. Wanna-be-rocking my natural hair days came, but not too often, especially considering once my tresses grew about six more inches, it would brush up against my donk every time my head moved. My hair was hard to manage, but I'd *never* cut it.

I only took about five steps, but I could feel the burn. I scampered down the breezeway, inhaling deeply through my nose and exhaling through my mouth, which didn't do much except give me the feeling of heartburn. In my mind, I was on pace with Sonic the Hedgehog, but in reality, my speed matched that of a slow four-count dance routine. Whatever the case, I was determined to see what was so important that Yara had to drag me out of a deep "itis" sleep. I had downed about twelve chicken wings covered in ranch and some chili cheese fries, then washed it down with a thirty-two-ounce Sprite right before I crashed.

Of course, every possible scenario played on the IMAX screen behind my eyes. Seeing Taylor with someone in his apartment didn't necessarily mean it was inappropriate. Things between us had been going beyond well, and I trusted him 100 percent. No real issues in the year since we'd been kicking it. We were young college students about to graduate, and while we didn't have a pot to piss in, my wild imagination suddenly thought maybe he was about to propose. I didn't know what made me feel that, but I would scream yes if that were the situation. I pulled my ring finger close to my face and wiggled it. Good thing I had gotten my nails touched up earlier in the day. In fact, that very finger had Taylor's jersey number painted on it, surrounded by a heart in preparation for football season. He hadn't seen it yet, but he'd know that I would always and forever represent for number eleven when he did.

The smile that spread across my face exposed every one of my Colgate-whitened teeth and could've turned night into day.

"Oh shit," I said as I missed the last stair leading to the parking lot. "Damn blown lights," I scolded my surroundings as if they had feelings. I knew it was my fantasizing that caused my plunge, but in all fairness, the parking lot was scary movie dark. Some lights were out, and some were dim. Tuition was too damn expensive for Central Georgia University to have weak shining lights and unnecessary safety hazards.

After I picked myself up and cleared away some little rocks slightly embedded around my elbow, I brushed the bottom of my emoji sock, slipped my foot back into my Croc, and happily picked up the pace. I skipped for real this time, still breathing like I'd been taught to do in the exercise classes I signed up for. Let's just say I wouldn't be getting the perfect attendance award. More like a visit from a truancy officer. Who cared about any of that anyway? I was getting engaged to a man that accepted me for every Hawaiian roll that spread my body, and I wanted to hurry and accept my ring. It didn't matter the size. I'd love it, flash it, and polish it every day. I was already a good girlfriend to Taylor, so I knew I would make a great wife.

Yara paced in front of Taylor's apartment. "What took you so long?" she asked when I made it to the top of the other parking lot stairs leading to his building.

The answer to her question was obvious. "I'm out of shape," I huffed with all my might. Yara wouldn't understand. She was athletic, an avid spinner, and on a full tennis scholarship in college.

Except for "college student," none of those other attributes applied to me.

I bent over with my hands on my knees, not trying to get funky with it but simply trying to catch my breath.

Yara pointed to Taylor's door as if I didn't know where he lived. Apartment 155, room B. B for boyfriend. *My* boyfriend. Yet people claimed plump girls like me could never get or keep a guy like Taylor. A star athlete. A muscular, average height, fine-ass chunk of pecan football-playing meat. I was living proof it could happen.

What made fluffy girls unattractive anyway? Unlovable even? Nothing but a discriminatory society. I often wondered how those same judgmental people viewed overweight women in *their* lives. Are they ugly and unworthy of love? I bet those same people would be ready to fight if someone verbally assaulted their overweight grandmothers, mothers, sisters, or daughters—dumbasses.

"The door is unlocked. Come on," Yara said.

I knew that. Taylor's door stayed unlocked. I'd gotten on to him too many times to count, even going as far as printing out local burglary reports. He felt loyalty and popularity went hand in hand. I had personally never heard of invincibility to thieves. If anything, popularity attracted more of the wrong crowd.

When I didn't move right away, Yara pulled my arm, thinking she could move me. Featherweight to a heavyweight—not happening. Besides, I still had to get myself together, and I hadn't had a chance to work on my surprised proposal face.

"Re-dar-ra," Yara dragged my name out and shook her head. There was enough light that allowed me to see the water that pooled at the bottom of her sad eyes. "Please. It's bad." A lone tear fell that she swiped away with her knuckle.

When was a proposal bad? Yara deserved a BET award for acting, if not an Oscar because she played her role.

I pushed the door open with a smile that quickly faded at the sounds of sex noises.

"Call me daddy."

That wasn't Taylor's voice. That voice was too raspy to be his. Possibly porn. Or maybe it was his roommate or one of his homeboys. It wasn't my man. Therefore, it wasn't *my* business. Yara was overreacting and mistaken. I turned around, prepared to creep out just as quietly as I had crept in, but she was hot on my heels and standing in my way. Then I heard Taylor's voice in a sultry moan, "Daddy."

"What the hell?" I spun around like I was James Brown and every pound of me sprinted down the long entryway to the sex noises.

Yara was right. This was nothing she could tell me. I had to see it with my own eyes.

Chapter 2

Tie-dye. That's how people described my personality. Colorful, poppin', bright, and it all worked together to form a unified me. Not anymore. From now on, crazy would be used to describe me and tear me down. We all have a little of it in us, but it was never extreme nor a permanent resident for me. I may have said some stuff or acted a certain way that caused those in my circle to laugh and say, "You're crazy." Now when that's said, it will be true because crazy is ingrained in my medical records and attached to my name. I'm not just *Fat* Redarra Michaels anymore. I'm *Crazy* Redarra Michaels.

I may have gone crazy on Taylor, but I was *not* crazy. The crazy that I displayed was love-induced. He deserved every bit of it.

Crimes of passion should be justifiable. I couldn't think of one person that wouldn't have reacted the same way. I couldn't think of one person that would have sat on the couch and waited for the climax to have a civilized conversation with their boyfriend after catching him having sex with another guy. Not one person came to mind. Not even the weak-ass ladies in those Lifetime movies. They did some dumb shit, but I didn't see them calmly confronting their man when he's bent over the back of a sofa with one leg up.

Nasty ass.

"Knock, knock. Howdy there."

Relieved to be freed from images of Taylor's sexcapades, I exhaled deeply and turned from the window to the door. The institution's social worker and discharge planner, Ramona, stood there with her spiky pink mullet. "Morning," I muttered. I never added the good. There was nothing good about having my freedom stripped away or waking up in a mental institution every day.

"Oh, come on now, I come bearing gifts, so I *know* you can do better than that." Ramona jiggled her right hand that held the plastic bag with my clothes and shook her left hand with a clipboard containing my discharge papers. "You can't be grumpy. It's release day, and you've been ready to go home since you got here," she reminded.

"I'm sorry, Ms. Ramona." I added some fake cheer to my voice and greeted her again.

"That's more like it," she said and rested her right hand and the strings of the plastic bag on her hip. "And a half smile too? I hadn't seen that before." A cackle followed Ramona's words. It sounded like a rooster. She was everything country but the most genuine person I'd come across in a while. Southern Charm meets Garth Brooks, meets a Farm. That best described Ramona and what I imagined her life to be like outside of work. Milking cows, driving a tractor, and shit like that.

I guess the expansion of one of my cheekbones indicated a smile. I'd forgotten what smiling was since I'd been admitted and forced to swallow antidepressants.

"What's the first thing you plan to do when you get home?" she asked.

I shrugged. Because I hated everything about life, I hadn't thought much about the future other than flushing the meds down the toilet. It had been twenty-one days since I'd been confined, and the only thing I'd done during that time was thinking about the reason for my stay—Taylor Lawrence.

Since I didn't have an answer, Ramona asked another question. "Well, what's the first thing you plan to eat when you leave? I know the food here sucks."

My eyes lit up, realizing I'd be able to eat something other than the slop they fed us. "Häagen-Dazs. The cure-all."

"My girl," Ramona added in agreement. "Another Häagen-Dazs head. What's your go-to flavor?"

"Any coffee flavor or praline," I said. Although no amount will cure my broken heart, I couldn't wait to down a container just because I'd be free enough to do it.

"I love the Caramel Cone. I could eat it for break-fast, lunch, and dinner. I think I gained ten pounds just thinking about it." Ramona sighed and then shifted to the real reason for her visit. "All right, dear, I need to go over these documents with you."

I listened quietly to all of it until she got to the part about medication. As soon as I'm out of here, that medicine would be out of my system. I was *not* crazy. I didn't need it. The only reason that poison was in my blood was because of the swallow checks. I had never figured out a way to hide the pills in my mouth, so I figured I'd temporarily comply.

"Don't forget to register for the anger manage-ment classes. Do it as soon as you get home. In fact, you can do it while you're eating your ice cream," Ramona winked.

"Do I have to? I am not an angry person. Nor am I violent."

Ramona set the clipboard to the side and folded her hands in her lap. "Trust me, I believe you. I can tell you have a gentle soul. And based on what you've shared with me, I can understand your emo-tions at that moment. However, assault is against the law. Breaking the law has consequences. You caught a major break by coming here instead of go-ing to jail. You have so much life ahead of you, and you don't want to be ruled unemployable because you have a smudge on your record." She paused and made prayer hands. "Remember, a stipulation to not having criminal charges pressed against you and having a record hinge on the completion of anger management. So, please, show effort and take the initiative before a judge makes you. Get ahead of it and register for the classes."

I didn't have an anger problem, and the thought of being admitted into a mental hospital and having to take anger management classes pissed me off. Most would say the hospital was better than jail, but I think I may have preferred jail instead.

I paced in front of the window and cracked my knuckles. "I hear you, Ms. Ramona, but people would respect me more with a criminal record. Now, they'll avoid me out of fear that I'll do something to hurt them."

"Just because you were here does *not* mean you're crazy or that you'll hurt anyone. If you ask me, folks will find anything to goof off about no matter the circumstances. You've made so much progress, Redarra. When you first got here, you cried all day, every day. You wouldn't eat, talk, or participate. Let folks be and focus on yourself and move forward. Don't get worked into a tizzy. You got this."

"It's not fair. I didn't deserve what happened to me. It's bad enough that people make fun of me because of my weight. Now this . . ." I waved my hands in the air like an actual crazy person. "I didn't deserve to be here," I said and turned my nose up at my surroundings.

The institution wasn't as bad as people made it out to be. I'd just never admit to it outside of my head. It was nothing like the images taught to us in textbooks, internet searches, and movies. It didn't look like a spooky basement. There wasn't a lone lightbulb hanging from the ceiling of a dark room with water slowly dripping from a sink. People weren't chained to their beds or donned in straitjackets, screaming all hours of the day and night. It seemed like a regular hospital, and instead of getting healing for visible wounds, our invisible wounds were being treated.

"Remember, not everyone is Taylor. Not everyone will be careless with your heart. And I know it's easier said than done but try to move on from him. Replace thoughts of him with happier times in your life before he was in the picture. Think of life when you graduate and start your career. The places you can travel, the money you'll make, the house you'll buy. The lasting, lifelong friends. There are endless positive distractions."

I stopped pacing and scoffed. "Taylor was supposed to be my lifelong friend."

"There are genuine people in the world, and not everyone will place you in negative situations." Ramona walked over and set the plastic bag in front of me. "I will step out while you get dressed and walk you out to your parents." She smiled and excused herself. When she got to the door, she turned to me and said, "It may not seem like it right now, but this isn't the end of the road. You *will* heal from this, and it's okay to be scared. It means you want better."

I do want better, and while I was ready to go home, I was afraid of what I'd face on the other side of these doors now that people think I'm crazy.

Chapter 3

"Welcome home, bestie." Yara crept a few inches into my room with a container of ice cream and a spoon. She waited close by the door, silently requesting permission to enter.

"Hey, girl," I said, waving her in. "Why are you creeping? You scared of me now?"

Yara smacked her teeth. "Girl, yeah, right. I hope it's okay that I dropped by. Your mom said it would lift your spirits. I'd been calling Mama Michaels every day to check on you." She eased the ice cream down beside me and continued. "I've really missed you, and I'm sorry. Had I known this . . . I never—"

"No, ma'am." I held up my hand to stop her. I knew what she was about to say, and I was not about to let her blame herself. "You did what any good friend would do, and I will always appreciate you for that. Some women won't say a word. I'd rather know than not. So, thank you."

Other than the lid popping on the ice cream and me smacking, an awkward silence filled the room. One thing about Yara and me, though. We never fell short of conversation. I needed her to understand that I was not mad at her and I was still the same person I was three weeks ago.

I swallowed the cookie dough that sat melting in my mouth and cleared my throat. "So, what's new? You started back hoeing since I wasn't around to watch you, or are you still pretending to be a born-again virgin?"

Yara laughed and snorted like Miss Piggy was her nickname. "Shut up. You know I'm saving myself for marriage."

With the spoon stuck in my mouth and bouncing around, I said, "Still holding on to that lie, huh?"

I loved Yara to pieces, and my girl was not ashamed of her previous lifestyle. After surviving an attack by a stranger she left a club with, she changed. She slowed down, traded in her heels for kitty pumps, flats, and sneakers, and did away with her tight miniskirts, opting for pants and ankle-length dresses when she wore them. She even changed her major to theology and used her experience to reach other girls. She was the only victim I knew who encouraged us to remind her of the attack so that she didn't backslide into that life again.

"Theology student or not," she said before flipping me off. Her smile quickly faded, and her round brown eyes that constantly flickered dimmed. "How are you really?"

It took me a minute to answer. I shoved several spoons of frozen goodness into my mouth while I decided how much of the truth I wanted to reveal. Was it safe to tell her how I was all over the place? Do I tell her how I think about Taylor in a way that I shouldn't every day? Or how I blocked my number and called him as soon as I got home? He didn't answer, and since Yara had come over, I thought about asking her to call him. What would she think of me if I told her that I missed him and that sometimes I thought about forgiving him because, in my heart, I believed that he was just experimenting or drunk, and it wouldn't happen again? Do I mention that at times I'm so angry that I want to bash his face in again and again until the pain and memories subside?

See—all over the place. My mind was like an unorganized junk drawer.

Instead, I shrugged and responded, "I'm hanging in there." Then I felt the urge to convince her of one thing. "I am *not* crazy, and I do *not* have mental health issues."

Yara's bouncy, full-of-body bob swung back and forth as she nodded. "I know, Redarra. You don't have to prove that to . . . me."

I'd known her long enough to know she had something more to say. And with the way she paused and how the word "me" trailed off, it was something heavy.

"Just say it, sis," I encouraged.

She played dumb. "Say what?"

I smacked my teeth and cut my eyes. "Girl, I've known you for how long? I know when something is on your mind."

Yara's head tilted upward, and her wide eyes traced the multicolored LED lights that outlined the square of my bedroom ceiling at my parents' house like it was her first time seeing them. She was the one that helped me to hang them. "It's nothing," she said.

Liar! She couldn't even make eye contact with me. Trying to pull information from her was like performing a complicated tooth extraction. "Just say it," I repeated through clenched teeth.

She sighed and plopped down Indian style on my white furry rug. "You know I love you," Yara started, "and I don't want to hurt you any more than I already have, but I can't allow you to walk around unprepared."

I frowned, bothered by the word "unprepared." As soon as I swallowed the worry lump in my throat mixed with another bite of ice cream, I asked, "What is it that I need to be prepared for?"

Yara hesitated and stuttered, but she finally got it out. "Some not-so-nice things are circulating about you on social media, and I'm not sure if the right thing to do is to tell you, but as your nonbiological sister, I can't let you out there without a heads-up. So I just hope I'm doing the right thing."

Yara propped herself up on her knees and shuffled over to me with her phone in her hand while scrolling. My pupils jumped right along with my increased heartbeat the closer she got.

When she found what she was looking for, she handed me her phone and the box of Kleenex from my nightstand.

My mouth flung open and wouldn't close as I skimmed over a few comments. The tears fell, and no matter how much I swiped them, it was like a rainstorm against a windshield with broken wipers. Everybody had something negative to say under the video of me beating Taylor's ass. Bystanders had their phones out, so I knew there was a video, but I'd never been in a position to watch it, and with it staring me in the face, I still had no desire to.

I didn't remember the actual attack. Past seeing Taylor in a prone position getting . . . I couldn't even bring myself to say it. I blacked out after seeing what I saw, and, well, I whooped his ass.

Yara sat on the bed beside me and draped her arm over my shoulder. "I'm so sorry, and even more sorry that I'm the one that keeps sharing shitty news with you."

"It's okay," I said, attempting to convince her but mainly myself that I was, in fact, okay. "These comments are disgusting."

"Tell me about it," Yara agreed. "I'm just sorry people are too stupid to see how good of a person you are. You were amazing to Taylor, so it's his loss. He's a fucking coward-ass loser anyway. Every time I see him, I just want to jab him in the face. Trifling ass."

It was good to know that Yara still had my back and still looked at me as her sister instead of a lunatic like the people in the comments viewed me. Again, theology student or not, some of her ways I hoped she'd never changed.

The first comment I read said, Taylor and that fat girl probably be having threesomes and orgies. I can look at him and tell he likes dudes. She's fat; she knows she's serving as his beard. They always go after the fat ones.

I shook my head, confused. "Beard? What the hell is that supposed to mean?"

"What rock have you been living under, not knowing what that means?" Yara asked.

"You know what it is?" I asked.

"A beard is slang for chicks who date gay men in hiding. They ain't ready to come clean, so they swipe a willing participant. It's an arrangement," Yara explained.

"Get the hell outta here. I didn't know his ass liked the same thing I liked." Had I known Taylor wanted a man, I never would've swayed in his direction. I'm sure there were girls out there that wouldn't have a problem with it, but I was not her. I loved him. Hell, I still did.

Yara coyly raised her hand. "I knew he batted for the same team. At least I had a suspicion."

Her confession was no surprise. If she got a quarter for every time her eyes bucked or her lips pursed when Taylor said something or acted questionably, Yara would be a millionaire solely off collecting twenty-five cents at a time. There was the time Taylor had walked into my apartment and had his nails polished black. He said he'd seen it on some rapper and wanted to join in setting the trend. If said rapper caught wind of it, maybe he'd get an endorsement deal and expand his brand. Made sense to me, Yara, not so much. She clicked her tongue and let out the longest eye roll. I thought the girl had dozed off.

Then there was the time Taylor popped up with his nose pierced. I didn't make a big deal out of that either. Many men have done it. Tupac had a nose ring, and he was nowhere near gay. It's just that Taylor's choice of the ring was feminine-looking. A butterfly. I didn't sweat it, though.

Everything that everyone deemed questionable was justifiable to me. I supported my man, even when a few of his teammates teased him over his pants getting tighter and tighter—no big deal. Skinny jeans were the trend. They dropped a couple of inappropriate slurs and freestyled a few rap songs about him being "funny." Because Taylor was the star, they got kicked off the team, and the rumors went away.

I didn't mind the regular pedicures. Men should take care of their feet too. My eyebrows didn't raise over his gay friends. I wasn't bothered by the fact that he exfoliated or that his nighttime skincare routine was more detailed than mine. He had an image to uphold, and I understood that. Image was everything when stepping into the limelight.

I looked back at the comments. Another dis. Is she pregnant? Look how big her stomach is. If Taylor wanted an elephant, he would soon have enough money from the NFL to buy a real one.

Someone else commented, She only got the best of Taylor because all that weight she put on him cut off his circulation.

Another said, I heard Taylor got with that fat girl because she could cook, but then she kept eating all the food, and the fight was over the last piece of chicken.

These bastards.

I scrolled to another comment. That was not a fair fight. That chick has bat wings which make four fists to his two. I bet if she stumbles into a bat cave, they'd think she was one of them. I bet that ho sleeps upside down.

I knew better than to read the comments, but I couldn't stop, no matter how much they hurt. I guess I was looking for an ally outside of Yara. And I thought I'd finally found one.

"Look, Yara," I said and pointed to her phone. "Someone else thinks he's gay."

I read the comment out loud. "She probably found out he liked boys. My gaydar beeped heavily around him. Beep. Beep. Beep. Taylor must be around."

"Oh, girl, that was me. I created that fake page so I could send people in a different direction. Refuel the gay rumors now that it's confirmed."

I fell over and sank into the many decorative pillows that swallowed my bed. "Yara, why would you do that?"

She smacked her teeth. "Why not? I want everyone to know, and I won't rest until they do. People are doggin' you, and it's about time they start learning the truth about him and start doggin' his ass too. I've been lying low, waiting for you to come home so we can come up with a plan to expose his trifling ass."

"I'm not looking for revenge. I just want this to go away."

"Shittin' me. He shouldn't get to walk around playing the victim when he's not."

I didn't bother responding. No matter how much I pushed against it, Yara was gonna push back. I focused my attention back on the comments, and then came the exchange that made me sob so hard that I gagged, almost causing my ice cream to make an appearance. That bitch hovered over him like a feasting zombie. She tried to eat my guy. What in The Walking Dead is this?

In response, someone said, Noooooo, I watch enough zombie shows to know there aren't any fat zombies. Maybe an episode of when animals attack.

I told myself I'd never watch the video, but I couldn't help but press play because of the comments.

The video started with me straddling Taylor, just as the comments said. I screamed profanities and repeatedly punched him in the face. Spectators could be heard cheering, egging on the fight, and telling Taylor how to maneuver from under me. Yara could be seen trying to break it up. Just her. When she turned to the crowd to beg for help, she had droplets of blood on her yellow shirt. I punched Taylor until the police showed up. They ordered me to lie face down on the floor, but I didn't comply. Six officers tackled and restrained me. There was a knee in my back, an elbow pressed to the side of my face, and a few officers had my arms and legs pinned. I screamed for them to let me go as I tried to wiggle free. Officers threatened to slap me with resisting if I didn't calm down. They cuffed me with two sets of cuffs, ushered everyone out of Taylor's apartment, and then the video ended.

I sat in shock, holding Yara's phone. A part of me wanted to throw it across the room and shatter it, but that wouldn't make the video disappear. I was hurt and embarrassed. "I hate my life," I cried. Snot ran from my nose to my top lip, and what didn't run bubbled like that of a cold-infested baby.

After I calmed down some, Yara said, "I hate to ask you this, but have you been tested?"

I covered my face to hide the extra feelings of embarrassment. "Yeah. They diagnosed me with some bullshit. I don't even remember the name. It's on my discharge papers if you want to look at it." Without uncovering my face all the way, I pointed to my dresser. Now, every time I cry, people will think it's associated with my diagnosis.

I was *not* crazy.

"Not like that. I mean sexually. Like for HIV and AIDS?"

"Shhhhiiitttt!" I screamed and had a tantrum on my bed. I could take on any toddler in a toy aisle when their parent refused them a toy. So much had transpired in a short amount of time that I hadn't considered getting screened.

Yara waited for me to calm down again. "Tomorrow, make an appointment, and I'll go with you. I got you."

"What if . . ." Another statement I couldn't finish.

Yara shook her head. "Nope. We are not claiming that. It's just a precaution. We are *not* claiming that, you hear me?" She squeezed me and cried with me. Then she apologized again and tried her best to get me to agree to retaliation. "We can blackmail his ass. Get us some of that NFL money."

That was enough to make me laugh a little. "Blackmail him with what? It's our word against his, and who will believe me over Taylor Lawrence? Athletes get all the love, attention, praise, and leeway. I don't stand a chance."

Yara delicately pushed me off her. An evil smirk parted her lips. "I'm glad you asked," she said and reached for her phone.

I shook my head in protest. "Please, no more comments. I can't take anymore."

"It's a video, but one that will fuck up Taylor's world. Like I said, I was waiting for you to come home so we could figure out a plan. We have to be strategic, though. Press play whenever you're ready."

I caught the still shot. "Is this what I think it is?"

"Yes, bitch. We got his ass *and* the dude he was with on video."

I gasped. "How did you . . . Better yet, *why* didn't you lead with this?"

"Okay, so I needed to see where your head was before triggering you. Taylor has a head start. He's already painted the narrative, but with this video, we don't have to work too hard to turn it around."

When Yara took a breath, I jumped in. "Who are you, my PR person? And again, I ask, *how* did you get this?"

"I can be," she said. "And you never know. If we turn your reputation around, I might change my major again." She popped her lips and finally gave me what I was looking for. "While I was waiting on you to come to Taylor's, I snuck in, recorded them . . . you know, just in case. I'm glad I did. So, the first thing I plan to buy with my NFL blackmail money is a Birkin bag, biiiitch," she cheered.

The smoking gun to restore my reputation and life, but I couldn't do that to Taylor. Deep down inside, I believed he would make this right.

Chapter 4

Although I led Yara to believe that we'd devise a plan to ruin Taylor, I didn't mean it. He would make it right. Mediation was coming up; things were going to be okay. While I wasn't looking forward to sitting in a room with my parents, Taylor's parents, and the dean to discuss the attack, I didn't have much of a choice if I wanted to avoid criminal charges and expulsion, especially with a semester and a half shy of graduating.

Most colleges would've been done with me. Having attorneys for parents who also happened to be alumni and top boosters came with a few perks. The school didn't want to lose the Michaels's money, nor did they want to lose their star athlete. Luckily, my parents convinced the school to put me on an action plan, and in exchange, they'd increase their donation each year. Call it a bribe or unfair, but wealthy folks of another color do it all the time.

Still, I go back and forth over my punishment. That stain on my health record disturbs me.

Sometimes I think ahead, realizing, like Ramona said, that not too many careers require the applicant to disclose mental health records, but they certainly check for arrests. If I have a battery charge on me, they'll think I'm just another angry Black female. College graduate or not, I'd be a stereotype and never land a job.

The closer mediation got, the more I paced, chewed on my lips until they bled, and cracked the acrylic of my nails with my teeth. I'd see Taylor for the first time since that night. I had still tried to reach him to no avail. He probably thought I felt hatred toward him, or he was ashamed and didn't know how to approach me. Either way, I believed that once he saw me for the first time since the mishap, remorse would pour out like an upside-down container of salt, he'd own up to his wrong, and all of this would be water under the bridge.

After all, for the most part, I'd kept his clandestine affair from the world, including the video. Besides Yara and Ms. Ramona, my parents were the only other people on my end who knew what led to the attack. Yara knew because she told me, and I had to tell the other three. Mommy and Pops, as I called them, took the news better than I expected. They didn't jump immediately into lawyer mode. Instead, I was met with understanding and sympathy. I was grateful when the lawyer mode was activated. So far, they'd convinced officers that I had a mental health crisis when I attacked Taylor and that I needed to be escorted to a facility, not jail. I'd rather my parents continue to think I was perfect, but I was thankful that Yara called them when the cops showed up, or there's no telling where I'd be. Probably a sister jail wife.

The mystery behind who called the cops was still a mystery. My money was on Sammie, Taylor's secret lover. He had always been a punk and probably feared for his life when he grabbed his clothes and ran out of the apartment before he got his ass beat or before anyone could place him as the "poker." The handful of witnesses that recorded me putting the smackdown on Taylor may have called when they heard the commotion and came running. I doubt it, though. They were there for the entertainment. So, I wasn't sure. I wished that I could go back and undo the embarrassment, however.

My parents had informed me that I had to write an apology letter to read to Taylor during mediation. No sweat. I am sorry for what happened. I lost control of my usual docile self, and it was never right for a woman to put her hands on a man the same way it was never right for a man to lay hands on a woman. The apology letter was fair. No matter the circumstances, I owed him that.

The specifics of what the letter had to include weren't told to me. I didn't know if I had to type it, handwrite it, how detailed it needed to be, or how long it needed to be. My freedom and future relied partly on this letter, so I would give it my best. I grabbed my phone to Google some apology letter ideas and was met with something unexpected. I did a double take, and my eyes about popped out of their sockets. A message from Football Bae. That's how I had Taylor's name programmed in my phone. My eyes blinked faster than my heart thumped as I read it.

Can we meet? Yvonne's. Thursday @ 3:15. And don't tell anybody.

My eyes watered, and my hands shook like a good twerk as I responded:

I'll see you there. And I won't tell a soul.

That was all that needed to be said. That was enough for me. For weeks, I'd wondered why Taylor would do this to me and what was going through his mind since the fight. I'd finally get a chance to ask him privately. Yvonne's was the place Taylor and I went to all the time. Our little romantic getaway, if you will. It was quiet, thirty-five minutes outside of town, and we didn't have to worry about anyone recognizing him, crowding us, begging for pictures or autographs. But if they did, it was only one or two people. Plus, Yvonne's was cheap and fit a college student's budget.

I was as giddy as I was after I had experienced my first kiss back in seventh grade. Darius Montgomery was the only boy that showed interest in me. He was a little on the chubby side like me. Specifically, if he wore bras, he and I would've worn the same size. We practiced how to tongue kiss on each other, bonded over pain, ate our feelings, and vowed to become school counselors to end bullying. Bullies were the worst, which was why I decided to major in computer science instead of counseling. Sadly, Darius couldn't handle how callous the bullies were in high school compared to elementary and middle school, and he committed suicide. Continuing with the mission would've been the best way to honor him, but it wasn't the same after his death.

I will never forget the day my mother staggered into my room like my drunk aunt Pat and delivered the heartbreaking news. Darius had swallowed a bunch of pills, and he was never coming back. He and I would never attend the same college, study the same program, or conquer the world of bullying as we had planned. I hated everyone for a long time, including myself. I did carry on the tradition of eating away my feelings, though. By the time I graduated from high school, my weight had ballooned, and so did the remarks. Every time I walked the halls, pig noises followed me. Students even left pig stickers on my locker. When I got to college, it was a different story. I was accepted for my personality, and then I met Taylor. He needed tutoring, and we hit it off from there. Therefore, I knew he was going to make this right. The universe wouldn't let my heart break over another guy like it did when Darius left me. Surely this was all one big misunderstanding that would get worked out.

Another chime captured my attention. It was Taylor again:

Bet.

There was nothing special about the message, but it excited me enough that I started to send back the kissing emoji, but I decided not to follow through with it. I would kiss him in person if all went well.

"What are you doing, Redarra?" I paced and berated myself. "This man hurt you and embarrassed you, and all is forgiven just because he wants to meet? Don't be stupid. Don't be stupid."

Surprisingly enough, I answered myself. "You're not stupid. It's just love. It happens to everyone."

Maybe I was . . . Nah. I was *not* crazy.

I tossed my phone on the bed, and just like that, I had overlooked the conversation I had with myself. I raced to the closet to pick out the right outfit. Our meeting wasn't for another two days, but I wanted to look my best, and sometimes, that could take time when you're trying to make a statement. My look needed to say: *I still love you. I'm sorry for almost busting your head open to the white meat. I miss you. Was this a phase? How do we move forward as if this didn't happen?*

The hangers screeched across the closet rod, and garments either hung on for dear life or fell completely off as I hurriedly flipped through every 3X shirt I had. My room was ransacked. I pulled clothes from drawers and tossed shoes from racks and totes. Two days, but here I was acting like I was running late for a job interview.

Another chime, and I froze. I hoped it wasn't Taylor changing his mind. I stumbled over the clothes strewn over my bedroom floor and made it to my phone just as it started ringing.

"Hey, girl," I answered out of breath. Many things had changed over these last few weeks, but my weight wasn't one of them. Well, if it did, the scale added pounds, and I'd swear it was broken or conspiring against me. I was still out of shape and required an oxygen tank after doing anything more than a moderate to a brisk walk.

"Did you get my text?" Yara asked without returning the greeting.

"When did you send it?"

"Right before I called you."

I smacked my teeth. "Then no. You didn't give me time. By the time I made it to the phone, you were calling."

"Look at it while you have me on the phone." Yara's tone reminded me of the same night she called to tell me to get over to Taylor's apartment.

"Hold on." I put her on speaker and opened the message. I groaned when I saw that it was another video. Taylor's face was frozen on the screen. "Whatever this is, I don't care." I said that because I already knew this video would be some bull. Yara hated everything Taylor, and I knew that she'd share anything negative she saw going forward. The time stamp didn't show, but whenever it was recorded, I was sure it was before he reached out to me, which meant it didn't matter. I had faith that Yvonne's would be a positive turning point. I'd hear him out, and we'd start anew, even if it were only as friends.

"I hate to keep doing this to you, but Taylor is talking mad shit about you," Yara said.

"It's irrelevant," I replied without going into detail.

"It's *very* relevant, especially considering that he was live *just now* saying a whole lot of craziness about you."

Yara's facts were a little off, and I didn't want to hear any more. Taylor couldn't have been on live within the last twenty minutes talking trash about me.

"I'll call you right back. My mom wants me." What was one little lie to get her off the phone? I was sure Yara was well intended, but I didn't want any outside influence or incorrect information. I would see what's what when we met at Yvonne's.

My room was a disaster, but at least I'd narrowed down my 'fit—a tight, short dress with no panties for easy access . . . in case. I shook away that reckless thought. Taylor and I both still needed to get tested. I had yet to make an appointment because I didn't feel sick, and we always used protection. It was nothing, but I grabbed my phone to do a quick search on symptoms. Except for Yara, Taylor, and my parents having access to get through, my phone was on do not disturb. Multiple messages awaited me—all videos, and not just from Yara. I finally pressed play to see what all the hype was about. I gasped and choked on air and saliva. Yara's facts were indeed facts. Taylor had reached out to meet and then hopped on social media and said some inappropriate and embarrassing bullshit.

Chapter 5

"Taylor, what the hell?" I immediately started in on him when he finally strolled into Yvonne's almost an hour late. The meeting started much differently than what I'd envisioned days ago.

A few patrons sitting on bar stools turned and gave me some nasty looks over my outburst. Forget them and forget the small talk I would've had with Taylor. I even forgot about the short dress I planned to wear. Sweats and a raggedy-ass T-shirt covered me, but not my level of pisstivity. I was pissed-pissed.

First, Taylor had no regard for my time. Second, and most importantly, he needed to explain why he was telling the world lies on social media. This bastard casually said I was the chick he called when he wanted some head and how I got mad and attacked him when he told me that he was relieving me of my dick-sucking duties because, as of late, I kept scratching him with my teeth.

He shrugged. "My bad. Practice ran over." He slid into the booth and grabbed the basket full of used-to-be-hot bread. "I'm starving. Coach worked the hell out of us today."

We were not friends right now. I couldn't care less about what happened at practice. "Your tardiness is the least of my concerns." I pulled the video up and slid my phone across the table.

"What's this?" he asked and slathered a roll with butter.

Attitude deepened my tone. "Press play, and you'll see."

He scoffed at me and shook his head. "Y'all women are always trippin'."

Inside, I thought maybe that was why he got with a dude. However, I practiced restraint because I wanted him to explain his behavior. What was the reason for making a whole defaming social media post to his thousands of followers, knowing they would share it and give the world more shit to talk about me?

He watched the video and munched on bread like he didn't have a care in the world. That wasn't a random Netflix movie. That was my real life. When the video ended, the bastard laughed, which sent a jolt of anger throughout every crevice of my body.

I leaned forward and growled. "You *seriously* gonna laugh at that bullshit?"

He shrugged. "Man, chill. I was just talkin' a li'l shit."

"*Seriously,* Taylor?" Maybe I did have an anger problem because both my hands balled into fists underneath the table.

"What's the big deal? It was all in fun."

I smacked the hell out of the table, rattling the silverware and sending more eyes mixed with glares and frowns in our direction once again. If Taylor's face had been closer, I would have slapped the stupid off it.

"Easy for you to say. People aren't saying slick shit about you."

"Man, you trippin'. It's just words. Whatever happened to sticks and stones may break bones, but words will never hurt?"

Was this bastard *seriously* using some elementary school saying to justify another betrayal? He wanted to play the dumb jock card. "No big deal? If I ran around here making videos and telling people the *real* reason behind our fight, would it be just words then?"

He looked around the diner, and I followed his direction. A few people were finishing up their meals, waiting for checks, and uninterested in us. They seemed to be more disgusted with my boisterous behavior and were trying to escape before I set it off worse than I already had. Remember, I was an angry Black female, and it showed.

Taylor looked back at me and shook his head. He leaned in closer to make sure I was the only one that would hear him. "Watch your mouth," he demanded.

"Or *what?* My damn reputation and life are ruined."

"You'd have to have a reputation for it to be ruined. No one is checkin' for you unless I'm around. No one even knows who you are. So, like I said, chill, keep your mouth shut, and be grateful for the free publicity."

My neck snapped back. I eyed the butter knife first and wondered how much damage I could do with it. Then I eyed my glass of water. Instinct said to pick it up, throw it in his face, and then bust him upside the head with the glass. But I didn't. My annoyance was hard to hide, though, and the fork prongs looked really good to me. So did the saltshaker. Would it burn his eyes? Melt him like the slug that he was?

"Why would you say those things about me? Why not extend the same courtesy of protecting me like I'm doing you? You need to keep *your* mouth shut and not run around here talking junk," I aggressively replied.

Taylor pushed the breadbasket aside and re-laxed against the booth, unfazed since we prac-tically had Yvonne's to ourselves. "I'm Taylor Lawrence," he said and double-tapped his chest. "I don't *need* protection." He smiled, showing off all of his professionally corrected teeth. "I guess that nuthouse made you forget my power." He drew a circle around the team emblem and running back title sewn on his black hoodie.

My grip tightened on the glass. I squeezed it repeatedly like it was a stress ball. I imagined it as Taylor's neck, and the splash of water on my hand was a drop of his blood.

"Listen up, sweetheart," Taylor continued, "I asked you here to make sure we understand each other before mediation."

I knew what he insinuated, but I wanted to hear his attempt at blackmail. I narrowed my eyes. "I'm not sure I understand what you mean. Clarify."

He rubbed his hands together like he was about to feast on a Thanksgiving meal with a side of dick. "Keep your mouth shut, and I won't press charges. You think your reputation is trash now? Squeal, and me and my stardom will milk the hell out of this situation. Got it?"

I nodded, allowing him to think he had the upper hand. And he would have, had I not had proof of his extracurricular activities. Hell, without that video, I probably would've run out of the diner and into traffic over Taylor's threat.

"Got it?" he asked again, wanting verbal confirmation.

"I got it," I repeated but left the *all right* silent.

"Good girl," Taylor said through a slight snicker. "Now that we got that out of the way, how was the head pen? Did they get you stabilized?"

My leg bounced underneath the table, trying to control the urge to attack him again. He was asking for it, and I planned to give it to him. I wanted so bad to drop his sex tape on him and see him piss himself and possibly be the one to run out into traffic. But, strategically, as Yara suggested. "Far from unstable," I responded as cool as I could. "More like pissed off considering what I saw you doing."

"Still unstable, I see. You're still delusional and hallucinating. You ain't see shit."

I jabbed my finger in his direction. "I saw a lot, and I'm sure you *felt* a lot."

Taylor chuckled a little. "And who's going to believe you? Your word is worth the value of a McDonald's fry."

"It doesn't matter. Apparently, you're shook if you needed to call this meeting before our official meeting."

He laughed some more. "Nah, I just wanted to remind you who you're up against in case that nuthouse boosted your confidence and made you forget who you *really* are."

I gritted my teeth. "And *who* am I?"

He tapped the side of his temple, pretending to think. "Nobody," he finally said. "Don't forget, I did you a favor. It's not like anyone was or is knocking down your door." He shrugged as he added, "No one wanted you, and after seeing some of those memes, that won't change anytime soon."

If "strategically," like Yara suggested when dealing with the sex tape, didn't come soon, I didn't
think I would last much longer. Taylor's ass was
too cocky. I tossed my recently flat ironed hair over
the back of my shoulder so it wouldn't fall into my
chicken when I leaned forward to cuss his ass out.
"Fuck you. At one point, your bitch-ass wanted me.
You were calling, texting, bringing me ice cream,
and spending time with me. So, what you said
makes no sense. I can't even believe you're acting
like this. The Taylor I knew would never be this
much of an asshole, but it's cool."

"And here I was thinking you were smart," he
retorted.

If it weren't for the deep wrinkles of confusion
between my eyebrows, they would've touched. "Oh,
so, now I'm dumb? I was smart enough to help
your dumbass with your assignments."

"No, you were smart enough to get me passing
grades, and up my GPA with the assignments
you *did* for me," he corrected. "You were dumb
because you didn't see how I played you. Look at
me and look at you. You think I would've wanted
you for any other reason? You were the easiest one,
by the way. All I had to do was show you a little
attention, pretend, make you feel special to me,
and keep feeding your chunky ass Häagen-Dazs.
That's it. Easy and cheap. You did everything I said.
Had you eating out of the palm of my hand, and I

appreciate you for being so naive, catching feelings, and making it to where I could get a restraining order against you if I wanted to." Taylor celebrated with a handclap. "All the red flags were there; you just didn't pay attention."

"You know you won't get very far with that attitude. Karma is a bitch, and she *will* get your ass."

"One of the reasons I'm headed to the NFL is my speed. Karma will have to catch me first."

I shook my head in disgust, which Taylor mistook for something else. "Don't look so defeated," he added. "I'll keep you on speed dial in case I need another favor."

"So, this is it? You're not going to take any responsibility for your part? You're not going to come out and be your authentic self? Gay, bisexual, bicurious, experimental, whatever the case may be. You are gonna keep carrying on like *this?*"

"I ain't gay, so you need to watch your mouth. Matter of fact, you need to worry about yourself, *not* me. Worry about unclogging your arteries and lowering your blood pressure."

Another fat joke. I had heard them all before. Because of his arrogance, I thought about killing him, but I realized how dumb and weak that sounded. Plus, I needed him to stay around a bit longer to watch his demise. Karma would catch him because I planned to work with her to ensure they came face-to-face.

I was done talking, but Taylor wouldn't stop. "Thank you. If there was any doubt about my future in the NFL, your tantrum increased my popularity and solidified my place." He stood, kissed two of his fingers, and then touched my cheek. "See you at mediation," the bastard said and headed toward the door, signing two autographs for some giggling teenage girls that had entered on his way out.

He asked me here and left me with the bill. He really thought he was God. However, no ego formed against me shall prosper. Taylor just flipped a coin and settled on tails—what he was comfortable giving away. I chose heads, and I was coming for his. *Strategically.*

Chapter 6

"All the red flags were there; you just didn't pay attention."

"What red flags?" I screamed and pounded on my steering wheel as I recited Taylor's words. My horn accidentally blared a few times, which caused some angry drivers to give me the finger. Road rage wasn't what I felt, just solid rage mixed with a little bit of confusion and sprinkled with a little bit of disgust.

That damn sentence had taunted me ever since he said it.

When did Taylor become this person? The better question was, how did I *miss* this person? Was this the real him all along, and I didn't see it because I was blinded by love? Or was he triggered by something I said, therefore becoming defensive?

What happened at the diner bugged the shit out of me and had me frazzled. I had to figure it out. My mind was preoccupied with that damn statement on replay on the drive back home. I had run two red lights, almost side-swiped a parked car, and almost hit a cyclist when I swerved out of my lane. He had followed the bicycle law, yet I almost ended his life because I had once again allowed Taylor to get to me. Imagine if I would've run that man over. The adjectives would've piled in the front of my name: *"fat, crazy, killer."* I could envision the comments. Remember what was said about me during Taylor's smackdown? Just imagine what the internet trolls would have said about me then. And rightfully so.

Before I inched my car along any farther, killing someone or even myself, I had to calm down. I pulled into the first empty parking lot I saw. It wasn't the safest, but whatever. Homeless people slept feet away under a bridge. One even approached my car, but I hit the locks and turned my head, pretending not to see her. I was usually not like this, and if my parents knew what I'd done, they'd probably try to knock my head off my shoulders.

The safest thing would've been to call someone. Emotional driving was up there with drunk driving. However, I needed alone time, not a listening ear or a ride. I had to figure this shit out myself. I turned the radio down and tapped into the unsafe territory—memory lane with Taylor.

The entirety of our relationship replayed on fast-forward.

We first met because his dumbass needed a tutor, and I served as a tutor for the college. Typically, the student picked a name from the database of tutors specific to the subject they needed assistance in and set it up on their own. Imagine my surprise when I got a call from the dean, Dr. Richardson, to set up sessions for Taylor. I didn't second-guess it. All I knew was that a student needed my services in more than one subject. That was probably why Dr. Richardson suggested mediation. Guilt or a cover-up. Athletes and their favoritism. Hell, they could've been lovers too, for all I knew.

I'd never been into sports, and while I'd seen Taylor around, he never gave me a second look. The most I knew about him were the basics: his name and that he was a jock. Nothing more. We'd never had a single conversation before he walked into the library with his head covered in a green hoodie and dark shades. So much for trying to be inconspicuous. I recognized him right away.

"Hey, Taylor." I remember smiling to put him at ease and let him know that he was in good hands, but he took it to mean something else.

"What's funny?" aggressively exited his mouth. He slumped in the chair, pulled the strings to his hoodie tighter, and lightly drummed his fingers against the table.

He didn't know the difference between a laugh and a smile. I thought it, but I didn't say it.

"I'm Redarra, your tutor." I didn't know whether to smile or sit stone-faced. The problem was that I smiled all the time, and that would have been a hard thing to change.

"What kind of name is that?"

Wasn't sure how to answer that, but I tried. "I'm named after my grandmother."

"Yeah, it does sound old-lady-ish."

Not the start that I anticipated. Dr. Richardson had made me aware of Taylor's needs without revealing who he was. He never told me I'd be dealing with an asshole. At least that's what I thought about him before he let his guard down, and we became close.

"Since we will be working together three days a week on three different subjects, I figured we can focus on one subject each day to avoid throwing so much information out there at once. What do you think?"

Taylor was nonchalant and slow to respond. He was too busy periodically watching the door and the table across from us.

"Oh, shit!" *Red flag.* It was so obvious now. I hit the steering wheel at my discovery. My horn sounded again. This time, *two* homeless people appeared at my window like genies. I wished they'd leave me be. I fanned them off and promised myself that I'd make up for it before I spun wheels out of the parking lot. A lightbulb had gone off, and I couldn't risk it blowing.

It didn't dawn on me before, but I remembered who was at that table. Sammie's ass. That's who Taylor watched. His ass assaulter. The more I pondered, the more I started to see. Yet, I was inundated with questions created by me that I didn't have adequate answers to.

Then I wondered if they were already a thing or became a thing after that. I thought and thought. I really needed to pace, but I was in the middle of what looked like a war zone, and a nasty storm was brewing. The sky had darkened to match my mood. With all the hazards around me, I couldn't bring myself to get out of the car. Instead, I hummed and rocked back and forth.

Shortly the rocking stopped, and the humming turned into words. "No, the hell this bastard didn't," I jeered as the lightbulb illuminated brighter, showing me the light to how much of a sucker I was.

Taylor had become highly stressed and irritable between daily practices, daunting coursework, lack of sleep, and not having enough time in the day to breathe. With that, I stepped in and occasionally did some of his assignments. I'm guilty of bailing him out. I'm guilty of growing so in love with him that I did anything to make him happy, including completing assignments for Sammie. Taylor straight up used me to do his work and his lover's work. Not all fault could be placed on him.

I was too blind to see it. My dumbass willingly did everything he asked of me, and when we became a thing, I did even more for the extra love points.

It didn't start that way. Strictly tutoring. After getting past Taylor's tough exterior, he began to warm up to me. He spoke instead of barely waving, asked personal questions, and shared personal experiences. We talked about football, home life, plans after college, and more. Our thirteenth session was when things shifted between us. Taylor had grown frustrated over his lack of retaining information that he snapped a pencil in two. I had reached across the table, rubbed his hand, and whispered encouraging words to calm him down. No romantic implications on my end, but to him, it was. Everything changed, even the look in his eyes. He looked at me like he felt something for me outside of being his tutor.

"You want to get out of here?" The way he asked that question, I couldn't resist.

I nodded. "And go where?" I asked, blushing.

He leaned over and pecked my lips right there in the library. "Your place, my place. Anyplace where I can study *you* instead of *this*." He pushed the notebook toward the middle of the table and continued staring at me.

A soft giggle escaped my lips as I licked off the spearmint flavor he left behind. When I started packing up my things, he knew what time it was.

He too started packing up his things. He followed me back to my apartment, and that's when I learned he and I lived right across the parking lot from each other.

Once inside my place, the door hadn't closed before he grabbed me and sloppily tongued me down. Slurps filled the room for a while. I was one of those girls that liked to kiss and explore with my hands. Every time I reached for Taylor's package, he pushed my hand away. The fact that he prolonged it turned me on even more.

He pulled away from my mouth and rolled his tongue in a circular motion across my cheek and up to my ear, licking it like it was an ice cream cone. "Taylor," I whispered. He wasn't even inside me yet, but I was already calling his name.

"Shh," he whispered back, then wrapped a handful of my hair around his hand and lightly pulled it. My head tilted back at the tug, exposing my neck and both chins. He licked over all of it like it was dirt, and he was the washcloth. Ecstasy had me wobbling, but I held on and reached for his junk again. Same reaction. This time when he pushed my hand away, his voice registered low. "I'm about to punish you for disobeying me."

I didn't know what that meant, but I played along and begged for it. "Punish me. Punish me."

"Say please."

Before I could get the words out, he had stuck his hand down my pants and started rubbing my clit. I leaned forward to kiss him, but he jerked his head back and refused to connect his lips with mine. He stared at me hard like the sound of my moans was satisfying enough. The rejection and teasing drove me so wild that all I could do was close my eyes and intensely beg for him to rub me faster.

Right before I climaxed, he stopped. I gasped and opened my eyes. "Why did you do that? I was right there," I said, with weakness in my voice.

"I know." He smirked, snatched his baseball cap off his head, and handed it to me. "Put this on," he demanded. I wanted to say no and argue over why he pulled back, but I was too eager to see what else he had up his sleeve.

"Why?" I asked over the odd request.

"Because I said so. Are you disobeying me again?"

Ah! His pulling back was my punishment. I put the cap on without any more lip.

"Tuck all that shit in," he said regarding the straggling strands of hair. I didn't think anything of it at that time. Shit, I was about to have *the* Taylor Lawrence up in my guts, so who had time to care about his freaky fantasy, fetish, or whatever it was. Little did I know, it was another *red flag*.

"Now what?" I asked once every flyaway was completely hidden.

He slowly lifted his shirt showing off a nice, toned stomach. My eyes immediately shifted from there to the piece of him that I'd been dying to see. A nice-size bulge poked through his basketball shorts. When I tried to grab it a third time, he smacked my hand away.

"Bad girl." He pointed downward and instructed me to get on my knees. "Good girl," he said after I obliged. Taylor pulled his shorts down but stopped just shy of exposing his wood. He had a headful of hair, and it was driving me insane—in a good way.

Whatever he had in store, I hoped he'd hurry up and make it happen. My knees were killing me. Years of carrying excess weight had damaged my cartilage and joints.

"Let me see," I said. This begging shit was sexy and annoying all at the same time. My vagina pulsated and felt like it would explode into a million coochie pieces if Taylor didn't enter me soon. I wanted penetration, and his ass was purposely making me suffer. Then again, the waiting and begging built up my anticipation for the official act.

"You wanna see it?" he asked.

I nodded. "I do."

He pulled his shorts down a little farther, exposing his shaft. "You want to taste it?" He allowed his shorts to fall to his ankles when he asked that. It was humongous and beautiful, yet scary because it was so long and thick. I closed my eyes and parted my lips, prepared to receive him. "Close your mouth."

I was confused. How was I supposed to perform like that? Better yet, how would all of that monster fit? Everything on me was big, *except* for my mouth. But I closed it like he told me and awaited further instruction.

He moaned while he slowly traced around my lips like he was my makeup artist applying lip gloss. I let out an extended groan when he picked up the pace.

"Play with my balls."

I did. I gently caressed them with my fingertips. Taylor's breathing became labored as his moans grew louder.

"*Now* open your mouth," he said and jammed himself inside as soon as I did. I gagged when it hit the back of my throat. "Don't do nothing; just hold it open."

I did as he said.

Five quick pumps (yes, I counted) and a few grunts later, Taylor's juices exploded in my mouth. I felt violated yet intrigued. Confusing as hell. If his stroke game was anything like what just happened, I was in for a treat.

I didn't know whether to swallow or spit. I looked around, dazed, trying to figure out what I could grab like we weren't in my damn apartment. I knew where everything was, but I felt out of place. I removed my shirt and used that to collect the waste.

Deep down inside, I wanted to ask what now. Since I was on my knees, was he expecting me to get on all fours or roll over on my back? To my surprise, Taylor pulled up his shorts, told me how fun it was, pecked my lips, and left, promising to call me later. I didn't know how to feel about what had happened or how he had left.

Everywhere I went, I made sure my phone was in my hand just in case he called. And he did. He asked if we could get together more often outside of tutoring.

I'd always heard women say good sex would make you lose your mind, and I was starting to understand that concept. Taylor and I had one oral encounter, and I was already addicted. He purposely toyed with me because he knew I'd come back for more. How could I resist? The teasing itself drove me wild. I'd never experienced anything like it. Past encounters for me weren't many. The experiences themselves—*meh,* at best. Mainly wham, bam, thank you, ma'am, and short-lived. Usually, it was over before I could blink.

I jumped when another homeless person tapped on my window. Finally, I did what I said and slid them a few dollars before driving off.

As I drove home, I pondered some more. Thinking back on everything, Taylor wanted me to wear that ball cap so that I'd look as much like a boy as possible. *Red flag.*

Chapter 7

"Come on in," Dr. Richardson waved my parents and me into his office and then got up to shake our hands. I'd never stepped foot into his workspace before, but it was the size of my entire campus apartment. Filled-up, built-in bookshelves aligned the walls. A glass globe sat on one of the shelves, along with a few other random glass awards. Degrees and inspirational quotes covered the other walls. I noticed all of that in seconds to avoid making eye contact with Taylor or his parents.

A small glass table separated the three of us from the three of them. Even though I won against Taylor, I'd never been a fighter. If his mom decided to unleash her noticeable fury, there would be nothing the table could do to prevent it.

The tension in the room was as thick as my thighs. The air smelled as if a storm was heading our way. Taylor coughed, and I mistakenly looked in their direction. By the way his mom glared at me, she was about to bring all the bad weather. She scooted to the edge of her seat. Her eyes narrowed, and her top lip curled. Behind her colored contacts was a rabid animal ready to attack. Rightfully so. I harmed her baby boy, but she might want to beat his ass if she knew the *real* him.

I noticed the sling holding Taylor's arm and his puppy dog eyes. Unless he got hurt in practice or recently got his ass beat again, he was putting on. At this point, I knew it was about to be some more bullshit, so I'm glad my ambulance-chasing attorney parents were here with me after all. They'd get the truth out like this was a courtroom.

"Can I interest any of you in some water before we get started?" Dr. Richardson asked.

I shook my head. My parents verbally declined, and so did Taylor's parents. Taylor didn't. I guess he needed to hydrate the lies he was about to tell. My mouth flung open when I saw his mom untwist the cap from his bottled water, hold it up to his mouth, and practically bottle-feed this bastard.

She rubbed his leg as he drank and then asked, "Is that enough?" When he finished, his mother proceeded to dab his mouth with a napkin.

Internally, I had all kinds of thoughts, and I think my parents did too with the way they fidgeted in their seats. I hoped they were ready to fight for me.

Dr. Richardson sat in his oversized brown leather chair and crossed one leg over the other, revealing a pair of football socks. Because he was a retired professional football player, I came into the meeting already believing he would side with Taylor, and his socks confirmed it.

"How is recovery going, Taylor?" Dr. Richardson inquired.

"Slow," he answered in practically a whisper.

"That's a lie," I yelled.

My mother tapped my leg to hush me.

"I'm sorry, Dr. Richardson, but this ain't gonna work. My son ain't safe around this . . ."

Taylor's mom stuttered, trying to find a clean term to call me in the presence of others. I knew "bitch" was what she wanted to say, but she forcefully hollered, "her." Then she added with disgust written all over her face, "I'm not sure her tantrums are under control." She kept her eyes on me to let me know that she wasn't scared of me. Her nose carried the same wrinkle as Taylor's anytime he got amped up like her.

"May I?" my mother asked. I got excited because she was about to scorch their asses. "I can assure you, Mr. and Mrs. Lawrence and Dr. Richardson, that our daughter will not be a problem going forward. Her father and I will make sure of that."

"It's Mrs. Epps," Taylor's mom corrected. "This is Taylor's step-daddy, and y'all better make sure she stays in her lane, or we *will* press charges and send her to jail where she needs to be. Football is all my son has, and your daughter almost took that away from us."

Us? I'd never seen her at one game. All this hood rat wanted was an upgraded lifestyle.

"My apologies, Mrs. Epps," my mother corrected.

I glared at her. That was not the heat I expected, but I thought maybe she was warming up to it. For the remainder of the meeting, Taylor's mom and her long, fake fingernails pointed in our direction, repeatedly flipped her two-toned blond wig, and disrespected us, while my parents just sat there and took it. Every time I tried to interject, they stopped me.

After an hour of disrespect, Dr. Richardson finally stepped in. He cleared his throat and pulled out a manila folder with multiple papers inside. "Both of you are great students and examples of Black excellence. I would love to see you both graduate and be productive citizens and role models. The incident that happened was unfortunate and cannot and will *not* happen again, or there will be tougher consequences." He then directed his attention solely to Taylor and his people. "I have been in constant communication with the Michaels family, and we have set a few things in place for Taylor and Redarra to coexist without further incident."

Special conditions were placed upon me—sucky conditions at that. First, eight sessions of anger management classes, which Ramona had already warned me about, but I didn't realize they had expected me to complete them in a month. Two classes a week. How was *that* fair? I was not angry, and the fact that people felt I needed to manage my anger boiled my blood. Just because I was upset and reacted to being cheated on did *not* make me an angry person.

Taylor raised his hand. "Can we get updates on her anger management progress? I don't want to feel like I must constantly look over my shoulder when she decides to get upset again."

This bastard really played the part of the victim.

"We can arrange that," Dr. Richardson agreed.

From there, I learned I couldn't live on campus anymore. I didn't necessarily mind that. The accommodations weren't the best, and while I had the option to live elsewhere before the fight, I wanted to experience the whole college life and not rely on my parents to pay my rent or extra bills outside of what my scholarships didn't cover.

"I hope you realize we are doing you a favor, young lady, by allowing this slap on the wrist," Taylor's step-daddy commented. My parents loved Ron Isley, and Mr. Epps reminded me so much of him. He appeared much older than Taylor's mom, which was why I was surprised when he was introduced as the stepfather instead of the grandfather. "My son was attacked and is in a sling because you couldn't control your emotions. I'm sure there's more to offer us for the inconvenience." He dropped his hand beside his knee and rubbed his fingers together.

"We are willing to pay for all medical bills, as well as pain and suffering, up to $2,500," my mother replied.

My posture straightened as I attempted to protest. "But—"

"Enough, Redarra," my mother said and tapped my leg again.

Next, the apology letter came up. I couldn't read what I didn't have, and if I did have it, I would've ripped it up before allowing Taylor to hear one word. Besides, how would I have started it? Better yet, why should I have to apologize for him betraying me? *Dear Taylor, there is nothing wrong with being gay. Hurting people to hide it is.*

"I started on the letter," I said. "However, my train of thought was interrupted when I was sent a video of him inappropriately bashing my character to the world."

Taylor cleared his throat. I knew that was his way of reminding me of his demand to shut my mouth. Fuck him and fuck his demands, though. The only reason why I didn't mention his sex tape now was that I had bigger plans for it.

"Do you have the video present?" Dr. Richardson asked and tugged at his solid blue necktie that matched his gray suit but not his green and orange football socks. I didn't know if he was uncomfortable with what I was about to expose or if it was because his neck looked like it was made up of three other necks and the collar to his shirt was a little snug.

I nodded and felt the imaginary laser from Taylor's eyes trying to burn a hole in my face. Of course, I didn't want to play this in front of my parents, nor did I tell them about it because it was humiliating enough, but it was time to stop allowing Taylor to play this innocent victim. That sling did it for me, and so did the attempt of a money grab from the fake Mr. Isley.

In the video, Taylor starts with, *"What's good, y'all?"* He took time out to respond to a couple of people that had hopped on. Then he said, *"Y'all have been hitting my line like crazy asking me about the attack. It's like this. Shorty got mad when I told her I was cutting her from my rotation. She lost her touch, and I can't have my shit all scratched up. You feel me? Now, if she has all her teeth pulled, she can latch back on. Until then, it's a wrap."* He swiped his hand across his neck. *"Your boy is good, though. You know how psychotic bitches are? Takes more than a psycho chick to break me. I hope y'all come out to the game."* He ended the video by drawing a number eleven in the air and flexing his muscles.

"Mr. Epps, a moment ago, you stated that Taylor's football career almost ended and that he was in a sling because of my daughter. However, that video paints a very different picture. Perhaps you misspoke, and Taylor's injury is from football practice and not attempted extortion which is punishable by jail time and fines."

Suddenly, I was no longer afraid to make eye contact with anyone on Taylor's side of the room. If my eyes could change colors like a mood ring, they'd be yellow to symbolize laughter and joy. I smirked, and my insides screamed, "Get 'em, Mommy."

Mrs. Epps remained quiet, but the look of loathing on her face told me that when she caught me in the street, she would fuck me up and have me in a sling like her son, if not *two* slings and a *full-body* cast.

Mr. Epps stammered over his words. It took a minute, but he finally managed to say, "We don't want any trouble. We will take the original pain and suffering offer."

My mom smoothed out the sleeves of her dark corporate pantsuit and snickered. "That offer is off the table."

"Well then, we are pressing charges," Mrs. Epps threatened.

Sweat formed on Dr. Richardson's bald head as he tried his best to gain control of the meeting, but it was too late. My mother had switched from polite parent mode to pit bull attorney. She stood, summoned for me and my dad, who'd been quiet the whole time, to grab our things to leave. "Press all the charges you want. By the time I enter this video into evidence, I will make an argument so good and bring to light the *real* reason why my daughter attacked your son. His NFL days will *never* come." She went Clair Huxtable nice-nasty on everybody. She then looked at Dr. Richardson and added, "You can shred those documents. We won't be needing any action plan."

When my mother ushered us out of the room, I heard Taylor's parents asking what she was referring to. I wonder if he told the truth for once in his life.

The outcome of the meeting should've been satisfactory enough for me to leave it alone, but I considered it only a tiny victory, and I wanted so much more.

Chapter 8

Taylor's words still nagged at me. *All the red flags were there; you just didn't pay attention.*

Relationship flags were inevitable. I decided to overlook a lot of what Taylor waved. I didn't consider any of his questionable behavior red flags because I was Stevie Wonder, blinded by love. Call it corrective eye surgery or bifocals because once the blinders came off, I saw it all. I realized that if other relationships were missing flags, it was because they were all in me and Taylor's fraudulent courtship.

It was safe to say that I was downright abused. Not physically. Taylor never laid a hand on me, but he served me with every other form of abuse, though. Emotionally, mentally, and even spiritually. He gave it all.

In recognizing my naivety, I took some of the blame. I fell into the "big girl" stereotype of taking what you could get when you didn't look like what magazines and movies portrayed as sexy. I allowed Taylor to mistreat me. Consider it my initiation into being a woman in love and left with a nick on the heart. Every woman I knew had been through it, so it was only a matter of time before it happened to me. I had heard countless excuses, and they all went the same way: I thought he loved me; I thought I could change him; I tried to give him the benefit of the doubt, and my favorite, he would never. I thought the same . . . but he did. What was the adage? Do unto others as they do unto you. I planned to. Not only strategically but secretly. That's why when Yara called to ask about mediation, I left out the part where I had a change of heart.

"Dang. You must've smelled me leaving Dr. Richardson's office," I said as soon as I put my phone to my ear. Yara was relentless. She had called multiple times during mediation, and I planned to call her back the minute I got some alone time, but I wanted to talk freely, not in code, since my parents were around.

"Yes, girl. The smell of the air changed from pollution to victory," she responded. "Please tell me I'm right, and Gay Tay got put in his place."

I laughed so hard that it took me a minute to answer. I excused myself to the bathroom so that I could relive my victory one more time and put my anxious bestie at ease. I pushed the door open, just as eager to spill it all. I started talking and immediately stopped when I saw a lady and young girl at the sink. I pretended to push up the fly-away hairs around my two French braids to the back. Because the lady and child lingered a bit, I adjusted the floral calf-length dress that I purchased from Old Navy. Even though it covered my body like a muumuu, I snapped a couple of pictures anyway. One to buy time but also to record the look of a winner. As soon as they left, I checked under the stalls for feet. When the coast was clear, I turned back to the mirror and watched a smile part my lightly glossed lips.

"He did get put in his place. You should've seen him squirm when I pulled out that video of him bashing me," I said through chuckles and then filled Yara in from start to finish.

"That's what his trifling ass gets, but I still don't feel like that's enough." Little did she know, I didn't feel like it was enough either. Maybe it was greed. "What's the move now? We gonna get those matching bags or what?" Yara pressed.

I knew she wanted to help, and as much as I would've loved to grant her the satisfaction of helping me take down Taylor, he was something I needed to handle myself. "No. I'm good with what happened today. A small victory, but satisfying," I lied.

"If you change your mind, just say the word."

"Gotcha."

"Since I won't be getting the purse of my dreams, you can make it up to me." Yara's tone was sinister.

I laughed nervously. There was no telling what would come out of her mouth next. "I'm sure whatever you're about to say is gonna be some bull."

She laughed in return. That too was sinister sounding. "I have a date, and I need you to entertain his cousin." She raised her voice over my objections and added, "And before you settle on no, it would be good to get out and celebrate your victory. You know, move on."

"Not ready, friend. Right now, all guys are trash."

"There's someone out there for you, and Dre's cousin may be it. God removes trash and replaces it with treasure. He could be your treasure." Yara wouldn't let me get a word in as she went on and on about her new flame's cousin, who was visiting from South Carolina. They didn't want to cancel their fourth date, nor did they want the cousin to feel like a third wheel.

Against my better judgment, I allowed Yara to talk me into going on a double date that I knew I wasn't mentally ready for. "I guess I don't have much of a choice," I reluctantly agreed.

"I'm so glad you see it that way because I already told him you said yes, and I sent him a picture of you."

I choked on my spit. "Yara, what the hell?"

"Don't worry about it, girl. He is definitely interested."

I stared at my reflection. My mouth hung open in utter shock. "I could kill you right now." But I wouldn't because I was too curious. "What picture did you send, and what did he say?"

"I sent the one of us freshman year at homecoming."

I never knew I could open my mouth as wide as I did. My jaws popped, and I could see my bottom molars. "Yara Marie Santana!"

"What?" she asked as if she were innocent and had no clue why I called her by her full government name.

"I look *nothing* like that picture anymore. I was already chunky then and have since packed on freshman fifteen, sophomore twenty, junior ten, and senior thirty."

Yara snorted. "That ain't even a real thing. Anyway, he said you were beautiful, and he likes them thick and meaty. Stop worrying about everyone prejudging you because of your weight. I've told you that a gazillion times. You're the cutest."

Easy for her to say. She had never suffered a tragedy involving weight like I had, nor did she know what it was like to wear double-digit pants. Nothing jiggled on her when she walked, coughed, sneezed, or waved. Yara was toned and had long legs like a model.

"You're my sister. You're supposed to say that."

"No, the hell I ain't. I tell it like it is. If I thought you was ugly, I'd say it and mean it."

I blew out a breath and fogged up the mirror. "The scale is creeping toward three, and you know I eat my feelings."

"We can work out and diet together."

"Hell no. You eat leaves and berries and practically drink rainwater like you're stranded on an island," I teased as I often did. This girl was disciplined to the max with what she put into her body, and it showed. "Plus, you're an athlete. I don't want to slow you down."

"Forget you—always talking shit. But seriously, you can start with walking. That's a good way to clear your mind too. Or you can hit up that trainer I told you about. I heard he's outstanding, but I couldn't afford his prices. So no pressure, and if you change your mind, we can tackle it together."

"I appreciate it, sis."

"And, Redarra," Yara's tone suddenly filled with compassion, "you *will be okay* and bounce back from every bad thing that has happened in your life. There will be blessing after blessing, and one day, you're gonna look up and become so overwhelmed by all the good happenings that anytime you hear 'Taylor,' that name will only be associated with the person who makes sure your clothes fit right—not trauma. Karma is going to eat Taylor up and swallow him. Just trust me."

"I do trust you." Yara had 99 percent of my trust, which is why I couldn't tell her why I was so confident in knowing that Taylor had some not-so-pleasant things coming his way. That 1 percent is what might have gotten me caught.

Chapter 9

"Welcome to Dollar Tree," the cashier greeted from lane number two.

Because I knew I was up to no good, I froze in place a few feet from the entrance like a dumbass. *Run back to my car and spin wheels out of the parking lot or proceed with the mission?* It was a simple one. Shop for basic everyday supplies. Yeah, it was for a covert operation, but nothing alarming to anyone who didn't know my intentions. For some reason, I felt caught already. I felt as if the jury had returned a guilty verdict and sentenced me to life in prison solely for *acting* suspiciously.

"Can I help you find something?" she asked. I'd been in this store quite a few times over the years with Taylor buying composition books and writing utensils, and I'd never encountered an associate like her. She was Chick-fil-A pleasant, and it worried me. I'd now convinced myself that she knew what I had planned and had already alerted the SWAT.

I shook my head at her question. Crime shows were my guilty pleasure. I had watched enough of them to know that the sound of my voice could be used against me. I was not about to be the girl in a lineup, holding a number and being forced to step forward to repeat a sentence.

Damn. Nerves had my mind playing tricks on me.

I hopped like a bunny when the automatic doors opened for an incoming customer—another potential witness. I glanced at the cashier and noticed her raised eyebrows. A male employee stood beside her, his face stiff with worry. Then it dawned on me. It was pitch black outside, a little warm for this time of year, and I had on shades and a black hoodie pulled so tight that it could have cut off my circulation. Plus, I stood in the middle of the store with my hands stuffed inside my pockets. I could see how my appearance could be misconstrued. They thought I was a robber. I quickly snatched off the hoodie and shades. The low-profile disguise was only intended to be worn while I ran into The Sex Hole to grab a little something for Taylor.

Even though it was probably a little late to change the impression the store associates had of me, I cleared my throat and tried to sound as friendly as possible. I smiled, showing every tooth, cavity, and my healthy pink gums. "Um . . . Where are the hand shopping cart basket thingies?" I asked, sounding like a dumbass.

The manager pointed. "Right behind you." They both continued to stare at me like I was up to something. Technically, I was, but it wasn't targeted toward them.

I snapped my fingers and made an explosion sound that I instantly regretted. A dubious person referencing a deadly sound was probably the equivalent of saying the word "bomb" on a plane.

"I'm sorry," I said, attempting to relax the atmosphere. "It's been a long day, and I swear my mind is all over the place. If my head weren't attached to my neck, I'd probably run off and leave it somewhere." So much for keeping quiet to protect my voice. And the worst part of all, my mouth continued to run like a leaky faucet. "I have some projects I promised my nieces and nephews I'd help them work on. And you know kids, they will hold you to your word and bug you each and every day until you do as promised." All lies. I had no nieces or nephews.

Note to self: criminality is not your forte. How hard would it have been to be cool, grab some items, and get the hell on? Just my luck, they had already activated the panic button, and the SWAT team was waiting by my car with a helicopter on standby in case my fat ass tried to run. I shook away that thought. I was losing it for real. For one, everything was a dollar and not worth the hassle. Two, them needing a helicopter to keep up with me was utter bullshit. A turtle could outrun me.

"I can relate," the man added. "No kids of my own, but I have a nephew." I wasn't sure how to respond to him, so I nodded in place of words. "Well, I'm the manager," he continued. "Let me know if you need help finding anything." His stare lingered.

Eventually, I got over the extreme scenarios I had wasted time creating, scooped up a green handbasket, and ventured on with sealed lips and a semi-relaxed stroll around the store. Every time I looked up, the manager lurked nearby, pretending to organize shelves. I grabbed everything I needed, plus some, including a couple of those cheap flashlights the campus security guards used, and headed to the line.

After I flipped my basket over, dumping out all the contents, the manager emerged from thin air and started lollygagging around lane three. He clandestinely scoped me out, casing me like he thought I did when I first arrived. Again, everything was a dollar. If I were to put myself in jeopardy, it would be at a high-end store in Beverly Hills somewhere.

"Chasity, go ahead and straighten up the aisles. I'll take care of this young lady," the manager instructed.

What felt like a large lump of salt slid down my throat. Why send her to do something he had already done? He had to have perceived me as a thief, and I hadn't done anything. My tastebuds became bitter. "Is something wrong?" I asked nervously.

"Not at all. You find everything okay?"

I didn't like how he asked that when he had practically profiled me the entire time. Nor did I like how he continuously stared at me. He should've been paying attention to my items rolling down the conveyor belt. Instead, he scanned and stared. It was creepy, so I unzipped my wallet and pulled out cash to show him I planned to pay.

"Looks like you and your family plan to have some fun. What are you guys making with all these flags?"

None of your damn business. Only I didn't have the heart to be rude and say it out loud. "Just kid stuff. Nonsense projects," I replied.

He held up a pack of flags. "These are marked down, by the way. They are being discontinued in case you need to grab some more."

"Thank you for the information. I think I have enough." Three packs of 500 self-stick flags should be plenty . . . I hoped. I only intended to use the red ones. Even still, that should be enough. If not, I'd get creative and make my own. I shouldn't have to wave that many in Taylor's direction. Then again, he has a God complex. Time will tell.

Manager Man just had to provide stellar customer service. "How old are your nieces and nephews?"

All this lying on the fly was too much for me. No disrespect to my parents, but I would've gone to law school if I wanted to be a liar. "Really little," I responded. He might've thought I was dumb before and a thief, but now just a smart-ass.

"It's ironic that you're here," Manager Man said. "I've wanted to reach out to you, but I wasn't sure how you would take it."

I frowned. "*Excuse* me?"

He inhaled deeply and chuckled a bit, but I didn't see shit funny. "I'm sorry if I freaked you out. We don't know each other, but I know what happened with you and Taylor Lawrence. I—"

I held up my hands. "Whoa! Let me stop you right there. I don't know what you are about to say, but I don't want to discuss *anything* regarding him. Now, if you can please give me my total so I can pay and go, I would appreciate that."

"I don't mean to offend you. It's just that—"

"Total!" I'd abandon all this shit if he didn't shut the hell up.

He did what I asked. As he gave me back my change, he blurted out, "He and I were lovers."

My lips spread like puberty hips, but no sound came out. I dropped the coins Manager Man had given to me. His words echoed. *He and I were lovers.* His confession had me catatonic. *Say something—anything.*

Remorse wore on his face heavier than the black guy-liner outlining just the top of his eyes. "I'm really sorry to drop this news on you like this." Manager Man kept apologizing and dropping bomb after bomb. "I'm not the only one. We have a whole group chat dedicated to Taylor. He's a total prick, and he gets away with it because of his star power."

I took a couple of steps back and bumped up against lane one. My airway felt constricted. My hands trembled as I fumbled through my purse for my inhaler and hit it twice. I was gonna pass out at any minute.

"Please. Please. Let's talk in my office. I will tell you everything." He yelled to Chasity to come back and operate the register.

The office space was little as shit. It was about the size of a deep freezer, with a large window for viewing pleasure. It was so small and congested that all of me wouldn't fit inside, along with a desk, file cabinet, and a folding chair. Although Manager Man was as thin as a pair of white women's lips, he barely fit himself. Half of my body chilled in the office, and the other half waited out in the store.

He handed me his phone and permitted me to scroll through a group chat until I couldn't handle it any longer. It didn't take long. I shook my inhaler and hit it like a pipe.

"I'll get you some water," he graciously offered.

I didn't want any more water. Quarts poured from my eyes already. By the time I left the store, I had way more than I had come for in the first place. Manager Man's name was Dalton, and Taylor used him too, as he did with Jalil, Francisco, and Gentry.

Before I pulled out of the store, I checked Taylor's social media accounts and the accounts of other players. The team was away at a community fundraiser that started earlier in the afternoon. From there, dinner. One thing about Taylor, he told his every move for the world to see, and so far, he hadn't let me down. I hoped he managed to alert the world—mainly me—to what awaited him. It would tarnish his reputation, so I doubt it.

Dollar Tree didn't disappoint. I grabbed a pair of surgical gloves from my purse and put them on. The gloves might've been a bit extreme because I didn't plan to kill Taylor, but he's a popular athlete, and I couldn't take the chance of having my fingerprints on anything if the police went above and beyond to search for the culprit. I even cleaned everything with disinfectant wipes and the gloves too.

I sifted through the shopping bags and found the flags. I peeled back a red one, wrote the letter H with a Sharpie, stuck it on the dildo, dropped it in a gold bubble mailer, sealed it with gratification, and wrote his name on the front of it to make sure his roommate didn't think it was for him. Because

I'd left many sweet handwritten notes for Taylor, I wrote everything with my left hand. Next, I put an extreme amount of tape on the envelope to avoid the weight ripping it down. It was just a tiny dildo, but still . . .

I started the car and pulled into a spot closer to Taylor's building with my headlights off.

Chapter 10

Ever since the ambulance carted me off from Taylor's apartment, I hadn't been back in the area. With the help of Yara, my parents had packed up my place and moved all my belongings back to their house while I was on an extended stay at The Wellness Center.

According to my unfinalized stipulations, I wasn't supposed to step foot on campus unless I had a class. And although my old residence was considered campus apartments, it was several miles from my classes. Plus, it was after nine p.m. on a Saturday. So, bottom line, I had no business being on the property. If caught, there would be no valid justification for my presence.

I grew more nervous the closer I got to Taylor's, but I took solace in knowing that I wouldn't be on the premises long. Besides, what I was about to do needed to be done.

I drove my granny's older model Cadillac. It was black, polished, and resembled what a car service would use to chauffeur clients. The best part of all were the tinted windows, and no one could place me in it, not even the bastard I planned to destroy. When my granny passed, my parents took ownership of the car, and all it did was take up a section of their two-car garage. Occasionally, my dad would hop in and give it a spin to the store to keep the battery alive, but that wasn't very often. So, he was all for it when I asked to drive it.

When I turned into the parking lot, the first thing I noticed was how dark it was. They still hadn't fixed those damn lights. I wasn't complaining this time. It would work to my advantage. I backed the Caddy into my usual spot in front of my old building and killed the lights. That way, I could scope out the scene without detection.

My heart knocked against my chest like the beat was produced in a music studio. Once again, my airway felt constricted, and whatever was going on with my stomach felt worse than period cramps. Forget a growl here and there. It roared like a mad lion. I undid the button on my fitted black jeans like I'd just feasted on one of the biggest Thanksgiving meals of my life and let my stomach hang, hoping that would bring me a little comfort.

I covered my tracks pretty well, but I was still shaken. At times, I held my breath. I didn't want any sightings of me around, not even a hint of fog on the windows. The surveillance cameras never worked, so they weren't my concern. Actual eyewitnesses were. I made sure to come when traffic around the complex would be close to a snooze. It was the weekend, and everyone either went home to visit family, to a party, a club, or out to eat. As I said, crime shows were my thing, and I took extra precautions, even powering off my cell phone long before I got to the complex. I had an alibi too. It all timed out perfectly like it was meant to be.

"Let it go. Ignore them. Give it time. Don't compare. Stay calm. It's on you. Smile," I recited the seven rules of life that I fished from the internet one day, hoping they'd help me cope. I had tried to let it go and ignore it, but every time I turned around, another reminder. I had given it time, and while time may heal wounds for most people, I settled on the need for revenge to heal mine. I did plan to smile, however. I hoped to drive Taylor insane with these little clues that he'd grow so uncomfortable in his own skin. I wanted him to experience admission into a psych ward and lose out on the opportunity of a promised NFL contract. That smile would stay on my face for the rest of my life.

Once again, I tried to control my breathing before tackling the stairs. In through my nose, out through my mouth.

I stuck the envelope on Taylor's door and somewhat bolted through the breezeway leading to the backside of the building. Taylor never went that way.

"Oh shit." Not again. Karma for me. I missed the third to the last step, and booty bounced down the last two. I imagined I looked like a slinky on steroids with the way I fell. I landed on my side and was met with an ungodly pain. I moaned and groaned and rolled around on the ground. Either I broke something or landed on a knife. The pain was sharp and intense. There was no way I could deny trespassing if I needed an ambulance to cart me off again.

"You okay? Do you want me to call for help?" someone asked.

Now my lungs stung worse than my side. I was caught and couldn't breathe. It wasn't a voice I was familiar with. Still, my ass was straight busted. Too afraid to look at the person, I shook my head and turned it as close to the concrete as possible.

"Let me help you."

This time I lowered my voice, trying to disguise it as much as possible, and added, "I got it." Seriously, I didn't. I was hurting and on the verge of having a panic attack. More embarrassment was coming, and so was jail time. This time, there was *nothing* my parents could do to save me.

"Please don't take this as me being rude, but if you had it, you'd be up by now," he said. "I'm a premed major. At least let me take a look."

Premed stranger, who may also be a serial killer, or an ambulance, where my parents may find out? It didn't take long to decide. Either way, I'd be killed.

"Thank you," I said and extended my arm for him to pull me up.

"Okay, well, first, my name is Julian. I'm going to roll you over to see how bad it is before I move you too much." Then he went on to tell me everything he planned to do before he did it.

Eventually, I ended up in his apartment, which was directly behind Taylor's. Julian talked a bunch of doctor talk, but ultimately, I'd live without the need of an experienced doctor delivering the same prognosis. My side was just bruised and badly discolored. So was my ankle.

Everything went well until Julian slipped up. "All set, Redarra. I'll send my final bill in the mail," he joked. Only I wasn't laughing. I never told him my name.

"Humph." I eyed the door he helped me to limp in. I'm not a fast runner. Plus, I'm injured. He'd catch me in no time. Same with the kitchen if I ran to get a knife. Nothing around me was sharp enough to do any serious damage. The décor was the epitome of a bachelor pad. There were no pictures on the wall, no dining room table, and no decorative throw pillows covering the couch to where it left little room to sit. The entertainment center was dusty and filled with every game console that had ever been invented.

"Do you want me to drive your car around the back for you? Or are you going through the front?"

I played it cool. "You've done enough. I can handle it from here."

"That's not a good idea," Julian retorted. "As your free doctor, I order you not to put any pressure on that ankle. Go right home and ice it. Now, let me help you out." He attempted to put his arm around me, but I pushed him off. He rubbed the top of his head, confused.

"Don't touch me," I roared.

"Whoa, whoa." Julian held his hands up and retreated.

That made me feel a little better, knowing that if he planned to kill me, he wouldn't have backed away when I got aggressive.

"How do you know my name? And don't lie." I shook my finger around like I was his momma, punishing him.

Julian still had his hands raised in the air like I was the police, pointing a gun at him. "Don't mean to be rude, but everyone knows who you are. Your face is all over the internet. And since you said don't lie, I heard you fucking up Taylor through the walls that night. Even saw you in the ambulance."

I dropped my head in shame. "Damn. So much for honesty."

"It's okay. I feel your pain."

I scowled at him. "You have no idea what I'm dealing with. What do you want to keep quiet about seeing me over here?" I asked and prayed he wouldn't ask for sexual favors. He was cute, but I'm not a one-night stand kind of girl. "Money?" I added that to sway him in case he did want that type of favor.

Julian slowly lowered his hands but stayed feet away from me. "I can assure you I understand, and I'm not looking for anything."

I smacked my teeth. "Yeah, right. Everyone wants something."

"Not me. I'm not everyone," he said and walked into the kitchen. He came back with a bottle of liquor and two glasses. After I declined, he poured himself a drink and continued. "Don't mean to be rude, but why are you giving him the time of day after what happened? Why waste your time on a dude that likes fucking around with other dudes?"

My eyes lit up. "Wait a minute, you know?"

Julian nodded and sipped. "Who doesn't know? People ride his coattail because he'll get drafted, no doubt—dollar signs. Just know you better hurry up and do whatever you plan to do before *I* catch him. You're a beautiful girl. You can do so much better than settling for him."

"Hold on. I am not *settling* for Taylor. That's not why I'm here. Me and you are on the same page when it comes to getting his ass." I'd gotten so comfortable knowing I had an ally that I'd said too much.

"You don't have to worry about me saying a damn thing," Julian said, trying to convince me that I had his loyalty after realizing I'd told on myself. "As a matter of fact, take down my number, and I'll even help you."

"A little young to be playing bodyguard, aren't you?" I asked, taking in his youthful appearance. He looked more like a short, stout, middle school student with big black glasses and no facial hair. With his weight and my weight, the floor to his apartment might cave in with a sinkhole any minute. He was still attractive, though.

This time he guzzled and refilled. "I'm old enough to drink legally." He raised his glass in the air.

Neither of us said anything for a while. I stared at him, wondering why he'd risk helping a stranger unless he was setting me up. He didn't strike me as gay, but neither did Taylor. Or at least, that's what love convinced me of anyway.

"I don't mean to be rude," I said, adding in a little of Julian's flavor, "but what did Taylor do to you? Trick you into thinking y'all would be in a relationship too?"

"Hell naw," he snapped. "Let's get one thing clear. I love women. It isn't what Taylor did to *me*, but what he did to my brother, Jalil."

I choked on my spit. Julian rushed over and patted me on the back. "I take it you know him?" he asked, now rubbing my back.

For some reason, I felt comfortable spilling the beans. "Never met him," I replied. "I so happened to be in a store, and the manager recognized me from the video. He showed me a group chat of guys that Taylor had messed over. Jalil was one of the names. Not too many Jalils in the world, so I assume he's your brother."

"More than likely."

Silence lingered again. Julian's blank expression had me wanting to ask exactly what he planned to do to Taylor. However, the deranged look that expanded his eyes and the cracking of his knuckles that sounded like fireworks scared the spunk out of me. Taking him up on his offer to help was enticing, but was he talking a simple ass-whooping or murder? I damn sure didn't want to be implicated in his premeditated scheme. Plus, I wasn't so sure I wanted an accomplice. Then again, working with Julian would at least eliminate potential trespassing charges.

After deliberating briefly with myself, I extended my hand to seal the deal. "Partners?"

"Partners," Julian replied. "Just don't tell my brother. He's already bitchin' over my threats and begging me not to hurt him."

"My word."

Julian had no reason to worry. My lips were sealed because I had no clue about the extent of his threats. The less I knew, the better.

Julian took a long chug before burping and slamming his glass on the counter. "What was in the envelope?" he pried.

"You saw that, huh?"

He nodded. "I did. I was looking out for Taylor, actually. I had ducked off, waiting for you to leave to see what you left, when I heard you fall." His face contorted, and he coughed a little before he busted out laughing. "I'm sorry. I don't mean to laugh, but that shit was funny as hell."

I couldn't help but laugh in return. When the laughter subsided, I told him what I had left. "A dildo and a red flag with the letter H on it."

Julian's frown let me know he was confused. "I get the fake dick, but . . ."

"Once upon a time, Taylor said to me, 'All the red flags were there; you just didn't pay attention.' Therefore, I'm leaving him some flags of my own to torture him." A proud giggle filled the air. "They so happen to be red."

"Nice," Julian said and nodded. "The H?"

I laughed. "Just a little extra to see if he'll put it together. H is the first letter in Häagen-Dazs," I admitted and explained how Taylor mentioned he only needed to feed me ice cream and I'd do anything he wanted. "I want him to know it's me, but in a way where no one can prove it." I shared most of the plan, except the video. That would serve as the grand finale once I figured out how.

Julian drove my granny's car around back like he suggested, and once he helped me to it, I promised him that I'd call later to meet up and brainstorm on how he could help. One way I could use him is to leave the clues at Taylor's door. Them damn stairs were plotting to kill me.

The more I thought about my fall, the more I laughed. How in the hell did I manage to fall on my last day there and my first day back? And how in the hell did not one but two of Taylor's secrets cross my path? Karma and fate rolled into one.

When I powered my cell phone back on, it tinged, pinged, and chimed. Yara had blown me up in every form possible. Multiple calls and messages, including social media. Not that I expected anything less from her, especially since I'd agreed to this double date. I was late and looked and felt a hot-ass mess.

Chapter 11

Yara waited for me at the entrance of the bowling alley. She looked at her watchless wrist, demanding an answer.

I held my hands up in surrender and yelled over the commotion, "I had an errand."

"What did you have to do that caused your ass to be this late?" she yelled back with her hands on her hips. Yara had five younger siblings that she parented. Sometimes, she swore she was my momma or I was one of her siblings.

I tapped my Apple Watch. "I'm only twenty minutes late."

"Try forty, and even if it *were* twenty, it's *still* twenty minutes late of making a great first impression." Yara looked me up and down and turned up her nose. "Seriously, what's going on? Why do you look like you just got off work at the landfill?"

"None of your nosy business," I sassed. "But if you must know, I took a fall. And last time I checked, I was grown."

"And last time *I* checked, you had a fine-ass man waiting to meet you." Yara pointed toward the bar at a small group of guys lingering. "Did you break your phone in the process because you could've called," she fussed, interrupting my scout.

"Yeah, I'm fine, thanks for asking," sarcasm laced my tone.

Yara dropped her head in shame. "I'm so sorry, Redarra. Are you okay?"

I rolled my eyes. "I'm here, aren't I?"

"Come on, friend. I'm sorry." She batted her extended lashes at me, but I didn't fall for it.

"The least you could've done was ask if I was okay before you started in on some bullshit. I'm doing you a favor, *remember?*"

"You're right, and I apologize. I was stressed because you weren't here. I called multiple times, and your phone went straight to voicemail. I thought you were gonna stand me up. You know how much I like Dre."

"I know you do, so I agreed to come, even though I didn't want to. But apology accepted, and I apologize for being late." I turned my head to the bar. "Now, which one is he, and he better be cute."

Yara directed my attention to a muscular, chocolate guy carrying a pitcher of beer, headed toward the lanes. Everything around him blurred out, and his movement slowed down like the slow-motion part of a movie. Judging by the way he dressed, he looked like he smelled amazing. His dark jeans were a little baggy, which put me at ease. I was not open to dating anyone that wore tight pants, especially skinny jeans. He rocked a Hawaiian button-down floral shirt that he paired with Vans. Bright orange highlighted the tips of his neatly styled short locs.

Yara's snap in my face brought the world around Mr. Chocolate back to regular motion. "Did that fall give you a concussion? You're being weird as hell," she laughed.

A concussion wasn't too far-fetched, considering how I was standing in the middle of a crowded place lusting over a stranger. I nudged her. "You did well with my date."

"Of course, I did. I already got your shoes. Now, come on before Dre thinks I ran out on him." She looked me up and down again and frowned. "We need to make a pitstop to the bathroom first."

My ankle throbbed, but me and my limp followed Yara. When we emerged from the bathroom, I looked a lot more presentable. She had adjusted my T-shirt that read *Curvy Badass*. The knot she tied rested underneath my double D breasts and showed just a little of my stomach. I was big and all, but my stomach wasn't too bad. Looked like a little puff of bloating. My jeans were already ripped up to my thighs, and if any extra tears came from the fall, they fit right in. With dirt wiped from my jeans and debris brushed out of my hair, I was ready for some tasty chocolate. Yara never sent me a picture of Dre's cousin, and I thought it was because he wouldn't be easy on the eyes. A straight-up, busted-up frog, but I stood corrected. Sir Chocolate was fine fine. The test would be if he were an asshole and really into girls my size as Yara claimed he was. Taylor's nice-looking but also a cruel, confused, brutal asshole. At this point in my life, all men were probably assholes, except for my dad. Hell, he may be one behind closed doors. See how confused and all over the place I was? Even I secretly questioned if I didn't bake long enough in that psych ward.

As Yara and I got closer, Mr. Chocolate watched me, and I watched him. He stared me down over the rim of his plastic cup.

"Myron, this is my good sis, Redarra. Redarra, this is Dre's cousin, Myron." How nice of Yara. I could've done that myself. I'd never been a shy individual, especially when meeting guys.

He hit me with a head nod and refilled his cup. Okay, that was a little rude. I'd expected a hug, a handshake, something besides a homie nod. Maybe he was the bashful type, and if so, I could respect that.

Myron pointed to a tray of food. Chicken wings, tater tots, spring rolls, and nachos sat untouched. "I went ahead and ordered for you a while ago. It's probably cold now."

"That was sweet. Thank you," I said and sat beside him. When I did, his scent engulfed my nose. He smelled like I imagined—expensively tasty. I didn't recognize the cologne he wore, but I planned to ask before the night was over. If accurate, there was a hint of Lever 2000.

"You can order more if this isn't enough," Myron smiled, showing off his baby teeth.

Ordering me a variety of food because of my size was a significant blunder, not something to be complimented or to feel proud over. People automatically assumed I was overweight due to a poor diet. Don't get me wrong, I didn't eat as many servings of fruits and vegetables as I should, nor did I work out, but what if my weight had *everything* to do with a health condition, not food? Yes, ice cream was my guilty pleasure, and while I was no dietician, that isn't the only contributing factor. What if it were genetics? My mom was shapely, and my dad was stocky.

Rather than saying anything, I gave Myron a pass and kept my comments to myself. Not without a mean side-eye, however.

After a while, Yara and Dre ditched Myron and me. I knew she was trying to give us a chance to get better acquainted but making small talk with him was difficult. I asked about everything from his college experience to his five-year plan to his views on marriage and family. The conversation lasted about ten minutes. I asked most of the questions, and he responded with mainly one-word answers.

Then finally, I thought we were about to get somewhere when he leaned closer to me and said, "Your face looks so familiar."

I had taken in his features when I first laid eyes on him. I stared more, trying to see if anything stood out. Nothing. "You're from Carolina, right?" I inquired.

He threw out location after location, and then his face lit up. "Yo, I got it," he said like a jackpot would follow his discovery. "You're the girl that molly-whopped ol' boy." He started laughing, clapping, and stomping his foot. "Dre didn't tell me that's who he was settin' me up wit'." He laughed harder.

I dropped my head in shame, hiding my face with my shirt. It wasn't that damn funny. This was my life, and my face was known everywhere, attached to some bullshit—no wonder why people took extra-long looks at me when I first walked in. Or maybe I was paranoid and making that up now that Myron had recognized me.

"No need to be ashamed, sweetheart. Soak it up. It took me a minute to recognize you. You look different from the video, but I guess that makes sense because that was some fatal attraction shit."

I eyed the exit. My ankle still throbbed, but I could try to make a run for it.

"Yo, you mind if we get a picture together? You're campus famous in a scandalous way," he rambled on.

No, this fool *didn't*. "I'll pass on the picture."

Myron scooted a little closer to me. "I will show you how a woman should be treated. You're bigger than what I'm used to chillin' wit'. But you're cute for a big girl, and you have just the right amount of crazy in you."

Talk about offended and confused on whether to slap his ass or walk out. Why couldn't I just be cute? Sexy? Charming? Stylish? Fun? Why did it always have to include: "for a big girl"?

"That's a disgusting thing to say," I said, hoping he'd misspoke.

"I don't mean it in a bad way."

"If not bad, how else?"

"I'm just sayin', you're bigger than the picture your homegirl showed me. I thought you were about 175, but . . . That's not necessarily a bad thing. Not what I'm used to, but I can rock wit' it. And that ounce of crazy is a turn-on."

The only time I'd been 175 pounds was at birth. It was not my fault he couldn't gauge a roundabout weight without a scale. I held up my finger in his face to stop him from further insulting me. "Please quit while you're ahead," I said. "I get it."

"I'm just sayin', I heard big girls got that bomb-ass pu—"

Before I knew it, the back of my hand met with his baby teeth. I didn't want to hear another snide remark. In fact, I didn't want to listen to his gruff voice at all. I'd suffered enough disrespect to last a lifetime and was *not* in the mood tonight or any night.

"You fat bitch," he said and grabbed a napkin to dab the speck of blood from his lip.

I'd been called worse. All guys were clowns. They all had a God complex. Too much work and sacrifice go into them, only for women to be left sad, crying, and suicidal. Depression was what it's called. Black folks call it weak. Myron was not about to send me over the edge and have me eat away my feelings again or not eat at all, only to reemerge looking like a crackhead. The funny thing was, as long as I was skinny, the world would overlook what I did to get there.

"You better be glad my cousin is into your home-girl, or else I'd send your ass off again like ol' boy did."

I stood and grabbed my things. Myron could sit there and do the negativity thing by himself.

"Wait, before you go . . ." he calmly said.

Good, he needed to apologize. I stared him square in the eyes, waiting for it.

I frowned when he pulled out his phone. I was not giving him my number if *that's* what he thought. "Is that a calculator?" I asked when I caught a glance at his phone's screen.

"Yeah. You need to cover your portion of the bill."

"I didn't realize we were going Dutch on this date."

"This ain't really a date since I was catfished," Myron said and kept doing math on his phone.

"Catfished?" I scoffed but let it go. "No problem, I can cover my half of the bill."

The inside of my fat rolls tingled. *That's* how mad I was. When he gave me my total, I stormed about five feet away before realizing I'd forgotten those damn to-go plates. Might as well. I paid for them. Sometime during my inquiring about Myron, he'd asked our server for to-go boxes. I pivoted, snatched up the container, and said, "I'll eat these for dinner."

Chapter 12

Gentry Tucker. The suave guy with the rainbow tattoo on the front of his neck. According to the group thread Dalton presented, Gentry and Taylor met in an online chat room called *Males Seeking Men*. I stalked Mr. Tucker's social media account the first chance I got, and there were several pictures of him and Taylor. The last one dated about four months ago. At first glance, one would think nothing suspicious of the photos: two friends, maybe even two relatives, creating memories. I would have thought that too had I not seen the screenshots on Dalton's phone.

Taylor and Gentry were physical. Distance prevented it from happening more often as many miles separated them. But Gentry had come to visit Taylor a time or two. Seemed like Taylor never returned the favor. My brain worked overtime trying to figure out if I'd ever seen his face in passing. I didn't recall Taylor ever mentioning his name around me. Never even a slip. None of his lovers' names that I could remember.

I saw no canoodling or questionable body language as I analyzed the pictures. Not even a single caption to reference any type of relationship between the two of them. It was evident that Gentry was comfortable with his sexuality and wanted the world to know Taylor was his guy without saying it. Taylor must've convinced him with the same lie he used on me—he wanted to keep his relationships private because envious people will do everything in their power to divide love. I had respected that and went along with it. It made me feel as if he wanted longevity with me.

According to the exchange between Taylor and Gentry, Taylor used distance as the reason he felt the relationship wasn't working out and felt it was best to separate. Valid point, even though I knew it was just an excuse to disassociate himself from Gentry, who agreed to relocate to our area to save the relationship.

The breakup must've happened when Gentry posted a picture of himself wearing dark shades, Zebra striped pants, a red shirt, and suspenders. The caption was simply a broken heart. I checked the date, and it was during the time that Taylor and I were together. I'd never seen Gentry around, nor could I recall a time when Taylor traveled anywhere outside of with the football team.

Assembling the puzzle of lies was all a perplexing mystery, to say the least. The more I tried to figure it out, the more my head throbbed. Aspirin and wine did nothing to soothe the aches anywhere within my body.

I moved on to Francisco. He reminded me of a chunky Bruno Mars but with a ton of piercings. Unorthodox piercings, might I add. I cringed when I saw the one in his gums. Who would think of that? Hell, who would *want* that? I barely tolerated dental work. Yet, he had a silver stud just above his two front teeth. As if that weren't crazy enough, Francisco also had his hairline pierced. That hurt *my* hairline just *looking* at it. I swiped through his photos, taking in every jewelry-filled hole on his body. Well, what was in view. Septril, eyelid, nose, ears, lip. *Ouch*. Imagine what was pierced that clothes *hid*. Made me wonder if he owned a shop and just sat around poking holes in random parts of his body for the thrill of it. Hard to tell.

With everything he posted, there was never a mention of a profession or Taylor unless he scrubbed away the remnants of him when they parted ways. However, Francisco looked like he was a lot of fun. He modeled some insane outfits, wore heavy eyeliner, and often traveled abroad. He seemed like he enjoyed life to the fullest, all while single.

I wondered what happened between him and Taylor. Although he participated in the group chat, the most he said was, "Taylor's old news."

Jalil seemed to be the most hurt out of everyone. Crying spells, loss of appetite, and depression. There wasn't much information I could find on Jalil. All I knew was Taylor cheated, but I didn't know with whom or when. Story of all our lives. It could've been with me for all I know. After his breakup with Taylor, he deactivated his social media presence. Without a digital footprint, the only way to know was through Julian, but those were waves I wasn't ready to ride.

Lastly, there was Dalton. Manager Man. He too was in love with Taylor and thought they'd be together. In fact, he was the one to orchestrate the chat. Hurt feelings would do that to you. Hurt feelings would make a person lose everything. I had been there. Well, sort of. I didn't lose everything, but I lost my dignity, which could be considered everything depending on how you looked at it.

According to Dalton, he met Taylor first at a gay bar about an hour outside of town. They were never physical. Taylor told him due to religious beliefs, he wanted to "wait until marriage." Like all of us, he believed whatever Taylor had told him. Dalton said they took long walks in the park and that he had helped Taylor financially when he feared he'd have to quit college because he couldn't afford tuition. And after that, anytime he needed money, he'd come to the Dollar Tree and pick it up—*red flag*. Taylor played him. He was on a full athletic scholarship. He didn't want for anything.

And because he was so popular, people used to hook him up with stuff all the time. I didn't inquire into the amount he'd given, but I do know Dalton never got his money back.

They broke up when Dalton started catching Taylor in frequent lies and calling him out on it. Then our scandal hit the internet, and that's when he found out about me. Dalton said he chose to keep quiet because when he confronted Taylor, he told him the same thing he told me . . . "No one will ever believe you," and then blocked him on everything.

Seemed like our boy used us to his benefit, controlled us like puppets, and instilled so much fear in us that we couldn't expose him without serious ramifications.

I think back over every day that I could remember with Taylor, and I was still baffled at how well he played the part of a loving, straight boyfriend behind closed doors. Even more, I was disappointed in myself for not recognizing that I was dealing with a true narcissist, user, abuser, and straight-up asshole.

Breakups suck, and even though I was hurting myself, I felt for these guys like I'd known them all my life. What I do to Taylor won't just be justice for me, but for these poor fellas he hurt along the way. The only problem was that they wouldn't know that I was representing them, but I hoped they would appreciate the takedown.

Chapter 13

"What brings you in today?"

Dr. Sharp held my chart, so she knew good and well what brought me in. Why make me say it out loud?

I cleared my throat and stammered over my words. "I . . . I . . . um . . . need to get checked for . . ." I stopped shy of stating HIV. I broke down and begged Dr. Sharp not to make me say it. "I'm 22. I know better than this," I said instead.

She handed me some tissue and watched as I dabbed away at my tears. "It's not the end of the world. Breathe," she said.

"What if the test comes back positive? What am I supposed to do?" I cried harder. Snot ran from my nose.

"What if the tests come back *negative?*" Dr. Sharp countered. "I think the best thing to do right now is to try *not* to worry about it until you have concrete results. You haven't experienced any symptoms, and you stated you and your partner took preventative measures outside of oral, so don't work yourself up over what very well may be nothing."

I nodded, sniffed, and continued to wipe away the flood.

"I'm going to step out. Go ahead and get changed and hop up on the table." Before Dr. Sharp stepped out, she rubbed my shoulder and assured me that everything would be okay no matter the outcome. Those words rang hollow in my ears. Surely the degrees she earned that were encased in expensive frames were well deserved and meant she knew her stuff. And while I wanted to believe her solely based on the words that exited her full, black-painted lips, it would be impossible to rest until I got the results. Even then, rest would only come in the form of death if they returned positive.

Dr. Sharp was one of the few Black female gynecologists in our area. I was on a waiting list for nearly two years to get in with her as my primary care women's health doctor. She was patient, delicate, and kind. She wore her hair in a huge natural Afro, and she always wore a statement piece T-shirt that coordinated perfectly with a pair of Jordans. The shirt she wore today was neon green with white cursive letters that said: *Black History is the Best History*.

As soon as the door shut behind her, I changed, and instead of climbing on the table and putting my feet in the stirrups, I dropped down on my knees and prayed.

"Dear God, I know you haven't heard from me in a long time, and I'm sorry about that. I promise to do better if you please help me out of this jam. I have no right to ask for any favors, but I need a miracle. Please let my test come back negative. Amen."

Crappy prayer. Every human had thrown in that good ole bargaining prayer, knowing good and well we would eventually revert to our old ways. God knew it too, but I had to try. One thing was for sure. I didn't deserve any blessings. I got myself into this position, and I should have kept my legs closed or at least been smart enough to use protection with oral sex. After all, I was an honor student. Common sense got lost behind book smarts and was slow to catch up. Nonetheless, I had enough sense to pray anyway, and I tried my best to hold on to hope that everything would be okay.

When I heard the light tap on the door, I rushed over to the bed like I would be in trouble if I weren't wide open and ready. Dr. Sharp entered with her nurse. She was also a woman of color—another reason why I loved this office. Everybody was Black, and I was always pro-Black.

Dr. Sharp went through the usual process, making small talk while she examined me. Then she gently swabbed inside my vagina, and it was over before I knew it. The doctor removed her gloves and started washing her hands. "Keena will draw some blood, and then you can get dressed. After that, I'll be back in to talk with you some more."

"Thank you, Dr. Sharp."

Keena stepped out and came right back with a blood-drawing kit. I watched as she wrapped a tourniquet around my arm and filled tubes with my blood. The whole time I prayed it was clean.

"You can get dressed. The doctor will be back shortly," Keena said and exited.

I thanked her and wondered what she and Dr. Sharp thought about me for being in this position. Were they judging me? Did they think I was nasty? A ho? I even wondered if they had ever been in a similar situation and could understand how scared I was of the outcome. I switched from that thought and over to the pamphlets on the wall. There was one on everything under the sun, including myths and facts regarding HIV and AIDS. I was scared to touch it. Somehow, if my fingertips grazed it, it would become true. Or everyone would know I was awaiting my status. Like a tattoo would show up on my forehead. Silly thoughts, but I couldn't help but think the worst.

"I see your weight is up almost ten pounds from the last time you were here six months ago," Dr. Sharp pointed out as soon as she stepped foot into the room. "Other than the reason for your visit today, is there something else going on?"

"A lot is going on. Nothing I care to talk about, though."

"I see," she nodded. "Well, there's a weight loss medication on the market I think will help jump-start some changes. It's called Saxenda. Do you think maybe you'd be interested in trying it?"

Look, I knew I was considered fat, and although I hadn't dared to step on the scale, my pants snitched. They were snug, hard to button, and the zipper stripped from the forceful resistance my FUPA put up. However, my weight was not the reason for my visit. The wellness of my vagina was. If Dr. Sharp was deflecting, I bet it's because she was at a loss for words on how to deliver the bad news. "No, I'm not interested in any diet pills."

"It's not a pill. It's a self-administered injection."

"Oh, heck no. I can't do that."

"You need to work on getting healthier before diabetes is a thing and you're *forced* to inject yourself for survival."

The good doctor had dropped the mic. I heard her, but diabetes would have to take the back burner. So I brought the conversation back to my results. "Am I okay or not? What did my results say?"

Dr. Sharp looked at me like I knew better . . . and I did. "Ma'am, it does not work like that. This is not a box of mashed potatoes. The results aren't instant," she said. "I wish it worked like that. It will take several weeks for the HIV results to come and a few days for the other screenings. Either way, you *will* be okay."

How could she sit so calmly and assure me that I'd be okay without results?

"And if not?" I asked. There was no glimmer of hope from my end. In my mind, I already had it simply because I had to test for it.

"We will discuss it at that time. Remember what I told you? Breathe. Try to find ways to keep your mind busy while you're waiting on the results."

"What do you suggest? How do I wait, unconcerned, to find out if I'm dying?" Just being in this position was killing me.

"Reconnect with or find new hobbies that you enjoy. Read, dance, self-care, join an exercise class, yoga," Dr. Sharp shrugged. "Whatever makes you happy and will keep your mind occupied with something *other* than the results."

I had hoped to walk out of Dr. Sharp's office feeling relieved, but it was just the opposite. I could see myself disabling my phone and locking myself in my room until the day I got the results back. I didn't fret as much over the treatable STDs. But waiting on those HIV results had me immediately binge eating, unable to control my bowels, and on the verge of going back into that damn mental institution.

Chapter 14

Days into awaiting the results, I couldn't take any more. I swung by a bar nearby my parents' house. I needed a drink. *Multiple* drinks. Probably some street drugs too, but hard liquor would have to do since I'd never dabbled in illegal drugs before, not even weed unless you count contact highs. Besides, everything seemed to be laced with fentanyl. I was suffering from a broken heart, not a broken brain.

There I was, sitting at the bar, tipsy, minding my own business, drinking away my sorrows when a disgusting pervert sat in the empty seat beside me.

"Grand rising, Queen. Looking good." He pulled the toothpick from the corner of his lips and sucked his teeth like I was a porterhouse.

Oh, hell no. I groaned in his direction and waved him off, so technically, I created the negative vibes. That greeting alone was a red flag in itself. If the bar had a *do not disturb* sign, I would have gladly put it up to drink in peace. Granted, getting drunk in the middle of the afternoon was not cute, but neither were the thoughts that had trekked miles across my brain.

"Must be man problems," he continued.

I looked at him and rolled my eyes hard. Had I known I wouldn't have peace, I would've gone to a gay bar. Besides Taylor, gay guys were the coolest, and I would have walked away with some free therapy and genuine friends.

"Seems like you've had one too many drinks," he added. "Let me take you home or back to my place to sleep it off." He laughed so hard at his stupid comment that he started coughing and wheezing. I should've offered him my inhaler, but his choking excited me. I hoped he would've swallowed that damn toothpick.

"I'll pass," I replied and downed another shot.

"Whew! Sexy, sexy. They call me Boogeyman."

I gave him the meanest look. "I can see why." His ass looked like a monster. Boogeyman should've been *my* name. The fact that my eyes were red from bawling and mascara had bled and stained my face made me look sadistic. Not even evil was enough to make this creep leave me alone.

"Whew!" he celebrated and whistled. "Them crazy, shit-talking ones are a turn-on."

Ugh. He was too old to be acting like this. My speech was heavily slurred when I nicely said, "Please, stop accosting me."

"A, what you?" he tried to repeat my word but failed. "I don't even know what that shit means. Hell, I can't repeat it," he laughed. "I apologize for whatever man hurt you, sweetheart. Let Boogeyman make it better. See, I can pick all that body of yours up and drill you against the wall without dropping you." He laughed at his inappropriate yet stale joke.

A handful of witnesses either shook their heads in disgust or pretended as if they didn't hear him. Who *couldn't* hear him? He yelled as if we all were hard of hearing. The '90s R&B music played softly throughout the bar, and there was a little rowdiness from the game of pool going on, but Boogeyman only wanted to draw attention to himself. "Bartender, another round of whatever the crazy lady is drinking on me." He smiled, revealing one gold tooth.

I was *not* crazy.

Through hiccups, I told Boogeyman, "No, thank you."

Maybe the liquor I guzzled was watered down because it did nothing to suppress my thoughts of Taylor. I couldn't stop seeing and hearing him with Sammie. The pending results wouldn't stop bugging me either. Despite wanting this annoying jerk to disappear, I did drink the two shots of Crown he ordered for me. In fact, I drank so much that the bartender cut me off. How embarrassing was *that?* Story of my life.

"Is there anyone I can call for you?" the bartender asked. I was a little wobbly sitting on the stool, but there was no need for that. I had it.

I broke down in tears, which was enough to send Boogeyman out the door. "Never mind. You might just be a little too toxic for my liking."

"No one loves me," I yelled. Spit flew across the bar. I smacked it and begged for another round, to which I was refused again.

In an attempt to stand up, I lost my balance and crashed to the floor. If this bar wouldn't help me, I'd find another one that would. After being helped up, I couldn't find my keys. That triggered my emotions even more. I told all my business for enough sympathy that they'd keep pouring me drinks. "My boyfriend cheated on me with a man. I walked in and saw him. Why would he do this to me? Is it because I'm fat?" I let out a few more hiccups and added, "You wanna know what I think sometimes?" No one seemed interested in knowing, but I told them anyway. "What if I start dating another guy who once dated Taylor one day?" I dramatically dropped to my knees. "What if I have HIV? What if I'm dying?"

The people in the bar had no clue what to do with me. Someone eventually grabbed my un-locked phone and called my mother to pick me up.

I broke down more over the hurt in her face. She had no clue what to do with me herself. I cried. She cried, and I think half of the bar patrons cried after I confessed my pain.

Life was too much to bear. I was afraid that I'd do something to hurt myself if I went home. And I was sure a video of this night would surface soon. That's what people did. Record everything in hopes they'd go viral instead of helping.

I begged my mother to take me back to the mental hospital. She did. For seventy-two hours, I was able to detox from alcohol and hurt. I wasn't mad about it this time around. Institutionalized is where I needed to be. Padded walls and all if needed. I still wasn't taking the medication, though. And after what I pulled off at the bar, I probably needed AA too.

Chapter 15

"Welcome to Sweat N' Shrink. Coming in to enhance your gorgeous body?"

"Um . . ." What else could I say back to all that extra-ness? I'd never been made to feel this good entering an establishment that had nothing to do with food. I could be hungry, but as soon as I smelled what I was about to devour, all was well with my soul. Surprisingly, the aroma in the gym wasn't what I thought it would be. I just knew they all reeked of corn chips, sweat, and musk. Finally, I answered. "Something like that."

"No no no. Let's try that again with a little more enthusiasm," she said and repeated the original question, expecting me to respond like her.

Nothing changed on my end—still monotone. I was depressed and not about the workout life. However, I took Dr. Sharp's advice to get my weight under control. My weight was recorded during the second admission, and the scale whimpered when it registered a smidgen over 300 pounds.

"We will get there," she said before telling me her name was Skylar. "What changes do you want to make to your body?"

I shrugged. Wasn't expecting a gym interview. I expected to show up, talk, and possibly tour the facility, but I fired off a wish list. "Well, you see this flabby stomach?" I pinched it. "I want to get rid of it. I don't necessarily need abs that I can count, just something smaller that won't sit on my thighs when I sit. And I want to keep my curves. I just want them to look like curves instead of speed bumps. I don't know if this is possible, but maybe my breasts will shrink to look more like breasts instead of floatation devices. Bottom line, I no longer want to be flabby and soggy like cereal that sat in milk too long."

"If we are going to work together, you must start seeing value in yourself and not deflect by trying to beat everyone to the punch with jokes to demean yourself. You are a courageous, beautiful girl. Unfortunately, more people walk past the gym than into it." Skylar slid me a sheet of paper. "Let's start with a little nonphysical exercise. If there is anything you like about yourself, write it down. We are going to update this every month. That way, we can see your confidence grow on paper."

I wasn't expecting that either. It hurt my feelings when I realized the only thing I liked about myself was my personality. I wrote it, slid the paper back across the counter, and then asked a question that shocked even me. "What fundamentals do y'all teach?"

"Wow! Great question," Skylar said. "You are *definitely* going to be successful." She went into her spiel about how they encourage slow dietary changes while increasing movement. Then she pointed to a picture hanging up behind her. It was of an extremely obese lady wearing a muumuu. "This was me a few years ago. I put in the work and lost the weight, and now, I'm proudly rocking this healthy zaftig."

I squinted to make sure I indeed saw it right. Then my eyes bucked. "Get the hell outta here." It was like someone had pried my mouth and eyes open. Skylar had gone from a potential contestant on *The Biggest Loser* to a baddie. "What's a zaf . . .? Whatever that word you used." I sounded like Boogeyman's monster ass.

She laughed. "Zaftig. It means having a full, shapely figure."

"I still can't believe that was you."

"Believe it, honey. It can be done. And naturally with the right amount of dedication and patience," Skylar said. "And not to sound cliché, but if *I* can, *you* can. I was lazy, ate the unhealthiest foods, drank soda, had diabetes, and what finally made me get up and do something about it was when my family started complaining about my body odor. I was so heavy that I couldn't clean myself good. So now, I'm a personal trainer and love *every* minute of it."

"Say less. I'm in." At first, I thought Skylar was blowing smoke, but seeing her transformation made me believe I could do it too.

"Yeeeessss, honey. Let's get a before and after shot. You are going to be so impressed with the final results. All I can say is, stick with it. Brb, doll."

I studied the nutrition wall while I waited for Skylar to come back. Powdered protein jars, snack bars, and healthy chips lined the shelves. Some shit I'd never heard of a day in my life. The packaging was cute, but I bet it was nasty as hell.

I envisioned myself in a bikini, thick but toned. Hell, I even imagined myself in a Drake video as the sexy vixen. I danced on him, and he smacked my ass. Then, after the director yelled "cut," Drake whisked me away on a helicopter to a private island where we had dinner and mind-blowing sex. Afterward, he'd tell me how sexy I was and ask me to be his one and only lady.

"All right," Skylar said, startling me and making Drake disappear.

I jumped at her voice and knocked over almost every product on her nutrition wall. "Oh my God. I am so sorry."

With her help, we restocked the shelves. I was out of breath. She wasn't. This working out thing had to work. I wanted to breathe quietly like Skylar.

"Since you already have on workout gear, I assume we are starting right now?" my new trainer suggested.

I wasn't prepared for that, but no backing down. I wished I had. Skylar kicked my ass and gave me homework. I'm sure it was mild to a person who was used to physical activity, but to me, I got my ass kicked like my trainer had something against me.

When I finished my workout, I stood in the full-body mirror of the gym to see if anything looked different after the work I'd just put in. "Gross!" I said to my reflection. My forehead and neck were shiny, and my hair was drenched with sweat. Because my stylist took walk-ins, that was my next stop. Maybe I'd get sisterlocks like Skylar had, but I liked to change my hair up too much.

I had to wait an hour for Kita to squeeze me in. I looked like a wet cat, so if she needed me to wait five hours, I would have.

She frowned as she ran her fingers through my wet mane. "Did you get caught in the rainstorm from last week?"

"Ha-ha, you got jokes. I just left the gym."

"If you're going to be a regular at the gym, you might want to keep some braids or wear a head wrap or something." She referred to her appointment book and added, "My next opening for braids won't be for another three weeks."

"I don't want braids anyway."

"Well, what am I supposed to do with this?"

I shrugged. "I don't know. Chop it off," I said without hesitation. In all of my twenty-two years, I'd never once considered parting ways with my hair until that very moment.

Kita didn't ask any questions, nor did she make me repeat myself. Instead, she grabbed the scissors and went in. She cut, shaved, washed, cut, and shaved some more. When she finished, she spun me around to the mirror. It was drastic, but I *loved* it. Kita gave me a dyed sponge top. Just the top was red, and everything else remained black. The secret to getting the top to curl was beyond me. The part design she added to the shaved sides set it off even more.

I felt free. And because I was no longer hiding behind my hair, I felt seen.

"I'm calling you Red from now on because you are hot and on fire," Kita said.

Red? I like it. Short for Redarra, and the name matched my mood every second of the day. I felt either love or a fiery rage. Mainly rage. Red will be who Redarra couldn't be—a sexy, confident badass.

Chapter 16

Okay, so I changed my mind even though I had agreed to step back and allow Julian to do product placement. A part of me felt as if *my* mission wouldn't be accomplished if *I* weren't doing the grunt work. I may change my mind one day, but clue number two was all mine.

A letter. It read:

Dear Taylor,

I'm writing to let you know that I know what you've been doing behind closed doors. You're entitled to privacy. However, have you ever considered that sharing your sexuality with the world, given your star status, would open minds and hearts? Instead of being on the down low, why not be an advocate and promote love? The guys you've been with do not deserve to be hidden and treated like they aren't good enough to be loved. And the girls don't deserve to be strung along just for you to hide your true self. Don't get me wrong. I understand the fear of possible backlash. Why not try, at least? Imagine if you were free to love out loud without a care in the world. So, what if people judge you for it? They're going to do that regardless. So, what if they try to cancel you or block you from going into the NFL? Stand up and be true to who you are, with or without the league's support. Michael Sam did it. People assume he got cut for his sexuality and not his skill set. We all know you have the skills to dominate on the field. You've shown that. But please, also show people what it's like to dominate in your truth. There's nothing wrong with being attracted to the same sex. Stand proudly gay. That doesn't make you any less of a person. People will support you. I would respect you and your bravery if you started to live the truth.

Signed,

Z

Z was for obvious reasons. Another letter in Häagen-Dazs and also a representation for another word added to my vocabulary. Zaftig. I thought about writing out the word, but just in case Taylor was bright enough to look up the definition, I decided against it.

I hated that it had to come to this, and I hated that I would never witness the look on his face anytime he opened something I'd left for him. I knew he had to be wondering who in the hell left a dildo on his door. The possibilities were endless at this juncture. Every clue I staged would leave him more and more confused, especially considering he had played over way too many people.

Once the letter was typed and printed, I folded it and stuffed it in an envelope. Again, all while wearing gloves. Call me a coward, but you can't deny my brilliance in the matter.

In true Taylor fashion, things remained the same. His routine of blasting his every move hadn't changed, and I was banking on that to help me pull off this drop.

Just like last time, I drove the Caddy, killed the lights, parked away from his unit, and studied traffic. Then when it was safe, I walked right up to the door, and instead of dropping off the package and disappearing, my dumbass tried the handle. As usual, it was unlocked.

"Hello," I called out into the pitch-black apartment. What the hell was I doing? Breaking and entering was not a part of the plan. "Hello," I called out again. Still no answer. "Anyone home?" I double-checked.

Silence. Then the fridge dropped ice, and it scared the shit out of me. Still, when I gathered myself, I overlooked my gut telling me to leave.

My eyes had adjusted to the dark and recognized the décor was still scarce. I tiptoed down the hall to Taylor's room. PTSD hit me when I passed the infamous couch. Even the darkness couldn't shield me from seeing it. Taylor and Sammie doing what they did. I sighed, dabbed a tear, and reminded myself of the mission.

Taylor's bedroom door was cracked open. A beam of light illuminated from the slit at the bottom of his closet door. That strip wasn't enough. I needed more. The flashlight clipped to my security guard utility belt would have been perfect but also a dead giveaway from the parking lot. I donned the security uniform that I purchased from the costume store to throw people off if someone spotted me near Taylor's door.

I had no choice but to flip the light switch.

Looking around the room, not much had changed. It still looked like a war zone. The queen-sized bed looked like a bunch of hyper kids had jumped on it, complete with a pillow fight because those too were scattered like hashbrowns. Clothes and shoes covered the carpet. Filthy clothes were mixed with what I assumed to be clean clothes. A laundry basket full of clothes and a couple of dryer sheets were tipped over, and grass-stained football gear was intertwined. I felt relieved that Taylor was no longer my problem. I hated cleaning up behind him, only to come back the next day for his room to look like I never added my touch. The wastebasket was filled to the rim. I kicked it over just to see what would come out—empty condom wrappers. I wondered if he used them on a boy or a girl. Whomever it was, at least he was protecting himself. Empty, open food containers lay on his nightstand with fruit flies hovering around.

"What did I see in this bastard?"

I made my way over to his nightstand and rifled through the drawers. When I opened the top drawer, I saw the envelope I had left on his door. He had indeed received it and opened it. I was surprised he hadn't thrown it away. Next to my envelope was another. My gut yelled for me to leave, but my curiosity told me to stay awhile, open the envelope, and see what was inside. A letter. A love letter at that. Not from me but signed with a simple letter J, similar to my style. Julian had never divulged what happened between his brother and Taylor, but I wonder if the J stood for Jalil.

The letter from *J* read:

Tay: I hope this letter finds you well. Since you have me blocked on everything, I had no choice but to write you. I won't fill this letter with dwellings from the past, but I wanted you to know that because of your constant infidelity, I decided it was best to get tested for HIV, and I feel you should do the same. I know what you are going to say . . . It didn't come from you. But as I explained to you before, ever since I was 10, I knew I liked guys. I'd never had any interest in women. You know as well as I do that you were my first sexual encounter and, believe it or not, the only. I was in love with you from day one and dedicated my entire existence to you, and when we broke up, I have not been in a space mentally to even think about anyone else. Before you berate me or walk your days in denial, at least make an appointment and get checked. If I test positive, I'm pretty sure you are the source.

I was mortified by what I read. Tears pooled in my eyes. I could feel the sadness in these words. If J was for Jalil, I could understand why Julian wanted to kill Taylor, and every bit of rage and anger he felt, I had felt myself. I knew what it was like to make an appointment and request to be tested for every possible STD, especially the big one.

I sat staring at the letter, still ignoring my screaming instinct. I wanted to start a fire and burn everything of Taylor's. Unfortunately, dropping torture clues wouldn't be enough to incite remorse. This bastard had no regard for anything or anyone but himself. Time he started to see what it was like to lose something, even if it was only materialistic. I'm no arsonist, but I could be a bleach-ist. I'd douse all his shit with Clorox.

My tears dried up over that thought. I started toward the laundry room but froze when I heard the front door smack against the wall, followed by talking. Fear punched every organ in my body. I hid in the first place I could think to hide—in the damn walk-in closet where I barely crouched behind a closet rod full of clothes and between another hamper and that dusty-ass wall. Anxiety controlled my breathing, and I tried everything in my power to prevent the sneeze from escaping. There was so much dust on the wall in the back of Taylor's closet that it tickled my nose. I pinched my nostrils to stifle the sneeze. Then I slowly opened my eyes and almost lost it. Staring back at me was a crusty sock and another used condom resting right underneath my nose. Did he not know how to discard them? He did with me. My hiding place reeked of hot sweat and corn chips, and I refused to ponder over the other scents.

Through the even bigger crack in the closet door and from my crouched position, I watched Taylor's feet walk toward the bed. I knew it was him because I purchased those shoes for him when we were dating. My heart thumped, wondering if he knew I was in here snooping. Another pair of feet followed behind him, wearing blue loafers. I bargained with God, of course, that if He got me out of this mess this time, I promised I wouldn't step foot back on the premises. I was starting to freak out. I could feel myself on the verge of hyperventilating. I begged, hoping Taylor or whoever was with him didn't look toward the closet.

The springs squeaked when Taylor plopped on the bed. "We need to make this quick so I can get back," he said. "You better live up to the bragging."

"Trust, honey," the faceless guy responded in a high-pitched tone and dropped to his knees.

I hid my face but was forced to listen in horror. Taylor's ass was so reckless, carrying on as if he hadn't been informed of such a possible life-changing situation. That letter was dated two weeks ago. I seriously doubted he had taken the time to learn his status.

I wanted to puke. I should've never brought my ass into this apartment. Of course, I knew better, but I felt like I had something to prove to myself. Karma for me once again.

Luckily, it didn't last long, as usual. They cleaned up, passed some small talk, and headed back out the door, thankfully shutting off the light. Taylor never noticed I was in his closet.

I waited awhile to make sure the coast was clear before crawling out and hauling ass up out of there. Finally, I got back to the Caddy and drenched myself in sanitizer. I felt disgusted, violated, and filthy. This was the wake-up call that I needed. Not to stop but not to get my hands dirty if I was going to see this through.

Because of the letter signed by J, I felt better knowing Taylor had it coming from multiple directions, which meant he would never be able to piece together how clue number two got left on his bed. Not what I intended, but I was sloppy. And since I'd been scared beyond straight and shitless, I got all the clues ready without hesitation and explained to Julian that he could drop them however he wanted as long as the letters were jumbled. I refrained from telling him what happened when I decided to go against the initial plan and sneak in another.

H and Z were done, so that left eight more letters. Three *A*s. That was a challenge in itself. Ultimately, I decided to keep it light and simple— no sense in putting Julian in jeopardy. However, I felt that once he helped me, he would help himself to Taylor in a Mafia sort of way. Still, I reduced my clues to printable references.

I printed and stuffed the lyrics to Diana Ross's "I'm Coming Out" into an envelope for the first A. Then I wrote on the flag, *A for admission*.

The second *A* was for acceptance. I attached a picture of Lil Nas X. He accepted who he was and was thriving in the music industry. Taylor could do the same and still succeed in the sports industry. I had high hopes that this particular clue would provide encouragement for him to love freely.

The final *A* was attached to a pride word search and a strip of paper asking Taylor to raise his hand and advocate for his truth.

Up next was the letter *G*. Obviously for gay. I attached a rainbow wristband in hopes he'd start to wear it.

E was for embrace, which is what I wrote on the flag. I also dropped an earring in there in honor of Francisco. Hopefully, Taylor wouldn't think it was him and react.

Naysayers represented *N*. I attached a quote from Matshona Dhliwayo. "If you listen to critics for too long, you will become deaf to success."

The letter *D* was a simple, typed definition of denial.

And finally, *S* was a picture of Sammie that I printed from social media. I started to caption it: *I know* who *you did, but I left well enough alone.*

I felt like a failure, a coward, even when I met Julian and handed the box over to him. It was like I was giving my baby up for adoption, not ever being able to see it grow.

Now it's up to Julian. And although I said I was done stepping foot on my old premises, I planned to sneak back in once the last clue was dropped. A part of me needed to know that Taylor received every single one of them.

People would wonder why I risked my life and freedom over this scumbag. Or even why I tried to force him to come out when it wasn't my business. I had asked myself several questions. Mainly, why I had placed so much importance on him announcing his sexuality when people didn't have to disclose being straight. I understood it, and I could live with that logic if he weren't being careless and hurting people in the process.

Chapter 17

The gym had become my happy place. From the first visit, I started to stare at myself in the mirror to watch for changes. Even though I hoped for instant gratification, I knew it didn't work that way. Still, I studied every piece of my flesh, every day, hoping to notice the differences as they happened. Every time I heard, "You look amazing," it motivated me to keep going. At first, I wanted to lose to gain respect. The more that silly idea faded, the more I was proud to be doing it for myself.

Eventually, the weight started to fall off. Every month, I had a new attribute to add to the list. My stomach flattened, my muscles defined, and thanks to the excessive squats, my booty was no longer a weeping willow. Instead, it sat up like it stayed at attention. The tension in my back eased up. My moon face became oval-shaped, and my dimple-laced skin smoothed out like I'd been using cocoa butter all my life. Stretch marks increased, but I could live with those. Two chins turned into one, and most importantly, I could finally breathe.

What started with fifteen-minute walks, two-pound weights, hitting the inhaler every thirty minutes, and not being able to do one push-up transformed into jogging miles, bench pressing, and knocking out at least fifteen push-ups. Of course, the inhaler was still a thing, but not as often.

Who would have ever thought me, of all people, would have stopped eating meat? If it wasn't fish, I didn't want it. In fact, the sight of meat made my stomach hurt. Likewise, the lack of vegetables was an insult to my tastebuds. Before, the only vegetable I recognized was collard greens, but by the time all the ham and sugar were added, it might as well have been cheesecake. Now, I fill my plate with spinach, broccoli—no cheese, and even Brussel sprouts. In addition to working out five days a week, I combined a vegetarian Keto diet with intermittent fasting. By month three, several inches and over forty pounds had melted off like butter in a hot skillet.

Pounds weren't the only thing falling off of shit. I was out jogging one day, and some guy on a bike rode past me. I guess I looked too good for him to turn away, and he crashed into a parked car. He rolled across the hood and hit the ground. Before I ran over to help him, I laughed because it reminded me of when I fell, and Julian had to come to my rescue.

I made sure everything was positioned correctly. My titties had bounced around so much I had to push up them girls. I didn't know this guy, but I didn't want the first thing he saw up close to be lopsided breasts.

"Are you okay?" I asked, jogging in place, careful not to allow my heart rate to drop too much too fast.

I could tell he was embarrassed. I was embarrassed for him.

"You are stunning," he said, looking at me from the ground.

I smiled hard to mask the laugh I held in. "Thank you."

"I'm Tutt," he extended his hand.

"Tutt? As in your last name?"

"Nope. McCormick is my last name."

"McCormick like the seasoning?" I joked and stared into his eyes.

When he laughed, I noticed his teeth. That was usually the first thing I noticed on a man. But, with Tutt, his dark eyes stood out first. There was a look of passion and sincerity in them. Hell, I may have been tripping and mistaken his look for what was humiliation. Either way, I liked how loving they were. Plus, his teeth passed inspection, including the tiny gap in the front. Barely noticeable, but noticeable. I looked at his large hand, which was still extended but left him hanging.

"You have some blood," I pointed.

He wiped the corner of his thick lips with the collar of his muscle shirt that clung to his pecs like the yoga pants that clung to my body.

"Can I have your name, or are you going to leave me hanging with that too?"

I shrugged. "Probably leave you hanging."

He laughed. "Wow! It's like that, huh?"

"Let me help you up," I offered.

"If you're not going to tell me your name, can you at least tell me what agency you model for?"

This time, I laughed hysterically at his cheesy compliment, the fact that he fell, and the memory of when *I* was on the ground.

"It ain't that damn funny," he said, brushing debris from his clothes.

When he rose from the ground, I knew then that God was real! He was *fwine*. He had to be at least six-five and all muscle. Forget my previous refusals to take a second glance at a guy with a man bun. Tutt's was neatly braided into one, and it did something to my freshly shaven girl. I envisioned the little ponytail part bobbing up and down, round and round, as he feasted between my legs.

"Thank you for your help, nameless woman."

"No problem," I said, stuck my AirPods in my ears, and prepared to jump back into my run.

"Where are you running to?" Tutt asked.

He was exciting, and I had no clue why, but I wanted to find out. "To your place, if you want." I'd never had a one-night stand before, nor had I ever been this forward, but there was something about Red that liked something about Tutt that made me bold. Redarra would never.

"Damn," Tutt licked his lips.

I got a thrill out of being Red. That person, combined with my new curvy body and short boy cut, gave me a heightened level of confidence and made me start to love myself like I did before I lost my innocence to worldviews. I could be fierce and fabulous with Red, but then turn it off and be the brainy, soon-to-be successful Redarra.

And who knows? My heart was starting to re-open to the possibility of getting back out there. Or a "no strings attached" kind of thing. *If* I were able. Just my luck, I'd get attached only to receive a bucket full of tears in return.

"As much as I would love to take you up on that offer, I'd rather be a gentleman. Can I at least take you out and get to know you first?"

"What man turns down a no strings attached rendezvous?"

"The man who plans to make you his wife."

I buckled over with laughter. This fool was corny. I remembered a time that would have instantly worked on Redarra. "Wife, huh? So, you know, just like that?" I snapped my fingers.

He nodded.

"Mighty funny how you know something I don't. I don't have plans of ever getting married or telling you my name."

He smiled. "I'm not worried. I'll change your mind, and I already know your name."

Shit. Another person recognized me from that dumbass video.

"It's Mrs. McCormick," he added.

When he said that, I went nuts. I hadn't laughed until I cried in a long time. I recited how that name would sound with every variation within my ears. Redarra McCormick. Redarra Michaels-McCormick. Red McCormick. Red Michaels-McCormick. Why was I following him up?

"I'm glad you're laughing," Tutt said. "This will make an amazing story for our children and grand-children."

"Oh Lord. Not only are we getting married, but we are having kids too?"

"Yep," he said confidently. "At least two, but because I know I wouldn't be able to keep my hands off you, it will probably be more."

Shit. I was intrigued, but I'd never admit to it. Tutt was the first guy that had ever pressed me this hard. "Are you a comedian or something?"

"Nope. I will tell you all about me on our date Saturday."

I shook my head. "Date? I can't agree to something that was never asked of me."

Tutt put his hands in a praying position. "You're right. My apologies, Mrs. McCormick. Will you do me the honors of attending a wedding with me this Saturday?"

My eyes widened. "You want to take someone you just met to a wedding with you and with only three days' notice?"

"Yeah, what's wrong with that? You wanted me to take you home with only five minutes' notice." He stepped into my personal space. "You want what you want."

My recently healed microbladed eyebrows touched. "Very valid points, sir. However, weddings are intimate. You don't bring a random chick."

"Random? Woman, you have my last name."

Once again, I couldn't help but laugh. His sense of humor was unparalleled. But truthfully, I wanted more of it. "What time should I be ready, and what should I wear?"

Tutt's lips spread, revealing his gap again. "Whatever you choose, I'm sure it will be worth seeing you in. And I know it will be hard to do for such a beautiful woman but try not to outshine the bride."

"You are something else. Can you send me a picture of what *you're* wearing? I'll see if I have something to match it."

"I'll need your number," he said. "Your Cash App too. I want to send you the money for your wedding attire if you have to buy something."

I chuckled, rolled my eyes, and held out my hand for his phone. I programmed my number as Random Wedding Date and gave back Tutt his phone.

He frowned when he saw it. "Still no name, huh? No Cash App either?"

"I can manage the purchase," I winked. "Text me the details, and don't forget to send me your suit." Then I ran off to keep the thrill in the mystery. Tutt never had to know my name as far as I was concerned.

The ultimate test would be learning to balance in a pair of heels before Saturday. I tried once before during my heavier days, and a little kid embarrassed me. I needed shoes for senior prom. It was in Macy's where I met that snotty-nosed kid who was with his mother. I had found the perfect pair of Cinderella-ish heels. They made me feel like I'd land my prince at the prom. Since I didn't have an actual date, I attended with a group of friends. I slipped on the shoes and imagined that I'd glide across the floor effortlessly, like a ballerina, once I stood. Instead, I stumbled a bit when I stood, trying to find my rhythm. The little brat saw me, giggled, and said, "What's the matter? You too heavy for those shoes or something?" I kicked them off, grabbed my flats, and hauled my tail out of the department store, never looking back—little punk.

I was ready for the challenge. I would live the life I shouldn't have been afraid to live all along. 3XL was gone for good. Size fourteen was here to stay.

Chapter 18

Tutt's last name fit him. He brought a variety of flavors to the bedroom. Damn good and damn satisfying.

We'd only known each other for three days, but the instant attraction, contagious love surrounding the wedding, and too much champagne from lots of unnecessary, random toasting led me back to Tutt's place. Specifically, the kitchen countertop. The sexual chemistry was so strong that a few shenanigans started on the dance floor and moved to the car before we made it to his condo.

The wedding party and guests raised glasses to any and everything . . . Just because the bride's hair was in two French braids, or because every invitee RSVP'd and showed up. There was even a toast to promote honesty in relationships. I hadn't drunk since the day my mother rescued me from the bar, and I promised myself that I wouldn't, but what was one little sip in good company? Plus, I'd gotten good news a couple of weeks ago that was worth celebrating. My HIV results returned negative. So little sips turned into *lots* of big sips.

When they finally opened the dance floor, Tutt led me to it, and we never sat back down. For every slow song, he held me tight, respected my booty by keeping his hands on my hips, and passionately kissed me. On every upbeat song, he showed me how much rhythm he had, which was way more than me, but he never made me feel like I couldn't keep up. Already, there was something about him that I wanted to hold on to for a long time. I had quickly changed my no strings stance, and I kept asking God to have allowed Taylor to be the frog and Tutt to be the prince.

The reception was still jumping well into the night, and so were my lady parts. I'd convinced Tutt to leave the party of 100 for a party of two. After all, I allowed him to do what he wanted, and that was to take me on a date first. We'd gone out, and now he could do what I asked of him days ago.

We listened to sexy, feel-good music on the drive to his place. One thing I learned: the man had pipes. He serenaded me, and when he didn't know the lyrics, he made up his own. It was cute. I giggled and blushed a lot.

"Thank you for taking me out. This was nice," I told him.

"You're welcome. Thank you for accompanying me."

I'd always wanted to suck my man off while he drove, and technically, Tutt wasn't my man, but I had reminded myself that titles and men stipulations were *Redarra's* desires. With Red, he didn't have to be my man to live out a fantasy. However, I did learn from my scare. Any sexual act would require a condom, including oral. That's why I came prepared. I didn't know what size to get, so I purchased a variety, including flavored condoms.

First, I leaned over and started rubbing between his legs.

He jumped. "Woman."

I smiled at his and his thick friend's response, which immediately woke up. "All right, woman, you better quit before I crash," he said.

"I'm not worried about that. The only thing that will be crashing is your balls against my ass."

"Damn, girl. You a *nasty* little something."

I pulled back the buckle on his belt, undid his pants, and wiggled his meat through the hole of his boxers.

Tutt quickly glanced at me and then back at the road. "You just gonna take it while I'm driving, huh?"

"Maybe," I toyed.

"Didn't I tell you I wanted to get to know you first?"

"No. You said you wanted to take me out first. We're out."

"You know what I meant."

"I know what you said." I leaned over and blew on the tip. "You can always tell me to stop."

A few seconds passed, and he never said anything. With the way he moaned, I didn't expect any objections. I retrieved a pineapple-flavored condom from my purse and ripped it open with my teeth. Tutt did a double take. "It's just a little flavor. Protect us both," I said.

Confusion filled Tutt's words. "Never had that before, but . . . okay."

"And I've never used one before. First time for everything. And look, we are experiencing it together."

"Is there something wrong with you that I should know about?" he eased out.

Now *I* was the confused one. "What do you mean?"

"It's just that as many times as I've gotten head . . ." his words trailed off. I knew what he implied.

"Complete transparency," I said. "I found out my boyfriend was on the down low. Because of that, I recently got checked. I'm all clear and want to keep it that way. I have the results on my phone if you'd like to see them."

"Damn. But that's good to know about your status. I'm good too. I have results on my phone as well if you would like to see them. The passcode spells out *McTutt*."

I stopped stroking in amazement. He'd given me the passcode to his phone without hesitation. Taylor would never. Most men would never.

"What's wrong?" Tutt asked.

"Nothing at all," I said and started slurping.

Tutt's head fell back against the headrest. The car swerved with just about every moan that sensually changed his pitch, but I kept going. Then I felt the palm of his hand on the back of my head, pushing it down so that every inch of him got some pleasure. Every time he pushed my head down, I felt him thrust underneath me. The pushing and thrusting quickened, and I knew what time it was. I matched his pace. Suddenly, the car came to an abrupt stop. I jumped up and looked when Tutt threw the gear in park. We were in the middle of a dark road, the car idling.

"What are you doing?" he asked, forcing my head back into his lap. He whispered how good it felt over and over until he shook his liquid out. "Shit, woman. I need a minute," he said and slumped over the steering wheel.

"Need me to drive?" I asked.

"Nah."

I wiped my mouth, sat back, and secretly gloated. I can thank Taylor for making me a professional sucker. That's all he ever wanted. Oral and anal. *Red flag*.

Once Tutt got himself together, we journeyed on. Comparing him to Taylor, who was one and done, I was surprised when Tutt pounced on me as soon as we made it inside his place. I'd become used to servicing and not getting much in return. For Tutt, oral was just the appetizer. He came up behind me and started kissing and rubbing every crevice of my body. He was muscular, but I didn't expect him to pick me up and carry me into the kitchen effortlessly. No struggle. No grunt. Not even a gasp for air. Although I had lost weight, I was still over 200 pounds. He didn't break a sweat.

"You are so damn sexy, Mrs. McCormick," Tutt whispered into my ear after sitting me on the countertop. Despite telling him that my name was Redarra, but I liked Red better, he still insisted on referring to me as his namesake.

I'd removed everything on Tutt from the waist up during our passion-filled kisses. Every inch of his upper body was well sculpted.

"Can I make love to you?" he asked.

"No lovemaking. I like it rough."

He moaned and then stepped back, dropping everything on his lower half. My girl throbbed, excited that she was about to get some penetration for the first time in . . . I didn't even remember. Since Taylor, of course . . . whenever he felt like entering the front instead of the back or in my mouth.

"By the time I finish putting this condom on, you better be naked."

With the demand in his voice, I almost ripped my dress, trying to hurry up and get it off.

"Spread 'em," he demanded and jammed two fingers inside me. "Damn, Mrs. McCormick. You're oozing, and I *like* it."

"How much?" I toyed.

Tutt's breath tickled my ear. "A whole lot."

"Prove it." That was my way of telling him to get on with it. I was eager to see what he would do with the nice-sized blessing he had in between his legs. It was not as big as Taylor's but still big enough to excite me.

He entered me with a moan, and I received him with a grunt.

"You feel so damn good," he admitted more than once.

I wanted to scream the same thing, but he rendered me speechless. His stroke was something out of a porn movie. Not only did it feel like it came from a professional, but I was able to watch him put his back into it, thanks to the mirror that hung nearby.

A million things went through my head. I never wanted this moment to end. Whatever Tutt laid on me caused me to experience my first orgasm without clitoral stimulation. I shivered, bit down on his shoulder, and dug my nails into his back before yelling, "Oh my God!" My thighs warmed right before my juices trickled down my leg.

His climax followed right behind mine. I lay back on the counter in awe. This was a moment I never wanted to forget . . . which scared me. The last time a man showed me an unforgettable sexual experience, I was addicted to him like caffeine, and I didn't see this time being any different.

My thoughts disappeared when I felt the warmth of the cloth. Tutt was cleaning me off. I'd never had anyone do that either.

"You good?" he asked, never removing his eyes from mine.

I nodded.

"Hanging out a bit, or are you ready for me to take you home?"

"I can stay awhile." But honestly, I could stay in his presence forever.

"Hungry?"

"No, I'm good. But I can use some water." And a nap, but I didn't confess that part. Tutt had done his job of sending the sandman my way.

He laughed. "I bet you can with all that moaning and splashing. You need at least three bottles to replenish."

I smacked my teeth and playfully swatted at him.

I may not have learned much about Tutt during the wedding, but I learned a heck of a lot after sex. We transitioned to the couch, drank some wine, and talked.

"I'm surprised you gave me your password. No man ever does that."

"I have nothing to hide."

"Nothing to hide as in nothing going on, or nothing to hide as in since we just met, and I said no strings attached, you don't care what I see?" I was afraid of his answer. I could see myself with him, and if he had something going on, I'd probably feel a hint of jealousy.

He chuckled a little. "Nothing to hide as in nothing going on."

Now, I was suspicious. Glad that he was single but still suspicious. Even though it had only been a few days, how could what seemed to be a great guy have nothing going on? "When was the last time?"

"The last time what?" he asked for clarification.

I smacked my teeth. "Now you wanna play?"

"I'm not playing. You could be asking when was the last time I had sex or when was the last time I was in a relationship."

"Answer both."

"My last relationship was a little over a month ago. So was the last time I had sex. Next question."

My eyes narrowed at his change of attitude. "Why all the sassiness?"

"What kind of shit is that?" he frowned. "Don't use that word to describe me. There's nothing sassy about me."

"Why are you so offended by that question? Are you a homophobe or something?"

"Hell naw. My brother is gay, and he's one of the coolest dudes I know. Sassy and Tutt just don't belong in the same sentence."

Suddenly, my tongue tasted like sulfur, and I developed heartburn. *Gay* brother? Please don't let one of the foursomes be related to him. Granted, none of Taylor's guys' last names were McCormick, but that didn't mean anything. They could have different fathers. My leg bounced as I eased into the next question. "What's your brother's name?"

"Carter McCormick."

I let out a sigh low enough that Tutt couldn't hear. "So, your parents have a thing with giving y'all last names for first names?"

I was glad Tutt laughed. "Silly. Tutt is my mother's maiden name, and Carter is my paternal grandmother's maiden name. Next question."

"Why did you and your girlfriend break up?"

"You sure ask a lot of questions for it to be no strings attached," he said.

That's how it was supposed to work before I started second-guessing that statement. "Problem with me asking?"

"Not at all. Just wanted to point that out."

"Avoiding the question?" I playfully rolled my eyes.

"Not at all. She wasn't as ambitious as I wanted in a partner."

"What does that mean?" I pried. I mainly needed to know if there were a chance they'd rekindle.

"Meaning . . ." he paused, took a breath, and said, "How can I put this?" He clicked his tongue a few times, thinking of his word choices. "She comes from a very wealthy family who spoiled her. I'm all for spoiling my lady but within my means. What I had to offer wasn't enough, I guess. We broke up, and last I heard, she had hopped into a relationship with a doctor."

"How does that make you feel?" I pressed.

He shrugged. "It was tough. All breakups are. I'm cool, and I hope it works out for them."

"How long did y'all date?"

"Hmmmm. Like four years."

"And a month later, you're over her? That doesn't seem like enough time."

"My life doesn't stop because someone chose not to be a part of it. I have goals. Nothing will stop that. There are times when she crosses my mind. That's to be expected."

"So, what am I, the rebound girl?"

Tutt let out an exasperated breath. "Outside of basketball, I don't believe in rebounds. Next question."

"So, if not the rebound girl, then what am I?"

"A woman who asks a lot of questions," he fired back.

"*Excuse* me," I said with an attitude. "How am I supposed to get to know you if I can't ask questions?"

He shrugged and walked into the kitchen. When he came back, he had a stronger drink. "Before, you weren't interested in getting to know me. Now, you are. Which one is it?" He peered at me over his glass that was filled to the rim.

"I don't like how you're talking to me. What is *wrong* with you?"

"I'm trying to figure out the same thing with you because I don't like playing these games."

I jumped from the sofa in defense mode. "Who the hell do you think you're talking to like that?"

"I apologize if it seems I'm being disrespectful."

"What's with the attitude?" I asked again.

"I don't have an attitude. I don't understand you. You say no strings. You didn't want to tell me your name, you didn't want me to know anything about you, but you can ask all these personal questions about me." He shrugged and added, "I don't get it. Make up your mind, pick a side, and act accordingly."

"So, *that's* what it is? You're down to earth as long as I'm only interested in sex, but since I regret saying that and want to explore something a little more permanent . . ." I paused. That kind of slipped out. There was a fine line between Red and Redarra. Sometimes, they crossed paths.

Tutt set his glass down and crept toward me with a huge smile on his face. "More *permanent,* huh? Stop trying to play hard to get. I told you on day one I wanted to get to know you before introducing sex. I knew once I put this thing on you, it would complicate things. I'm good at what I do."

I gasped and punched him. He didn't tell a lie. While I couldn't explain why, I knew I wanted him on day two based on conversation alone. Sex intensified that desire.

"Don't fight it, Mrs. McCormick," he said, wrapping me in his arms. "May we take sex off the table? I'd like to get to know you."

After what he just laid on me, that was an arduous task. Finally, however, I gave in.

Chapter 19

Yara and I had stepped into the pre-graduation party at The Caprice Lounge about an hour after it started. Fashionably late, might I add. The crimson lacy crop top and biker shorts fit that barely covered my body had me drooling over myself in the mirror while taking multiple selfies.

Red was way more fun in more ways than one. Computer science geek by day, vigilante flag thrower by night. Well, with help from Julian, of course. Still, my idea.

The lounge was packed from the bare white walls to the accented purple and gold wall near the VIP section that Dre reserved for us as his gift to Yara. Solo cups occupied just about every hand, and the smell of marijuana followed my every move. I was that smoking hot that even the smoke followed me.

Before Yara and I reached our reserved section where Dre and his slimy cousin Myron awaited, the crazies were tugging at my arm from every direction on a compass. Some inebriated dude, who

I'd never seen before a day in my life, had the nerve to grope me. Just bold. That got his ass slapped. Anger management, my ass. A girl had to be able to defend herself against these vicious, entitled men, which was why I never went to anger management classes outside of the inpatient facility. After mediation, everything just kind of disappeared. Plus, I didn't need to know how to control my anger. I needed these men to understand that I would fight back against their disrespectful behavior.

Where was all this attention when I was heavier? Perhaps it was the side boob. If I moved too much, an areola might have made an appearance. Before tonight, a nip-slip would have sent me into hiding, but with my newfound confidence, I would tuck, shrug it off, and keep it moving.

Since I'd gone on to drop nearly sixty-five pounds, things were no longer puffed out and splattered. Everything was toned, pulled, and snatched but jiggly where it mattered. I was for real thick, not the pretend kind. "Oh, you're not fat. You're *thick*." That was the bullshit lie people told to avoid hurting feelings. Now, the only thing plus size about me was my confidence. My body shrank, and my head swelled. Not in a bad way. Every day that my eyes opened, I was sure to check my ego in the mirror, right after I admired my new shape and the curves that came along with it.

I couldn't lie. It felt good to be noticed for my looks with a smile, a lingering stare, or a compliment instead of a frown, insult, or an offer of food. And I ate every bit of it up like I did my vegetables.

"Twelve o'clock," Yara said, calling out Taylor's position. "Pretend he's not here and do you extra hard. Matter of fact, sashay past his ass and flaunt all that shit." Her voice slurred a little as she waved her hand up and down my body like it was something she'd won. "Make sure he sees this side boob."

"Awkward and obvious," I said, lightly pushing her hand away from my right breast.

One thing Yara hadn't given up in her quest for change was cursing and drinking. She felt that since wine was in the Bible, it was okay. Only problem, Hennessey wasn't wine. My girl was multiple shots in and currently in the pre-drunk stage, which meant I was in for a long night. Alcohol had an immediate effect on her, and anymore she'd end up dancing the night away on a table until the lounge closed or until she was involuntarily escorted out.

"Shake them shits in his face like you at Mardi Gras. I will even find you some beads." Yara stumbled a bit and added, "And if Taylor gives you any problems, I'll have Dre throw his ass out."

Newsflash: Dre didn't *own* this lounge, but I'd let her think her man had the power to do whatever. No point in debating with a drunk person.

"I bet Taylor's gay ass wish he could tap that again. I would do you, and I don't even like hoes."

I shook my head. "Gee, thanks, friend." Just because I occasionally flaunted it didn't mean I was any less of a person. I was proud that I had the confidence to show a little more skin and was finally able to walk in a pair of heels. Right before the creeps stopped me, I strutted across the lounge floor like I had walked in New York Fashion Week a time or two. Not only did the guys survey me, but the girls too.

Compliments from the ladies felt better than receiving them from men. Females were usually envious and judgmental of one another, so I never took it lightly when one uplifted me. I'd heard girls say how proud they were of me for shedding the pounds and how they admired my strength by not laying down and allowing the *Taylor-stances* to destroy me.

"I ought to go punch his ass." Yara pointed at Taylor, making it even more apparent that we'd noticed him and were talking about him.

Taylor was the last person I expected to see. Ever since those mysterious flags started faithfully appearing on his doorstep, thanks to Julian staying dedicated to the cause, Taylor's game was off. He had been lying low. As much as he posted on social media, even that had slowed down. Guess there wasn't much to brag about when losing your starting position. Bench rider number eleven had nothing on second-string number thirteen except for a seat on the bench.

Good thing that bastard graced us with his presence. I could get into his head a little more. I started to blow him a kiss, but since he stood near the bathroom, I decided it was a good time to pee—without Yara. I pushed her over to Dre and disappeared within the heavy clouds of smoke and dim lights.

The closer I got to Taylor, the more I realized I wasn't missing out on a damn thing. Misery was in his eyes as he stood against the wall, looking lonely and out of place, like he wished someone would be his friend. Or he was scoping out some fresh meat to take home. Either way, he looked like shit. I could tell he'd had enough like he was over life. I promised myself that I'd leave him alone as soon as I did one more thing. The video would serve as the grand finale. I planned to finish him off with a bang—literally.

When I walked past, we didn't exchange words. We only looked each other up and down. There was tension in the stare down—same thing when I returned. The whole vengeance, tough-girl thing had me feeling sexier than my new look.

Before I made it to the VIP section, "When We" by Tank blared through the speakers. Everybody and their mama ran to the dance floor. I hurried and found a place at the edge where I'd still be visible to Taylor. I could see him watching me hard through my peripheral.

Slow song after slow song played. I gyrated and bent my body in ways I never knew were possible. I ran my fingers through my short cut like I had a head full of hair.

"Damn, Mrs. McCormick," Tutt snuck up behind me and whispered in my ear.

And just like that—another slow song. After planting a sloppy kiss on Tutt, I turned around, bent over, and started sensually grinding on him since the bastard looked on. *Take that, Taylor. Soak it all up. You'll never touch this body again.*

Occasionally, Tutt would whisper in my ear to remind me how good I looked. His breath smelled like a cigar and tickled my ear to the point where I could feel how wet my panties had become without touching them.

"I bet you taste delicious," Tutt whispered.

I rolled my body around to the beat of the music, licked his lips, and said, "I do. Would you like to find out?" and rolled some more. When the music picked up, I bent down in front of him and started twerking—the perks of looking back at it. I caught a few glimpses of Tutt licking his lips and was reminded of the power his thick tongue held. It usually sent me to the top in two minutes. Withholding sex didn't last long, and neither of us was complaining.

Tutt smacked my ass. "Come on, let's get a drink before we go." He grabbed my hand and escorted me to the bar. "Crown and Coke for me," he said. "Water on the rocks for my girl."

"Ha-ha, very funny." Alcohol made me just as crazy as it did Yara, so I gave it up.

Tutt and I laughed and made small talk while we waited for our drinks.

"If you're smart, you better hit it and quit it. She's crazy."

I could identify that voice from anywhere. Taylor had some nerve approaching my man and me with some bullshit. I was *not* crazy. And my man knew all about both hospital admissions and why. I made sure to be transparent because I wanted to keep him.

Tutt hopped off the bar stool. "Shut yo' gay ass up before you get your brains knocked out again."

It was like a record scratched in there, and everything got quiet except for the back-and-forth exchange between Taylor and Tutt. Heat from everyone huddling around us scalded my face. I stepped in between the two of them, as did a few others. As did those damn cell phones. Could things not be private anymore?

When someone from the crowd yelled in an announcer's voice, "In this corner, Taylor is fighting for the LGBT community," the onlookers went nuts with laughter.

Taylor stepped back, gave me the nastiest look, and stormed out.

Poor thing. Wait until he saw what I left for him on the hood of his car.

When I ducked off to the bathroom, one of the staff members had the back door propped open, smoking a cigarette and talking on the phone. I batted my eyes, flirted, and convinced him to allow me to go to my car and return through the back to avoid fighting the crowded space. I didn't go to the bathroom or to my car, but I did go to Taylor's car. For some reason, I always carried a pack of flags in my purse, and because Tutt and I had already agreed to leave the party for some fun, I had a small sex toy with me. Sex between Tutt and me was good enough that I could sacrifice for a night. I hated to duplicate a previous gesture. It was a spur-of-the-moment thing. No letter. Just a flag attached to a sex toy. Technically, this was a bonus.

Parked not too far from Taylor's Impala was Myron's tricked-out Denali. He and I hadn't spoken since the bowling alley, but I'd seen his truck in recent pictures with Yara and Dre. It wasn't hard to miss. He had his social media handles plastered across his car windows. *Wanna-be-rapper*. I owed him too. I had pins in my purse in case I had to adjust my clothes. *Oops*. I wondered how the pins ended up in Myron's tire.

I went back inside and partied like I had never stepped away to commit a crime.

After Taylor left, it didn't take long for patrons to start whispering and laughing. By the time talk made it to me, it was still intact.

Blondie, sitting next to me, said to her friend, "I heard someone left a sex toy on Taylor's car. It had a flag or something hanging from it."

I leaned in a little farther to ear hustle. I didn't want to miss any details.

The friend's eyes grew the size of cantaloupes. "Shut up."

"I think he's gay for real," Blondie added.

"Me too. Where there's smoke, there's fire."

"Sounds like a scorned person trying to send a message."

"One of his boyfriends, maybe?" the friend asked.

Blondie shrugged.

Yes, this girl was definitely sending a message. Once upon a time, I was all bark. Now, I bite.

Chapter 20

My heart jumped to the beat of the graduation music. I marched and second-guessed if I'd eaten. I did, but my stomach seemed to have forgotten about the fruit and bagel I had nibbled on while my cousin applied my makeup. Slow cramps crawled up, making it seem like my small intestine and stomach had traded places and had different opinions over their new living quarters.

I guess it was just nerves, and rightfully so. This was a big day. Not only because I was graduating, but because it was the Big Reveal. Taylor Lawrence was going down, and apparently, so was I.

Whenever nerves got the best of me, I turned into a clumsy, uncoordinated individual. I was lucky that the person in front of me and behind me caught me when I tripped over my gown. One block heel went to the left and one to the right, but I didn't miss a beat when I straightened up. I trotted on, and when I made it to my seat, I searched out my family, just as happy and innocent as could be. They had all traveled from multiple states to witness this day and celebrate with me.

I toggled back and forth on when to share the video on the screen. During the commencement ceremony? But then, there would be so much commotion that it would interfere with the ceremony's completion. Then I thought I'd have it play as Taylor walked across the stage. That would still cause disruption, which wouldn't be fair to those walking behind him. I still wanted payback, but not at the expense of causing the other graduates to lose out on an experience.

There was even a moment when I had a change of heart. Burning off calories and fat in the gym almost made me burn off the need for revenge. Looking at my list of attributes, I was better than anything involving Taylor. I'd grown past the past. I had convinced myself that Taylor had suffered enough torture. The video never needed to surface. I had planned to send it only to Taylor. I wanted him to see how I spared him. I was over the flags, the torture—all of it. But then, Taylor just had to run his mouth. Because of what happened at the lounge, he'd been the topic in the rumor mill again. He decided to shift gears and push the attention back to me. He took to social media and announced he'd be throwing an anniversary party to commemorate the day I attacked him. That told me he hadn't learned his lesson.

Game back on.

Ultimately, I decided to wait until after we turned our tassels. Then I just had to press one button on my phone, and Taylor's world would explode. A little trick I discovered during my computer science course. Kind of like a virus. I didn't want to refer to myself as a hacker, but it was brilliant. The forty-five-second video of Sammie and Taylor would play and then disappear like Snapchat. There was nothing anyone could do to stop it, nor could it be traced back to me.

The graduation got underway. Typical ceremony. A lot of boring talking. Recaps. Well wishes.

I spent most of the time texting back and forth with Yara, who sat on the other side of the field, and my family. She had no idea what I had planned. I even feared her reaction. Would she be mad at me for doing it this way? Would she celebrate the fact that I had finally exposed him? Would she be sad because she was omitted? I knew how amped she was to put him on blast. As far as I knew, Yara and I were still the only two people who knew about the video.

All Taylor had to do was apologize and begin to act like he had a little bit of sense. Then I would have stood down, but he just had to be an asshole.

Name after name was called. Then it was my turn. "Redarra Michaels." Cheers erupted as I shimmied across the stage. The support left me feeling like everyone was on my team and not Taylor's.

I exited the stage, posed for my picture, and sauntered back to my seat. I had to pass Taylor, and that's when the bastard decided to boo me. Sammie sat a row behind him and laughed, as did a few others. Suddenly, I reacted. I pressed the button . . . and it happened. Taylor and Sammie were on the screen doing what they did. Everyone looked on as administrators scrambled to remove the video. Impossible.

Faces displayed various expressions: shock, silence, laughter, and mouths were agape. Finally, someone from the audience screamed. Probably Taylor's mom. Now, she and everyone else would know the *real* him.

I gazed at the two stars. They weren't laughing.

"I knew he was gay," I heard. I didn't look to see who had said it. Then I heard, "Oh my God," and "Hell to the naw."

Taylor put those fast feet to use and ran his ass up out of there. Sammie didn't. He looked lifeless as a few people jumped in his face, pointing fingers, laughing, and taunting him. I wish I were closer to hear what they said.

Then the video disappeared, and so did everyone's voice. They either stood or sat stunned and speechless. Immediately, the administrators jumped on the mic and threatened to hold the person responsible accountable and withhold their degree. Good luck with that. There was no way it would trace back to me. A part of me felt that even if it did, I'd repeat another four years of college if I had to because this was worth everything that might happen to me.

The ceremony came to an abrupt close. Some moods were numb, some energetic, and some were still in shock as we exited the field to go on and start our lives as college graduates.

"This will go down as the best graduation ever," some white guy said that resembled Post Malone with the face tats and a ponytail.

Taylor was nowhere to be found. I didn't see Sammie anymore either. Finally, I caught Yara's eye. She smiled and winked at me, giving me her approval for what I pulled off, even though she could only *assume* it was me.

And when I finally heard, "That's probably why that girl beat his ass, and I don't blame her," roll out of someone's mouth, I felt vindicated.

Chapter 21

"Good morning. The usual, please." It felt good to step foot into an establishment where the associates already knew what I wanted. This particular Starbucks was en route to my job, and because I was a regular, I was usually in and out in under five minutes.

"Cinnamon dolce latte, and a spinach, feta, and egg white wrap, coming right up."

"You're the bomb, Stacy." They all knew me well, but Stacy knew me best.

"Hey, there, Miss Lady. Good to see you this morning," Ms. Cathy greeted me with the exact sentence she used every time she saw me, which was almost every day. Routine. The only thing different about this morning, she had stepped from behind the counter with an application in her hand.

"Likewise, Ms. Cathy," I returned the cheer and glanced at my watch. It was barely after eight. "Interviewing already this time of the morning?"

Ms. Cathy shrugged. "When you need people, you need people."

"Amen." I turned my attention to my phone and started checking emails.

"Taylor Lawrence," Ms. Cathy called out.

What the holy hell. You *gotta* be kidding me. I wasn't sure whether to look. It had to be a coincidence. Someone with the same name. After all, it's a common name, but I couldn't resist. I slowly spun on the toes of my Jimmy Choo suede heels. Taylor and my stare lingered. My heart knocked like it wanted out of my chest. Images of graduation flashed. How did I not see him when I walked in? Granted, I hadn't seen or heard that name since shortly after the graduation scandal, which was two years ago, but I could spot him in a stack of hay if he were a needle. A slight smile appeared on his face. I didn't know if it was intended for me or if he was putting on for his interview. I wished I could be his reference. I'd have a lot to say.

"Here you go, Red." Stacy's voice stole my attention. I've had so much fun with this name that I decided to keep it.

"Thank you. See you tomorrow," I replied and grabbed the necessities—napkins, straw, jelly, and whatever else I could find while figuring out an exit strategy. Taylor was too close to the door, and although he was interviewing, I didn't want to take any chances in case he was bold enough to forfeit the interview to mess with me.

If I didn't have on heels, I would have bolted to my car like I ran track all my life. Or used the other exit and walked around the building, but it had started drizzling. I couldn't wait to tell Yara who I had seen. I could hear her loud country ass now. Well, maybe not as hyper and team-too-much as before, but still worthy of some good laughs, cries, support, and telling all my business to. She'd toned it down several notches after we graduated. According to her, she had to start taking life more seriously as an adult and in her career field. Yara had stopped cursing and expected me to do the same. Of course, that was probably never gonna happen. Anytime I'd slip up and curse around her, she'd scold me like I was one of her sibling kids. She was so lame now, but I still loved my preaching, Lord-following, non-bio to death. I knew she would think I made up running into Taylor, but I couldn't make that shit up even if I were an author.

"Ms. Cathy, I need an override," Stacy yelled out.

Ms. Cathy excused herself from the table. Now, it was just Taylor sitting by himself, still watching me. I knew because my peripheral game was still on point.

I started toward the door, and just before I was home free, I heard, "Redarra, wait."

Damn. I hoped to have slithered out without us passing words. My Apple Watch vibrated against my wrist. I checked it before turning to acknowledge Taylor. It was an alert that my heart rate had increased without exertion. Of course, it had. I'd become skittish—a normal reaction in a situation like this. Hell, I'm surprised my coffee wasn't in a puddle on the floor. I prepared for Taylor to unleash on me. I prayed that he was weapon-free and would only assault me with his words or a single knockout punch.

I inhaled, soaking up the sweet aroma of everything brewing. Coffee was one of those things that instantly changed my mood. Not that I was in a bad one, just paranoid about how the conversation would go. I took a big gulp, forgetting this shit was hot as hell. The worst thing outside of a busted tastebud was a burnt tongue. And now a burnt throat.

"What's up?" I asked, sounding like somebody's hoarse granddaddy.

"You want me to get you some water?"

Well, this was embarrassing. Something as simple as coffee had knocked me off my bad bitch game right in front of my worst enemy. He's the reason I'd become her in the first place. I shook my head, cleared my throat, and held up a finger. I needed a minute to extinguish the flames throughout my body and get my status back.

I dreaded hearing what Taylor had to say, and I thought Ms. Cathy would've been back by now, but when I looked at the counter, she was nowhere in sight, and the line had grown. At least if Taylor tried anything too crazy, there'd be eyewitnesses. I just hoped the other patrons would be courageous enough to step in and help as opposed to standing by, recording. Recording devices during tragic situations have given me PTSD.

When I finally doused the internal flames, I repeated my question, "What's up?"

"How have you been?" he asked.

"I've been well." Short and sweet. Okay, I can go now.

"You look good. I like those shoes. I remember you always used to say how you couldn't wait to be able to wear heels, and now look at you." He smiled a genuine smile.

Awe, hell. Was this another red flag? Liking my shoes and shit? Being nice to me after I ruined him?

I threw my head like I was flipping my hair out of my face. Don't ask me why. I still wore it short. Nerves maybe. An SOS. I didn't know. "Thank you," I said.

Too bad I couldn't return any compliment, especially one about his shoes. They were an ugly pair of loafers, designs and all, and in my opinion, not appropriate for an interview. At least, that's what we learned in the interview prep course taught at our college. My eyes worked Taylor from head to toe without him knowing. His hair needed a cut, his face needed a shave, and his white dress shirt was a little on the dingy side. But at least his pants weren't tight, and his nails weren't polished. He looked downright stressed, worn out, and full of misery. Just what I wanted for him a couple of years ago. Since I had moved on, I felt kind of bad for him.

"I hear you're working at your parents' law firm and back in school. Congratulations."

The fact that he knew *anything* about me caught me by surprise. I frowned, which was supposed to be enough for him to explain how the hell he knew all this information about me when I knew nothing about him other than not getting drafted. Outside of that, Taylor had not crossed my mind in any capacity since we graduated. Eventually, talk of me faded, and so did talk of him and Sammie.

"Yeah, I'm there and there," I said, referring to work and school.

"IT, right? And law school."

I slowly nodded. Everything that came out of his mouth was alarming and made me wonder if our chance encounter resulted from stalking.

"How do you know all of that?" I quizzed.

"I keep up with you. I ask around, and I follow you on social media."

"Interesting. I don't recall us being friends."

"Yeah, I don't go by my real name. Unfortunately, I had to disable my account after grad—" he paused.

Uncomfortable energy seemed to circulate between us. Taylor rocked side to side, which made me even more nervous. I gulped when he stuck his hands in his pockets, thinking he had a knife and was about to gut me.

I reluctantly asked him a question to kill him with kindness and to fill the awkward silence outside of the patron chatters and the calling of orders. "What have you been up to?" I was being cordial until Ms. Cathy returned to make my departure easier.

"Just trying to find work," he sadly admitted.

"Here?" I frowned and immediately tried to clean it up. "Not that anything is wrong with working here, but you don't want to do anything in your field? Kinesiology, right?"

"Right, and, of course, I do." Taylor tightly shut his eyes like he was trying to fight back the tears. "It's been a rough couple of years, so I have to take what I can get."

"I understand. Whatever it is, be proud and work hard to be the best at it."

"True," he said. "Well, I'm glad we ran into each other. I wanted to message you but wasn't sure how you'd take it."

"About?"

"What happened between us."

"Don't mention it," I said, and I meant that. I didn't want to talk about it or trigger any uncomfortable feelings for either of us.

"Since we don't have time now, maybe we can meet up at Yvonne's like old times and talk?"

"Taylor, I don't think—"

He cut me off. "At least just think about it. And I know you're with Tutt. Congrats on your engagement, by the way."

"Thank you." I held out my ring to show him. Not to boast. It was out of habit because I was happy, proud, and could not wait to become Mrs. McCormick. Officially. Speaking of which, Tutt was still on that Mrs. McCormick kick.

"You're welcome," Taylor said and paused. It was apparent something else was on his mind. "About that thing with Sammie—"

This time, I cut him off. "Taylor," I said and shook my head. Although curious, I wasn't sure I wanted to hear it. Either he was too dumb to realize I had anything to do with his demise, or he was playing me.

"I owe you that and an apology."

He didn't know. He couldn't. If the shoe were on the other foot, there was no way I'd be apologizing to any person that ruined my entire life, no matter what I did to them in return.

"I would have loved to have walked away with my dignity, but it's okay. Apologizing to me is not necessary. Let's just leave the past in the past." I smiled, hoping that was enough to make him leave the subject alone. I didn't want the guilt of what I did to have me confessing and apologizing. I wanted to remain innocent in his eyes and everyone else's. Yara didn't even know about the red flags game I played.

"I have to do this. It's been bothering me for years," Taylor confessed.

Where the hell is Ms. Cathy? I wondered but nodded and allowed Taylor to get whatever he needed off his chest.

"From the bottom of my heart, I am so sorry for what I did to you. The disgusting things I said, blasting you to the world. You didn't deserve any of that. I was dumb, had all the attention and a promising future, and it gave me an ego. As far as that thing with Sammie . . ." Taylor dropped his head in shame. "I'm not gay or bisexual. I don't know what I had going on. Guess I was just experimenting." He scratched his head like he didn't believe his own lie.

That was a lot of experimenting. What about the others that he never mentioned? It wasn't just Sammie. A part of me wanted to remind him, but then he'd know more than I wanted him to. So I kept my mouth shut and let him believe that I believed him, just like I'm going to let him think I had nothing to do with the way his life turned out.

"I see now that you were the only person in my corner that wanted me to succeed on and off the field. I regret not seeing the value in what you offered," he continued.

Everyone had jumped off his bandwagon when he didn't make it to the NFL. My work wasn't in vain. Taylor learned something.

My watch vibrated. Perfect timing. Michaels and Michaels appeared on the screen. "It's my job. I'm sure they're wondering where I am. It was good seeing you."

"You too. My number is still the same . . . in case."

I nodded because there was nothing more to say. I knew I wouldn't be dialing it. When I got to the door, I turned to him. "Taylor . . ."

"Yeah?" Hope filled his drab eyes.

I'd been waiting for this moment, but guilt had rendered me speechless. Or maybe it was growth. Either way, I couldn't fix my lips to say it. I had told myself that one day I'd get the chance to throw Taylor's words back in his face: *All the red flags were there; you just didn't pay attention.* Plus, that would be my way of confessing but still leaving the mystery element to it. It would be up to him to figure it out. I actually thought he would have by now. I still couldn't believe I went through with it and got away with it. All Taylor had to do was unscramble the letters on the flags, and it would all trace back to me. For God's sake, I left a crossword puzzle as a clue . . . and nothing.

"Taylor," I repeated his name in an attempt to try again. Somehow, I couldn't do it. The words rolled back down my throat. "Take care, and good luck with the interview."

The End